Silver Bullet

Silver Bullet

by

Gaylord Whiting

Authors Note

This is a work of fiction. Characters, places, and incidences either are the product of the author's imagination or are used fictitiously. Any resem- balance to actual persons, living or deceased, events or locales is coincidental. Names, titles, and name brands used are personal preferences, and used only to enhance the story.

— Gaylord Whiting

First Edition June 2018
Gaylord Whiting

Second Edition May 2019
Registered © 2019 Authors' Niche
Gaylord Whiting

Third Edition March 2020
Empyrean Publishing
Gaylord Whiting

All rights reserved

ISBN-13: 978-1-7039959-0-9

Published and printed in the United States of America

Dedication

To my loving wife, Samantha and my caring daughter, Jessica; for their patience, input and unwavering support.

Acknowledgements

To my Beta readers and my good friends, Kenneth McKenzie and Hanna Podkowa; your generous accolades and valued opinions were extremely helpful. Thank you all; for being there when needed and to all of you that read this story for choosing Silver Bullet.

— Gaylord Whiting

Contents

Prologue — viii

CHAPTER ONE- THE PRICE OF LOYALTY — 1

CHAPTER TWO-ALLS WELL THAT ENDS WELL — 31

CHAPTER THREE-STORMING THE GATEWAYS — 64

CHAPTER FOUR-THE COST OF TRANSITION — 75

CHAPTER FIVE-CLANDESTINE BANKING — 114

CHAPTER SIX- UNION NEGOTIATIONS — 128

CHAPTER SEVEN- PRESS THE PAUSE BUTTON — 148

CHAPTER EIGHT- WHO'S WATCHING WHO — 160

CHAPTER NINE- THE PUBLISHER'S HOT PARTY — 185

CHAPTER TEN- THE TEXAS TWO STEP — 205

CHAPTER ELEVEN- REAL FAKE NEWS — 253

CHAPTER TWELVE-ALLS WELL THAT ENDS WELL II — 279

Epilogue

Prologue

MARIE GASTON wove her way through the airport crowds, feeling somewhat bewildered by a strange sense of peripheral movement she could not identify until she got to the gate. Through the picture window overlooking the airfield, Marie saw the blistering heat waves bouncing off the tarmac in the July heat. They rolled irregularly in a surrealistic ocean of torridity. It only contributed to the nervous anticipation she felt as she waited at the gate of the international flight scheduled for departure.

Her fiancé, Kurt Melton, owner and operator of Melton Archaeological Consulting, did not yet arrive. Marie had surprised him when she said she would fly to Houston to see him off. It would be his last trip to the Middle East before their wedding that was planned for September in New Orleans, Louisiana.

Marie's anticipation was somewhat distracted, by the myriad of events that had bombarded her life in the past few months. The wedding plans alone were daunting, but she had a tinge of guilt that gnawed at her because of her mother's passing and the neglect of her father, in his time of need. Marie did well to give her father the attention he needed, although it was exceedingly difficult to balance with all the extensive wedding preparations and her grief.

Kurt's trip could not have come at a worse time, and the fact that Marie had a primal fear of the Middle East anyway, did not help. Marie saw it as one of the unstable regions in this now, global society. Even so, Kurt deserved to see this through. Uncovering the newest and largest ruins site yet found in the Middle East was an enormous discovery. Kurt was determined to ensure the government took the proper steps to protect the ecological treasures surrounding the soon-to-be, over-visited site.

Marie was suddenly alarmed as a hand grasped her arm. A look of shock quickly turned to elation as she recognized her assailant.

"Hello, darling," Kurt said grinning, and he kissed her on the lips, " I still think it was silly of you to fly all the way to Houston to see me off, but I'm glad you did," he said, kissing her gently.

"It really wasn't out of the way. I just took a flight from Washington Dulles direct to Houston. It's only a puddle jump home," Marie explained. "Flights from Dulles aren't usually direct to New Orleans anyway. Besides, I had to see you. I'll miss you."

Once settled near the gate Kurt asked, "How are you and your father holding up?"
"It's slow going," Marie grimaced, her eyes welling with tears. "We're both still so

lonesome for her! And dad's been different. He doesn't seem to have the same passion for his service and is considering a big change. He's not eating well . . . his power and influence mean nothing to him without my mother."

Kurt squeezed Marie's hand gently. "You've got each other and with me gone for a week, you'll be there for each other. Unless you want to come with me, and we'll elope!" Kurt teased her, and then leaned over to kiss her.

The final boarding call for his flight crackled over the loudspeaker, and Marie walked him to the passenger service agent awaiting boarders. Kurt handed over his boarding pass and heard Marie shriek out in pain.

A large hand nearly crushed her left arm. "Stop! You're hurting me!" This time the assailant was not her fiancé. Kurt turned into the barrel of an automatic weapon that crunched into his cheekbone. The terrorists were not wearing Thobes over Serwals, or Ghutras held on their heads with Egals. They were in black Parachute Pants with short or long sleeved black t-shirts and wearing thin black Balaclava face masks.

The terrorist pushed Marie, lowered the barrel of the gun to Kurt's chest and ordered them both toward the boarding bridge. Looking over to the gate agent, the terrorist gave her a nod that told her to follow the frightened couple. Instead of doing as trained, the agent panicked and yanked a microphone to her mouth and screamed, "Hijack!" The AK-47 was trained onto her and riddled her with bullets. Blood splattered onto

Kurt and Marie as the killer shoved them further down the jet bridge, then through the craft's plug door.

Four other terrorist had already gained access to the plane, corralled everyone on board and were guarding with watchful eyes and assault weapons.

No one had a clue how the hijackers entered with the automatic weapons under the intense security of the Transportation Administration Service Center who had been in place since 9/11.

For two days following the taking of hostages, Louisiana Senator, Andre Gaston joined the fray as much as allowed, in what appeared to include every branch of the United States Military, half of the United Nations, and every branch of law enforcement and first responder. The list was endless. All were there in an effort to negotiate resolve and reunite Senator Gaston with his daughter, Marie and his future son in law, Kurt Melton.

The demands of the airport terrorists were the immediate release of any remaining prisoners at Guantanamo Bay. As expert hostage negotiators tried to facilitate their release, the ISIS sponsored cell were only positioning themselves to carry out another senseless, violent jihad, on infidels and on American soil. At the end of the second day, two hostages ended up on Houston's tarmac, slashed and riddled with bullets: Marie Gaston and her fiancé, Kurt Melton. Despite Andre Gaston's vocal opposition to the United States position on negotiating with terrorists, the terrorist refused to surrender, and their demands re- fused. While hard at working on a way to free the hostages, one hundred ninety-three bodies spread across the tarmac of the Houston airport. The massive explosion cremated the plane's occupants and spewed the terminal and tarmac with debris, shattered glass and human remains.

His devastation could not have been deeper. Senator Gaston was still mourning his wife. And now his only child. Senator Gaston along with the nation stood appalled, astounded and frightened. Well aware America was facing a new reality.

1
The Price of Loyalty

SCOTT SILVER sat in his Chief Executive's Office at the Chicago Union Building. Silver was in his mid-thirties. Short mousy brown hair capped a substantial torso the likes of Orson Wells in the classic movie, Citizen Kane.

Silver insisted on being known as Scott at an early age because he hated his given name, Alexander, and Alex sounded prescribed. He hated Al more. Al sounded so sleazy to Scott. He didn't consider himself the former but thought he may pass for the latter. Had any of the people with the Chicago Union been aware of the reason behind using his middle name, they would have made a point to call him Al or Alex, to annoy him. Scott wasn't the most likable guy in the building.

The Chicago Union Building was located on upscale Michigan Avenue in the shadows of their competition, the Chicago Herald.

Scott's office was filled with back issues and specific articles dating back through decades of family ownership which came with his recent purchase of the Chicago Union newspaper. Most of the furnishings were original or were authentic pieces purchased to complement the existing furnishings.

The decor looked more like a Victorian period parlor than an office. Generally, everyone who entered it seemed fairly impressed, in spite of the current occupant.

The contents that came with the purchase approached an appraised value of three million dollars. During the negotiations, Scott jokingly, but assuringly mentioned if there were ever a problem making any of the payments, the contents of the office could be sold. Butch Logan, soon to be publisher of the Chicago Union, responded by suggesting, in his usual smart-mouthed manner, that if they ended up a little short on this deal, Silver should consider how much he'd take for his mother. Scott shot back with his infamous scowl and black hole eyes but said nothing. In an effort to break the ice, one of the bankers in the room re-directed the conversation to the closing. Months later Butch Logan had found himself sitting opposite of Scott. Now, Silver was seated behind the impressive antique oval cherry wood desk, nestled in a Victorian wonderland. Meanwhile, Butch was waiting patiently for Scott to finish a screaming match with the newsprint supplier on the other end of the telephone receiver. Butch, a crusty old ex-editor spent most of his newspaper career as managing editor of the San Antonio Beacon.

When he became too right-wing for the publisher, Butch was promptly promoted to executive editor. Of course, the publisher's intent was to push him aside, knowing so little about editorial, but Butch was quick to turn the opportunity into effective management becoming a highly respected executive editor in the newspapers.

When SCOTT SILVER bought the San Antonio Beacon, Butch instantly hit it off and as quick was appointed the papers new publisher. Silver developed a great deal of respect for him. Men like Butch Logan commanded it.
While dishing out crap which Butch returned in kind, Silver relied heavily on Butch during his ownership of the Texas Daily. When Scott sold the failing paper un- ceremoniously, he brought Butch to Chicago with the promise of great things. Logan was also Silver's security blanket.

Butch Logan had it made. He could afford to do what he wanted, and he did! Butch had made a bundle in the stock market off of the stock options purchased from the San Antonio Beacon prior to the paper's sale to Scott Silver. Logan was close to retirement age and didn't really need a job in Chicago of all places, but came along, 'for the fun of annoying Silver,' he'd often say. When Lance McKnight, Scott's maverick investigative reporter turned executive vice-president of editorial, witnessed a blow up between Butch and Scott, Investigative Reporter Lance McKnight had been shocked over the verbal assault Butch laid on Scott. Lance asked Butch how he got away with talking to Scott that way and Butch's only response was, "What is he going to do? Fire me?"

Logan and McKnight shared a mutual respect for each other. Butch's demeanor and brisk attitude was well received by Lance, and Butch felt much the same way about Lance. In fact, the purpose of Butch's current visit to Scott Silver office was to talk about Lance.

Scott was finishing up the phone call he was on, "I don't give a crap if you can't find the tonnage to ship. You signed the contract and promised me eight thousand tons this month. You've only shipped five thousand so far. The last rolls arrived over a week ago. I don't want to hear your crap about having to ship to Chicago. Our agreement didn't specifically identify properties and you know it! Your obligation is to ship tonnage to Fourth Estate, so do it!" Scott slammed down the phone in a rage that Butch, saw as a second nature for Scott.

"Glad to see you in such a good mood today, boss," Butch teased.

"Screw you! What do you want now? I don't have all day to play with you."

Butch chuckled. He loved poking at Silver. "I want to talk to you about Lance McKnight."

"What about him? He's out of here! I'm having Tyson fire his ass, today."

"Scott, sometimes you couldn't find your nose for looking up your nostril. Lance is probably the best investigator in the business. Actually, he should probably have my job, but you're too ignorant to see it. Lance's done everything from delivering papers to managing editors. I know you want to get rid of him, but I'm in a bind here. If you expect us to be successful with this Yankee rag of yours, you need to give me some help." Logan gave Silver a moment to digest it all.

"I don't know anything about good investigative reporting. The only guy that did, left. Thanks to the schmuck that occupies this office!"

Scott Silver turned beet red, but Butch didn't give him a chance to respond.

"If you don't figure a way out of this, your smelly reputation only gets stinkier. Why not tell him he can keep his job until he finds a new one? Put McKnight under me. He could help us regroup and keep the place together. We work well together. Mainly because we both hate your guts."

"If I didn't think your barbs were just that, I'd have you shot. Listen, I'll call Burt and talk about our exit strategy. You call McKnight and do whatever you want to do with him. But, you keep him away from corporate editorial and further away from me. I don't want to see the guy's face. Capiche?" Scott stood. An indication he was ending their meeting.

"Scott," Butch began again as he stood, "those weren't barbs I was throwing at you. Lance and I really do hate your guts. You won't have to worry about him coming 'round to see you. By the way, drop the Italian act. It doesn't go well with your Southern accent." Without another word, Butch pivoted out of the antique chamber.

"Logan!" Scott yelled after him.

"Talk to the finger!" Butch replied, heading towards his office and ignoring Scott's protest.

Butch chuckled again, to himself this time.

Back at his desk, Silver's dilemma came to mind. A quandary Butch enjoyed creating. Butch knew Scott hated Lance and, at the same time, Butch knew Scott knew that Butch was right. Lance was the best candidate to fill the recently created hole at the Union for now.

Logan also believed that his manipulation would probably result in making his life a lot easier, since the McKnight and Silver relationship would result in their failure to communicate and, rather than fight Butch on making those communications better, Scott, and Lance, would keep their distance from each other. Butch and Lance would be left to run editorial together.

Butch had no intention of making Lance find another position outside the company, not until Butch was ready to retire himself. He thought Lance was a big part of the potential success in Chicago. Butch commended himself for pulling off what he thought was a major coup.

Butch Logan was interrupted by Bobby Scaletti walking into his office, then plopping down onto the couch. Scaletti could portray a convincing old country Italian at will. After all, he was a full blooded Italian, but not from Sicily, Italy—from Buffalo, New York.

"What are you doing here? They let you out of the New York State Pen on a weekend pass?"

"You ought to have a little more respect for your corporate superiors," Bobby replied jokingly. Scaletti was six feet tall. His trim build and salt and pepper hair accented refined, attractive features. Bobby Scaletti fostered a genuine affinity toward Butch. For that matter, everyone liked Butch, even his adversaries.

Butch Logan had the ability to disarm aggressors with quick witted, cynical or dry humor. Rather than get angry, Butch chose laughter. Bobby mistakenly set himself up again. "You may be corporate, but it's impossible for you to be superior. Wops and superiority, by definition is an oxymoron."

"Watch it, Logan. You're forgetting, I have friends in New York."

"You have goons in New York! It's unlikely you have any friends anywhere!"

"Touché!"

"Except for the fat guy in the corner office, right?" Butch asked referring to Scott's massive 350 plus pound body.

"You know, you at least ought to start showing some respect for Scott, if not for me," Bobby insisted.

"I will! As soon as he earns it!"

"No kidding, Butch. Someday you're going to go too far with Scott. He can joke around with the best of them, but if he starts taking your shit seriously, you can never tell what he'd do," Bobby warned.

"What's he going to do, fire me? I can only wish. Maybe some of your cement boots for my retirement?"

"He might." Bobby's face turned deadly serious for a fraction of a second and back to its good-natured, smiling mask. Butch didn't really notice the change.

"Okay, let's get real. How about backing my choice of McKnight to Scott?"

"I thought you said we were getting real. You're asking for the impossible dream. You been smoking something before work, Butch?"

Familiar with the need for horse trading when working with Bobby, he carefully stated, "I've lost my best investigative reporter. I need someone like McKnight to fill and whip up a system to make this paper more profitable."

"Sounds to me like your sales pitch should be to Lance first," Bobby said. "He's pretty P.O'd at Silver."

"Let me worry about Lance. The truth of the matter is, Scott has already approved, but I could use a little more reinforcement. You know how he changes his mind every couple seconds."

"When did he give you the okay?"

"About ten minutes ago. Just before you walked into my office."

"Yeah, well, then, I'm probably too late. By now he's already changed his mind. Fair warning, I'm not on his good side right now. I told him I'm getting a little tired of playing with his stuff, and I'm ready to get back to newspapering."

"Do me a favor and do what you can." Butch begged. "Deal!" Bobby got up to leave.

"Hey, you didn't say why you came to see me. What is it?"

"Yeah, I always come here first to cut my teeth, before I have to chew the fat with Silver.

Thanks!" Bobby headed toward Scott Silver's office.

Scott's cherubic beet red face and black onyx

eyes burned an imaginary hole through Bobby's approaching figure, while on a phone call with the same supplier he'd hung up during Butch's visit. "What do you mean you shipped the order to San Antonio? We don't own SanAntonio anymore! Who told you to do a thing that stupid?" Scott screamed.

As he listened to the answer, daggers shot from his eyes, all but piercing Bobby Scaletti's forehead as he entered. "Well, he's right here, so, I'll deal with him." Scott was straining to regain control. "Meanwhile, as far as I'm concerned, you still owe me three thousand tons. I suggest you ship it. And ship it now, to Chicago!" He lost the fight of keeping his frustration in check and slammed the phone down for the second time on his supplier who by now, must be suffering from temporary, although significant hearing loss.

"Why the hell did you ship the balance of the annual contract with Fourth Estate, Inc. to San Antonio after the sale?"

"Hey, it's good to see you too, Alex!" Bobby chided. "Don't ever call me Alex again! Look," Scott said, still blood red, "I'm getting fed up with your free-wheeling decisions Scaletti. I needed that newsprint here. We're down to only four days' supply."

"Well, you should have thought of that when you told me to ship it to San Antonio!" Bobby raised his voice, "Which, by the way, you were obligated to do, according to the sales agreement."

"I have never told you to ship that, or any newsprint to San Antonio," Scott lied. He remembered doing so but wasn't about to let Bobby off so easy. Besides, he felt like taking his anger out on somebody. Bobby was always a target. In fact, everybody was a target.

"Ya know what Scott? You have one hell of a selective memory." Bobby was heated. "Everyone told you not to offer the remainder of the contract to the seller during negotiations in Washington; that you'd need it in Chicago. You didn't want anyone to know you caved! That's why you told me to ship it to San Antonio. And speaking of Lance . . ."

Scott cut Bobby off in mid-sentence. "Who's talking about that jackass? What does he have to do with any- thing? Why is everyone so worried about him today? Is there something in the water that's turning everybody soft?"

"Lance is a good guy and an even better newspaper man. If you want people to believe you are running a respectable organization; you need a man like Lance McKnight. The industry considers McKnight one of the best. If you keep getting rid of the real newspaper folk, it will only be a matter of time before someone uncovers the Silver Bullet scam, and I don't want to be around when that happens."

Maybe you won't be around; Scott thought to himself.

"Look." Bobby continued, "It's not Lance's fault that you thought he was too close to everything. Hell, he's an investigative reporter, remember? He's the last person you want to nose around, especially now. Lance's a smart son-of-a-bitch, and frankly, made me uncomfortable knowing he was still at corporate. It's not McKnight's fault you got cold feet and want to can him."

"Get to the point, Bobby!" Silver was exasperated.

"The point is," said Bobby, "that you should t a k e Butch's advice and bring him over here. It will add to the legitimacy of this operation." Bobby always slipped back into a halfway recognizable New York accent when he got angry.

"Logan already got to you, eh?" Scott observed suspiciously. "Before or after he talked to me?"

"What difference does it make?" Bobby hesitantly replied, "After."

Silver took a moment to mull over Scaletti's concise recommendations. He'd already told Butch he could have Lance out of his desire to avoid a confrontation with Butch. The caveat was looking like the hero at Bobby's expense. Silver liked that.

"I already told Butch he could have McKnight."

"I know. Butch told me. We didn't want you to change your mind. Not that you have a tendency to do that, much."

"Oh, so now you and Butch are conspiring

against me? You, of all people, are supposed to be on my team," Scott pointedly said.

"As far as Butch is concerned, he's just trying to make the newspaper work. He doesn't suspect a thing. Logan thinks if he has Lance, he could relax. Figures McKnight may be the Union's only chance to become a real competitor and thrive in Chicago," Bobby assuringly added, "As for me? I am on your team, damn it! That's why I'm here."

Scott tugged on his shirt cuffs nervously; a crafted habit of Silver's while contemplating a response for an audience. It was a no-brainer, but he wasn't going to give Bobby the satisfaction of telling him so. Silver realized he was disenchanted with Bobby Scaletti, although he didn't exactly know why. Scaletti worked with him for what seemed like forever. Subconsciously, Scott envied Bobby's talent.

He wished he could conceive scenarios so perfectly orchestrated as Bobby could. Every angle, including his ass, were always covered.

The last thing Silver thought he needed now was this damn Wop giving him advice. "Like I said, Bobby, I have already given Butch the go ahead, so discussion's over. You just protect Silver Bullet for me! Do you understand?" "Gosh, boss, that sounds a little threating." Bobby joked half-heartedly, "You know, you shouldn't do that to me. You need me too much."

Scott chuckled as if he shared the jest. *I need you like I need a frigging' hole through my head*; he thought to himself. *We'll see how much I need you. We'll see.* "Let's get down to the real business," Scott commanded, "We need to move some of the funds."

Bobby was wary. It seemed to him that Scott was slowly becoming more and more disenchanted with him over the last several months, and the current discussion wasn't giving him any warm and fuzzy's. For whatever reason, Bobby sensed that Scott was purposely trying to distance himself from a longtime confidant.

Both men worked out Scott's calculations and agreed on the transactions that would need to be processed before Scaletti left town. Upon leaving Scott Silvers office, Bobby's feeling of unease increased. Earlier, Silver had asked him if they were square. Knowing Silver well, usually when he asked questions of that nature, Scott's normal demeanor was demanding, insulting or egotistical during their exchanges.

Moments ago, something else transpired. Something onerous; nevertheless, Bobby couldn't put his finger on why he felt that way. Maybe it was just the idea of being 'square' with Scott. He'd feel more comfortable if he had some kind of security plan worked out.

BOBBY DECIDED THAT IT WAS in his best interest to take precautions and to be on guard; to protect himself, in case he lost favor in Scott's eyes. He didn't want to believe that would ever happen! He'd been with Scott since the beginning, when Scott Silver bought the Buffalo Breeze. Bobby Scaletti had always been loyal to Scott and never shy about speaking his mind. He and Scott went at it like cats and dogs sometimes, but Scott would usually come to his senses and follow Bobby's advice before implementing one of his famous Silver hair-brained schemes. Scott was impulsive, and Bobby kept him practical.

One time Bobby told Scott, 'I can't keep you honest, but I can keep you realistic! We have a good thing going and there's no need to take stupid risks.' Scott agreed with him. No. Scott wouldn't get rid of him. Or would he? Again, Bobby didn't want to believe it, but he would still take steps to ensure Scott didn't get away with anything. Scott asked Bobby to transfer funds, funds from the Silver Bullet account. That meant Bobby would have to stop by their corporate offices before heading back to Buffalo, New York for the weekend. He thought about ditching the task and booking the next flight to Buffalo in an effort to take time to shake off surmounting concerns.

Bobby recalled a conversation he once had with his boss. "I could always transfer the funds from home," Bobby offered.

"That would be dangerous, too easy to trace these days. If anyone discovers Silver Bullet, I don't want to hand them a clear trail to follow," Scott explained.

"Yeah, you're right. Since I'm in Chicago now, it would seem odd if I didn't handle the transfers before flying back to Buffalo."

Bobby replayed the conversation in his head now, debating the possible outcomes. If Scott Silver was up to something underhanded, he wondered if he should tip someone off in Buffalo. No, that's a bad idea. He was in it as deep as Scott Silver, if not more deeply involved in Silver's fraudulent scheme. No, Bobby thought, and settled on using the office system. Transfers initiated from the office wouldn't seem suspicious.

Now all he had to do is make sure no one was there when he made the transfer. It was one thing to sit at the computer working on personal financial statements and spreadsheets, quite another preparing and transmitting funds over the Internet. Lance was sharp. If he noticed Bobby using the banking software, he'd ask questions.

Bobby had no valid reason to process financial trans- actions for the company. Scaletti had a set of keys to the Fourth Estate Incorporated suites. The building's security system was considerably weak, despite Lance's repeated protests. To prevent unwanted attention toward Fourth Estate, the building wasn't equipped with video surveillance. An access card system let workers into the lobby and common areas after hours. Unlike a key fob system, the archaic card reader currently in place didn't have the technology to record entries or exits.

"I'm not sure I like the lack of security," Scott had said to Bobby after renting the space.

"You and Lance both. But if we tighten up on security, someone's bound to think we're hiding something . . . like Silver Bullet, for instance. The more visible security we employ, the more it looks like we have something of great value or importance to protect."

"We do. In folders on the computer," Scott quickly pointed out.

"Nothing to worry about there. The files are all encrypted with a security program I wrote that can't be easily hacked,"

Since there was little chance he would be discovered entering the offices, Scaletti decided to wait for the office crew to go home. The last one would probably leave no later than 6:00 P.M. on a Friday night. Of course, that meant getting back to New York very late, but he was used to life on the road and unexpected delays. Bobby would be able to ensure that all FEI personnel had left by referring to the corporate parking list that he personally requested to be compiled for him.

The document identified every employee's vehicle information and assigned parking space. This knowledge would come in handy someday should he ever be asked to supply information to the new building managements for their records.

It was four o'clock, and Bobby decided to have a glass of white wine over at Gino's East to kill time. He walked up Michigan Avenue toward the Old Water Tower; one of the few buildings that survived The Great Chicago Fire of 1871 The fire blazed for three days destroying 17,000 structures, displacing one hundred thousand people and killing nearly 300. After getting to the restaurant he decided he'd take a cab back to FEI's Lake Shore offices about ten minutes to six.

As he sipped his wine, Scaletti was lost in thought, developing his protection plan against any unsuspected events.

MEANWHILE, SILVER had made his decision, after agonizing over it for two hours. Bobby had to go! Scott regretted it a little, but that's just the way it had to be.

Silver thought back on what Bobby had said earlier in their conversation, '. . . you need me too much.' "*I don't need anyone.*" Scott spoke out loudly to the mirror deep set into the cabinets behind his desk. One thing was clear, Scott thought, Bobby Scaletti knew too much about his off the books enterprises and could bring everything to a screeching halt. This would be the last time that Bobby transferred funds for Silver Bullet. Silver swiveled in his oversized leather chair, took his keys from his pocket, and opened up the bottom left drawer of his antique credenza. He wheezed because his obese body pressed firmly against the desk. Inside and nestled precisely in the center of the drawer surrounded in ruby red velvet, was a crimson colored smart phone. His hot line: he mused, a glorified prepaid burner phone making traceability nearly impossible.

Scott smiled as he admired his thorough and cunning planning of the enhanced point to point phone system. Scott methodically established the location to ensure he was the only one with access and the only one that would hear the ring through a blue tooth device. On the off chance, that he missed the phones ring, a dull, red, blinking light barely visible was recessed into the woodwork of the desk's exterior. If he were at his desk, the soft flicker would immediately gain his attention. Now that he had every detail formulated, it was time to enlist the services of the only person he could trust to install the elaborate, secret communication system.

Scott called in an ex-employee, Jack Creed, from San Antonio to install the jury-rigged system. "Jack, you're the best telecommunications guy around. I know you're not feeling well, but I could really use your help. I'll make it worth your while. The telecommunications group up here are light years behind the stuff you did for me in Texas."

Jack retired at fifty-six, not out of willingness, but, out of necessity. He had terminal cancer, fairly well advanced. Nevertheless, he agreed to come up as a consultant. Once there, Scott wondered if Jack would do him one more favor. "Oh! By the way, you're the only one I would trust to install my private line. I'd rather no one else be aware of it for security reasons."

Jack was flattered and installed it willingly. Scott knew Creed wouldn't dare betray his confidence and Jack would probably take it to his grave.

Scott calculated correctly. Two weeks after returning to San Antonio, Jack died.

He was very confident no one else knew the burner phone existed. Scott trusted that he successfully orchestrated the installation of the cleanest line available

Scott, with steadfast determination, dialed the Miami number.

"Yeah." A deep, raspy voice answered.

"I need you to take care of a problem for me, tonight!" Silver commanded.

"What's the problem?"

"Scaletti." There was silence for a fraction of a second except for, what may have been a barely audible gasp.

"Why Scaletti?"

"Since when do you ask questions? That's not what you're paid for. Just do it!"

"Alright." Warily the man asked. "Any stipulations?"

"Make it expedient," replied Scott. "I'll send the corporate jet right away, so you can get through Buffalo airport well before Scaletti."

Bobby called the cab to Gino's at twenty minutes to six. The dispatcher had told him it would be ten minutes, but it didn't arrive until two minutes after the hour. That was okay, Bobby thought, the later, it was, the more it helped to ensure that the corporate offices would be vacant.

When he arrived at FEI's new building, Bobby asked the driver, "Can you wait? It won't take long. I'm heading to the airport afterwards, so it should be worth your while."

"I'll wait," the cab driver replied.

Bobby entered the building; his first task was to ensure the corporate staff had left. That being done, he turned on the PC used for the funds' transfer. The computer was designated for his use, but he knew that others used it when he wasn't in the offices. Still, his security for a fund's transfer was impenetrable. In addition, he thought, FEI had no one on the IT staff that was technologically capable of hacking this transfer software. The information would bounce around the globe through multiple servers before connecting to the offshore bank holding the Silver Bullet account. Once he transferred the funds and received the transaction acknowledgement he could shut the system down. The next time the PC was started, no one would notice anything different or find the software folder because the executable file was a hidden file, and the encryption required a password.

I'm a genius, Bobby decided as he worked his way out of the building. Someone would have to be extremely knowledgeable to figure out what was going on with that program.

"Take me to Midway," he instructed the driver as he jumped in the back of the waiting cab. Bobby arrived at the airport about 6:45 P.M. for a 7:10 P.M. flight. He speed walked as fast as humanly possible toward the departing gate. At this time on a Friday night, the flight to Buffalo wouldn't be crowded or overbooked. The flight was likely to depart on time, and it did, without Bobby.

Scaletti missed it by only a few seconds. Now, he'd have to spend the night in Chicago. The layover wasn't a bad thing. He liked the city. It had great night life and tons of upscale hotels to choose from. However, he didn't like to paint the town alone and decided to give Silver a call to see if he had dinner plans. Perhaps they could come to a better understanding of the disturbing conversation that afternoon. Silver said he was busy and couldn't join him. Scott did verify that the transfer was made, and then rather abruptly hung up.

Bobby Scaletti booked a room at the Fairmont Chicago. The Fairmont Hotel's stunning skyline views were never tiring, and the location was close to the Millennium Hotel. After dinner, Scaletti would ponder his shaky relationship with his boss. He'd make it an early night in hopes of getting one of the first flights to Buffalo in the morning.

After hanging up on Bobby, Scott

immediately called Miami. "Little change in plans tonight. Scaletti is staying in Chicago tonight. I still plan to get the plane out there, but this should give you a little more time to plan your approach. Scaletti won't fly out 'till morning. I'll let you know the flight schedule. Scaletti always keeps me well informed."

EARLY SATURDAY MORNING Bobby started searching for available flights out, which were few and far between. Finally, he scheduled a 3:59 P.M. departure, landing in Buffalo Niagara International Airport two and a half hours later. This time, Scaletti would catch his flight using Chicago O'Hare International Airport.

For the first time that he could recall, Bobby had to leave his flight itinerary on Scott's answering machine. He made the bed, straightened the bathroom and checked out of his room. Bobby could think of nothing to do that would fit within the time he had to waste, so he loitered around the hotel shops until it was time to call a cab and head for the airport. The Taxi arrived about 2:00 P.M., that was cutting it close again, but he hated hanging around airports.

Out of breath from a two-pack-a-day cigarette habit, Bobby Scaletti sat in his usual seat; 1A, in first class seating. Long ago, Scaletti decided the sacrifice of his social life to that of a life on the road for Scott Silver, warranted first class bookings and service. Scott would rather see coach fares and fast food joints on his expense report, but always paid and reimbursed him the few times he had to use his own cash. One time, he told Scott he was too damn cheap for a guy, who is scamming millions.

"Welcome aboard, Mr. Scaletti! Can I get you anything tonight?"

Scaletti recognized the flight attendant, yet couldn't remember her name, and as unusual, she wasn't wearing a name tag. "Yeah, I'll have a white wine, no ice."

"I should have remembered," she scolded herself.

"I'm surprised you remembered my name. I can't say I did that as well. I don't remember yours."

"Candy," she said, "as in sweet." Candy's voice trailed as she entered the galley, peering around the corner facing Bobby as she prepared his beverage. When she returned Candy handed him a cup half-filled and set the rest of the wine in the tiny bottle onto the tray table.

"Candy, here's to a safe flight." With a smile, Bobby raised his glass in a toasting fashion. That was the extent of the exchange between Candy and Bobby until landing.

Bobby's mind remained fixed on his uneasy feeling about Scott Silver. Scaletti needed to protect himself from his mania, somehow. During the flight, Bobby began to formulate a plan. It was far too risky Bobby thought, to document anything. It had to be discovered by someone with a savvy mind, access to their corporate offices in a position to stumble upon it, and then know what to do with the data. On the flip side, if it was easily figured out, the documentation could get into the wrong hands. Bobby was healthy, wealthy, and wise and didn't want to find himself in the slammer for the rest of his natural life or dead.

Only one person would fit the bill—Lance McKnight. Scaletti knew McKnight had the capability to discover the meaning of what may seem to be, barely related pieces of information. Bobby witnessed McKnight in action plenty. Lance did this kind of thing in his sleep. He was that good.

Bobby would prepare a letter for Lance McKnight that would expose Silver Bullet. Claudio Falco, his attorney, could hold the envelope to only be sent to McKnight if something perilous happened. The note also had to be ambiguous enough to mean little to anyone who may read it through mishap or interception.

Bobby knew he could trust Claudio Falco. Claudio was outside the organization. He was an old friend and legal counsel of his fathers. After the reading of his father's will, Scaletti hired Falco to prepare a new will.

Retaining Mr. Falco to safeguard the letter and honor the terms of release was the best option because Claudio would be one of the first notified upon his demise. As far as Bobby knew, Claudio did not know of Scott Silver and was sure Silver did not know anything about Claudio Falco.

Scaletti planned to tell Scott to think twice before try- ing to mess him up. He didn't know how Scott would react. Or did he? Yes, he thought; he knew. Scott would be fuming! Scaletti wasn't about to let those thoughts deter him from doing the right thing. He'd worry over the consequences, if any, much later. The time came to look out for himself and not Scott Silver.

Bobby dug into the inside suit coat pocket, pulled out his smart phone and looked up Falco's number. After two rings, the familiar voice answered.

"Hello."

"Mr. Falco? Bobby Scaletti."

"Bobby. How are you? Where are you? You sound like you're in a plane."

"I am in a plane on my way back to Buffalo, from Chicago. I need to see you tonight. We'll land 'bout 10:30 P.M.," Bobby explained, looking at his watch and allowing for the time change.

"That's late for me, Bobby. Couldn't we get together in the morning?"

"No, I really need to see you tonight. It's urgent, please Mr. Falco?"

"Well, okay. Bobby, I'll be there. It'll take me a while. What flight are you on? What time did you say you'd land?"

"Ten thirty. The plane taxis to gate four. There's

a small service bar two gates down toward baggage claim. I'll meet you there. When I walk in, don't let on that you know me. I'll leave a newspaper on the bar. Inside, will be envelopes with instructions. Hopefully, later this weekend, I can explain everything more clearly,"

"What's all this cloak-and-dagger stuff, Bobby? It doesn't sound like something I want to get ..."

Bobby cut him off. "Please trust me Mr. Falco, I can't tell you now, I'll explain in person, as soon as I can."

"Alright, Bobby." Claudio agreed reluctantly. "I'll see you there, but I'll pretend I don't see you there, right?"

"You got it! Thanks, Mr. Falco." Bobby ended the call. Maybe I'm overreacting, he thought. Nevertheless, he went with his gut, and once he made up his mind about something, he wasn't comfortable until he saw it through. He didn't want to second guess his decisions, so the best thing to do was to proceed with extreme caution. Bobby opened his planner and started to write something he hoped would never be given to Lance McKnight.

Bobby quickly pulled an envelope from his briefcase and addressed it to Lance, using the information from his corporate list. He took another sheet from his planner and wrote to Claudio Falco.

Scaletti put Falco's note along with a sizable check into another envelope addressed to Falco and put both into a legal sized mailer. After stuffing the entire package inside his jacket, Bobby prayed that the FedEx would never be sent.

The pilot finally turned on the fasten seat belt light, and Candy announced the crew's preparation for landing in Buffalo. Ten minutes later, they were on the ground on time. As Bobby walked past Candy, he asked if he could have the copy of the Union that was sitting on the galley counter.

"We recently bought this newspaper," Bobby explained. "I think it's about time I read it."

Candy laughed, handed him the paper and said, "Goodnight, Mr. Scaletti."

"Goodnight, Candy," Bobby left the plane, entered the terminal and headed for the service bar. As he walked, he slipped both the envelope addressed to Lance McKnight, and the other addressed to Claudio Falco between the pages of the Chicago Union. When he got to the bar, he was grateful to see Falco, his thin, lanky torso propping up a stool at the far end of the bar. He looked fidgety. The bartender was leaning casually up against the counter making small talk with Claudio. The rest of the bar and floor tables were empty.

Claudio was the nervous type, thought Bobby, although his dad always claimed he was one hell of a lawyer and must be Sixty-five, seventy by now? Bobby sat two stools away but didn't acknowledge him.

"I'll have a shot of Wild Turkey," Bobby told

the bar- tender. He drank it in one gulp, left a twenty-dollar bill and the newspaper on top of the bar and headed toward the ground transportation exit.

Claudio took the last few swallows of his coffee, preparing to pick up the paper any second, but the bartender had decided to pick up the money and, at the same time, the abandoned newspaper which he was about to throw away. Claudio's heart pounded ferociously as he spoke,

"Excuse me, Sir; may I take a look at that paper?"

"It's a Chicago paper. Still want it?"

"Yes. I used to live there." Claudio lied. "Thought it might be interesting to read about the old hometown on my flight to Denver." Claudio was positive that he wasn't convincing and felt weak, as if he was about to faint.

"Knock yourself out." The bartender handed over the paper. "It's all yours."

Claudio accepted it, threw enough cash down to cover his coffee and a nice tip, and followed Bobby Scaletti. Not too close. Bobby was clear about being seen together. He kept a fair distance as he pulled out the manila mailer and the envelope addressed to him reading the note as he walked. Claudio didn't understand what was going on and wouldn't be satisfied until he knew Bobby was all right. Keeping his distance he watched Bobby exit the terminal.

O∪TSIDE THE TERMINAL DOORS, a Super Shuttle van was parked directly in front and a cab stand was to his right. No one was there, but two empty cabs with drivers waiting for fares. A neatly uniformed Buffalo police officer working the transportation line stopped briefly to speak with both cab drivers. Bobby Scaletti could faintly hear the officer telling the closest cab driver to keep things moving along. He was trying to decide whether to take a cab or the Shuttle. The convenience of the cab made much better sense. The police officer dropped his mag light. As he bent down to pick up the light, the officer also secured a mechanism to the undercarriage of the taxi. He was positive the guy heading toward him now, didn't notice and no one else was around. As he rose, the officer finished by saying, "Okay. Then!" as he tapped the door frame twice with one hand, to signal a firm, got it? The officer moved away from the door, nearly bumping into Bobby and said, "Excuse me, Sir."

"No problem," Scaletti answered and slid into the back seat. "2563 Oak Tower Lane, please."

As Claudio Falco exited the terminal, he noticed Bobby getting into a cab. Something seemed off about this whole evening, so Claudio decided to follow him. As he began to get in, the taxi Bobby was in started to drive away. He watched the taillights, and out of the corner of his eye noticed a police officer put a phone to his ear. Then came a deafening sound and the brightest of lights. The loud noise was that of a small heat-seeking missile.

Windows shook, nearly shattering. The canopy fascia rattled fiercely as the yellow cab Claudio Falco was watching, exploded right before his eyes! Flames ripped throughout the air! The cab driver's hair and upper body were ablaze as he struggled to free himself, but was trapped and burned to death, as did Bobby Scaletti.

"Oh, my God!" is all that Claudio could utter; he was paralyzed, gazing blankly, unsure of what he had just witnessed. Falco nearly lost his balance as he took in the scene and grabbed hold of the door of the cab. Oblivious to the screaming taxi driver, his heart was racing, like it was about to pound right through his shirt.

He looked around, and noticed the uniformed policeman was gone, probably in his squad calling for backup and emergency personnel. No one else was around. Slowly, Claudio released his grip of the cab and staggered back inside to the empty terminal. The only other human being he could see, was the girl behind the Budget car rental counter. He forced his feet to shuffle the twenty- five yards to the counter and fell upon it, barely able to make his request.

"Could you Fed-Ex this for me?" Claudio gasped as he dropped the envelope addressed to Lance McKnight onto the top of the counter and fell to the ground.

2
All's Well That Ends

LANCE MCKNIGHT GOT IN his Nissan sedan in the parking garage of a new building overlooking Chicago's Gold Coast that was littered with miles of upscale apartments and condos along Lake Michigan offering the rich and famous a glorious view of the windy city. Waiting to take his turn onto Lake Shore Drive, and absentminded, Lance watched the slapping of the waves against Lake Michigan's shoreline.

Mid-September was pleasant in Chicago. The humidity during the summer was gone, and a cool breeze came off the Lake. Temperatures were in the high sixties and low seventies.

However, all of this was lost on Lance as he turned South on Lake Shore Drive, toward the Eisenhower Expressway heading west out of Chicago's Loop. He was distracted by the whirling flap of a helicopter as it descended on the landing pad of the hospital two blocks north. Flight for life, thought Lance, how appropriate, that was what he'd be doing for the next couple months.

Whenever Lance got into an automobile, his reaction was virtually always the same. His hands and feet seemed to slip into an automatic pilot mode, and his brain concentrated on practically everything except the operation of the vehicle. For most drivers, and most of Lance's passengers, this seemed extremely dangerous. Lance, however, seemed to have perfected the feat. It was as if the right side of his brain took over while his left side operated on auto pilot. Lance did nothing but reflect on the loss of his job; convinced he would never find another like it. He was obsessed with feeling like a failure, even though in the back of his mind, he knew he wasn't. Everything would surely work out, one way or another. As he inched his way through rush-hour traffic, he considered his career.

Lance's fist job in the newspaper business was when he was ten. He delivered seven different publications, across the same Chicago suburbs where he had coincidently purchased a new home, many years later. There were times; Lance McKnight wished he had never started delivering papers.

During some of the grueling Chicago winters of his youth, when he was crunching through snow or twenty degrees below zero days, he considered quitting his routes. Had he done so, he wouldn't be in the same predicament he was in, or need of a job. On the other hand, he didn't know what else he would have wanted to do. Lance liked being associated with newspapers, loved the mystique and didn't mind the money newspapers made for him. The editorial department and investigative reporting were where his career led Lance. Generally, he was paid well, and above the standard rates because of his vast experience.

Early on he saw a chance for advancement and the money he could make would be up to him.

His father didn't make a great deal, and with a large family to support didn't have a lot of extra cash to pass around to the kids. Lance always liked what money could buy, the stuff some of the other kids' fathers could afford. He started delivering papers, which was the beginning of a well-rounded career in newspapers.

At THIRTY-NINE, LANCE accomplished a great deal. At least, he thought so. After working his way through four years of college with various newspaper delivery and administrative jobs at the local news agency, he landed a
job as a reporter at a small newspaper in California.

McKnight reported on newsworthy events for eight years before being promoted to managing editor and held that position there for three years. Since it was such a small newspaper, to many it sounded like more of a major accomplishment, than he believed it was.

Lance McKnight was a rebel with a cause, interested in only doing things his way, and in a fairly self-righteous manner. He had a tendency to resort to shoot from his mouth without giving a thought to diplomacy, landing him in trouble repeatedly.

Even when he was a kid, he didn't think the trainers in the news agencies knew how to prepare carriers for their routes. None of the instructors he came across, really knew the ins and outs of paper routes the way he did and doubted any of them ever carried a newspaper very far, let alone hundreds every morning like clockwork, day after day, year after year.

In the process, Lance learned the most efficient way to deliver papers. Sure, he'd listen to the trainers, nod at the appropriate times and acting all enthusiastic, then go out there and do it his way. Lance McKnight may have been a renegade but, for him, it paid off. His dedication and efficiency earned the respect of many, therefore he was presented with carrier awards in spite of his unorthodox methods.

As a district manager, Lance was given the chance to train carriers within his division and passed on some of the knowledge he developed as a carrier. McKnight's customized guidelines were noticeably appreciated by the carriers, particularly the training on collections and tip generation.

One of the things Lance's father taught him was how to procure a decent Christmas tip.

Before collections in November and December, he purchased holiday cards When he went to collect, he handed the customer their card and graciously wished them a Merry Christmas. Even Scrooges shamed themselves into giving Lance a tip. Lance modified this proven system further. Since he delivered numerous publications, he would also purchase several cards and make multiple visits to his customers. Many of the collections were from the same household.

After the third visit, customers would question him by asking, "Aren't you the boy who delivers the Shopper? I thought I already gave you a tip?"

"Yes," Lance would answer politely, "but I also deliver your Citizen." Nine out of ten times, Lance would walk away with another tip. One Christmas, at the height of his carrier career, Lance made fifteen hundred dollars on tips.

Despite the ingenuity, Lance was often in bad graces with his superiors. Lance's first big career blunder was in California, after being named the "Youngest Managing Editor" in one of the largest media groups in the United States at the time.

When the company decided to squeeze all of their management to earn more and better editorial awards and recognition during one of their meetings, Lance McKnight, stood, faced the senior vice president of the company and said, "Listen, I've delivered the best for community recognition of any of the papers in this group for the last two years and there's not much to improve upon. We're already recognized as one of the best in Investigative Journalism. You don't know 'Jack' about this property anyway. How could you? You just fly a couple thousand miles once or twice a year for a brief visit, and you think that qualifies you to make editorial calls?"

The entire room was still. Lance's immediate supervisor was dumbfounded. Later that afternoon, he suggested to Lance that he develop some polish.

That little episode got McKnight a one-way ticket to Oakland, California, and one of the company's dumping grounds for the bad boys. A promotion, they insisted, and told Lance that a one-year stint as an investigative reporter, under the publisher, Richard Wittier, would give him that sorely needed polishing of corporate moxie. To his misfortune, one year turned into five, with continual pledges of greener pastures to come, every year or so.

As fate would have it, Wittier was a good mentor for Lance. McKnight learned a lot about the inner workings of the editorial side of big newspapers in a competitive environment. And during his tenure, there McKnight efficiently ran the city desk and editorial page. After five years of empty promises, Lance started job hunting.

The San Antonio Beacon in San Antonio Texas offered Lance the vice-presidency of editorial. McKnight believed that the Beacon was a better newspaper company, and happily accepted the position. Shortly after his arrival, it became clear that the San Antonio Beacon was in worse financial shape than he was told, so Lance developed a plan that called for some very severe expense cuts in the editorial staffing, as a means to keep the paper afloat.

When he presented a restructuring plan, McKnight told them if they did not have the stomach to implement the cuts, they should consider selling the paper. He never thought they would do it.

Three months later, the San Antonio Beacon was sold, along with Lance McKnight, to Scott Silver, one of news- paper's best-known wheelers and dealers; the undisputed King of the leveraged buy-out.

Scott made all of Lance's suggested cuts and then some. The first year turned out well, financially but while the economy continued to worsen, Silver kept giving the advertisers deeper discounts. Discounts were the only way the paper could remain competitive and profitable, Silver would say. Lance had no idea Scott Silver cared little about the survival of the Beacon. Advertising revenues kept dropping, as did circulation numbers.

By the middle of year two, Scott grew disenchanted with the paper and the money it was losing. He put it up for sale and announced a move to Chicago, Illinois. In the interim, he asked Lance McKnight to be the executive vice president of editorial, for the corporate offices of Fourth Estate, Inc., containing headquarters for most of Scott Silver's business enterprises. The position would pay very well but would require relocation to Chicago.

Since Lance reorganized the San Antonio, many of his responsibilities there decreased, and centered more around support by way of guidance for other papers' Scott Silver owned. As needed, Scott would enlist his help to evaluate the editorial quality and area demographics of newspapers Silver was interested in acquiring.

"All you need to do is make sure the editorial is high quality for our current properties and give on call support for sales and delivery," Scott said, after Lance McKnight accepted the corporate position. "I never really have to see you much, and if you think you need information, don't ask. I'll decide if you need to have any," Silver added as he stomped out of the office.

Lance never really could figure Scott out. Even when he thought, he was anticipating Scott's needs, he'd find the opposite. Like the time he went into Scott's office to discuss a project in the works; "The paperwork for the refinancing is complete. Do you want to take a look before it's sent?"

"Do whatever you have to do with it!"

THE NEXT DAY, Scott came storming into Lance's office. "Where the hell are the refinancing numbers? I need to see them before they go out. We may not want to give them the whole story," Scott explained angrily.

"Scott, I asked you if you wanted to see them yesterday.

You told me to do whatever I had to do."

"And that didn't include letting me see them?" Scott scowled.

"Scott. . ." Lance threw up his arms. Throwing up his arms became a trademark for Lance nearly every time he dealt with Scott, that and staying away from Scott as much as possible.

All of this didn't allow for the best relationship between the two. But, Lance thought he was getting most things right, except for one—he was sure that he never handled properly in Scott's eyes; his relationships with Scott's bankers. When Lance tried to explain the editorial pluses and minuses to the bankers, Scott would follow behind him contradicting everything Lance had said.

One day Silver declared, "We're selling the San Antonio Daily paper and moving corporate headquarters to Chicago." Lance knew that Scott had to bail out of his bad investment in Texas and was fortunate to find an "old friend and associate," a sucker, more accurately put to buy the failing newspaper.

Lance wouldn't mind the move, mainly because he had grown up in Chicago. In fact, his mother and some of the family were still there.

Unfortunately, so was his ex-wife, Jill. Fortunately, his daughter Devon, was still a minor and they lived together just outside the city.

Another complication with the move to Chicago was Kait; Kait Adams. A striking woman as opinionated as she was pretty. She and Lance met while serving as board members of the Chamber of Commerce in San Antonio. They hit it off right away. By the end of their first week's acquaintance, they had dated three times. They fell in love and within months were living together with Lance's dog Rusty and occasional visits from Devon. Actually, Rusty was Devon's Cocker Spaniel, but Lance had fallen in love with the dog when Devon first picked him out.

That evening, Lance McKnight told Kait and asked her to come to Chicago with him. "Why would anyone want to go from San Antonio to Chicago? Its cold up there isn't it? It even snows there doesn't it?"

"Survival?"

"In the snow? Maybe for you, but not for me. I must be in love!"

So, Lance sold his house in San Antonio and closed on the offer for a home in Hinsdale, Illinois, a nice affluent western suburb of Chicago, before the actual move so they could get acclimated before his duties of executive vice president of editorial resumed.

Unbeknown to all, and also prior to the big move, Scott Silver hired another executive vice president for editorial of Fourth Estate, Inc., Burt Tyson. Although Tyson was still recovering from a blunder a year ago in New Mexico, Tyson was the kind of editorial type, who had failed repeatedly, but somehow managed to keep employed.

Silver was well aware of his history; it was one of the reasons he fit the bill.

Burt Tyson was really excited to be at the helm again. Mr. Silver had given him files on everyone he would need to know and the full authority to hire and fire as he deemed just. Abreast of the people under Scott Silver, he envied Lance McKnight's status and access to everything, especially Scott Silver. Lance McKnight would have to go; the sooner the better. And today, as it turned out, was his lucky day. Burt won't have to connive at all. Mr. Silver just told him to give McKnight notice of termination. Burt enjoyed writing the message left on McKnight's desk Friday morning; summoning Lance to his office upon arrival.

"This is typical." Lance told Tyson. "Silver never had the guts to do the messy things himself! What's his problem anyway?"

"You just piss him off, I guess. I don't know." Burt Tyson lied. "Mr. Silver never explains his actions."

"You mean to screw his employees like he

screws every- one else, don't you? And you're just the guy who came out of the blue to deliver the message. Right? I get it! I piss him off?" Lance was very outraged. Enough to set the record straight by pointing out, "I saved his ass in our newest buy, as I always do. Doesn't enter the equation, does it, Burt 'ol Boy? Want to know why I pissed Silver off? Because I pissed them off; The buyers who were trying to cheat us, the bankers that were after the interest and Mr. Alex Scott Silver only cared about dumping this rag!" Lance screamed.

"Let's put it this way, McKnight," Burt nodded and raised his brow, "Mr. Silver doesn't think he needs you anymore."

"No, I guess not, apparently he has you now. You're so eager to do his dirty work and applaud his idiotic whims!"

"Look, you can stay through the next few pay periods or so. You'll find another job by then. It's the best I could get for you. He wants you gone, McKnight."

"That supposed to make me feel better?" Lance said as he stomped out of Burt Tyson's office and out of FEI's building.

Alex Scott Silver and John Patrick Beecher started Fourth Estate, Inc., years earlier with the purchase of the Buffalo Breeze, in New York. Lance could never figure out why Beecher got involved with Silver to begin with. Upon reflection, Lance guessed it was because Beecher singlehandedly destroyed his family's newspaper. John Beecher was wealthy and either ignorant, careless or senile, but probably a mixture of all three. John Beecher put up the ten-million dollar down payment for their fifty-million dollar loan. Silver's investment was his expertise, which was management through intimidation and fear. The duo were fairly successful in spite of themselves, growing their prosperous newspaper empire into what it is. Lance knew he contributed to FEI's success, since John hired him and took advantage of his experience and Scott just used him as a fixer or a scapegoat.

McKnight wondered what John Beecher was going to do when he discovered Scott Silver terminated him. John, faults and all, was the only reason he decided to suck it up and cash the checks as long as Scott kept signing them, and Burt kept handing them over. He didn't care if "Burt and Ernie" excluded him on investment matters now. Beecher was little more than a well-paid handsome fixture, in a nice office with a view, to be used as needed. For now, McKnight decided it best to keep a low profile and wait for the fireworks.

To think, weeks earlier, he was on top of the world. After turning around his own pessimism about buying another number two newspaper in a truly competitive metropolitan market, they closed the Chicago Union deal. He married Kait

Adams and honeymooned in Cozumel, Mexico. Kait was his mouthy Southern Belle and life was great; until they returned to Chicago and Burt Tyson nudged him out the door.

Now Lance was depressed. He'd have to work around people he began to despise and cram job searching into a hectic daily routine. He didn't want to see his wife worry for him either and hoped Kait didn't regret marrying him and moving away from her life in San Antonio, Texas.

"What now?" Kait was sure her husband had a plan and would rely on his wisdom.

"I really don't know, Dear," Lance replied. "There's only one thing I'm sure of; Alex Scott Silver's parents must have known that their son would grow up to be an ASS. That's why they made sure his character could be spelled with his initials!"

Kait resisted the strong urge to giggle by forcing her lips together tightly wondering how Lance could be so clever and funny at a time like this, and not even realize it?

"I don't think he has any redeeming value as a human being, whatsoever! Like after divorcing his first wife; his teenage son got into serious legal trouble and thrown into a detention center. Scott filed a motion to challenge the child support order. The kid's incarceration meant he was 'otherwise emancipated' as stated in their divorce decree, therefore, he shouldn't have to pay child support to his ex-wife while the boy was locked up!" He paused and looked into Kait's eyes and asked, "Can you believe that? He lost the fight and also lost the boy. His son committed suicide while in Juvenile. I heard Silver actually said, 'All is well that ends well.' I mean really?"

Lance McKnight thought about how patient Kait had been with his rant and finished reveries just in time to exit to Ogden Avenue.

Off of the freeway he fought sixteen blocks with umpteen traffic lights leading to the McKnight residence. It was only nineteen miles from the office to his front door, but it generally took at least an hour during rush hour. Lance pulled down the driveway, shut the car off and then glanced into the rear-view mirror, efficiently combing his light-brown hair with his fingertips in an attempt to be presentable for his lovely, new bride. He then hefts his husky, nearly six-foot body out of the car.

Lance always claimed to be six feet tall. Somehow, the number made him feel more masculine. Silly as it was, the fact that he was never able to reach the six-foot mark made him feel as if he had failed somewhere along the way. So, Lance tried to convince himself and others that he was as tall as his aspiration. Lance walked over to the mailbox and grabbed the stack of envelopes and flyer's, mostly junk mail. He entered through the front door greeting Kait with a kiss.

"Your momma's here, we went to lunch, and then she came over to help unpack the stuff that's been sitting untouched, since the move. She is upstairs right now, reorganizing the extra bedroom linens and things."

"Well, I hope she's not bothering you,"

"Your mom couldn't bother anyone if she tried. And besides, when she's done I'll just rearrange it the way I want it. Now don't you go telling her I said that! It's not the way it sounds. I really appreciate your momma's help, but I just want the things the way I want them." Kait really did appreciate the help. The act of unpacking and wiping shelving down would be well worth extra rearranging.

"Wouldn't it be easier if you put the stuff where you wanted it in the first place?"

Kait smiled, "Not unless I want more to do, and hurt your mom's feelings."

"I get your point," then Lance yelled facetiously toward the ceiling, "Hey Mom, I'm home!"

"Hello, sweetheart." Janice McKnight echoed from somewhere upstairs. Janice moved next to the banister railing and stood looking down into the foyer.

She was a short woman with nice-looking features and an unbelievable ability to survive; Janice was tough but would rather people thought otherwise.

"You know, I keep getting turned around in this house. It's so big. I don't know where I am half the time. Could be a week before I turn up again!"

Indeed, the house was vast. Precisely five thousand square feet with a three car garage built on a third of an acre. "What have you guys been up to today?" Lance's curiosity was genuine.

"Oh, I've had those old warranty people in and out all day trying to fix up all their mistakes. I have a feeling that it'll never get all done,"

"I've been looking for myself since lunch," Janice replied loudly with a concerned tone, which came as no surprise to her son, Lance.

The McKnight's may have had a much larger home than necessary for the two of them, but after selling the house in San Antonio, Lance felt it was a great real estate investment that would build equity and a nice foundation toward their new life together. He had "inherited" the San Antonio house from Jill, along with all of the mortgage payments and tax consequences, when they divorced and Jill left San Antonio with their daughter, Devon.

"If you want them to finish the punch list, you have to get on top of them," Lance winked.

"I hope you don't mean that literally, You're the only one I want to get on top of."

"Really you two!" Janice protested, "Now pardon me for saying so, but you really shouldn't be talking that way in front of your mother."

"Mom, you've heard a lot worse. Besides you

shouldn't eavesdrop."

"You're right. I'd better finish up the fourth bedroom. I'll be down in a bit."

"The fourth bedroom," Lance mumbled to himself and tried to imagine what they could use the spare rooms for. Lance pulled Kait toward him, "and you're the only one I want on top of me," and he kissed her gently. "I love you, but I hate everything else." The minute he said it, he wished that he had stopped after the first three words.

"You really have to get out of this mood. You've been moping around since Tyson let you go."

"You'd be moody too, if you had lost your job right after getting married and buying a nice, three- quarter million- dollar house."

"You forgot the part where you moved across the United States. And I did lose my job due to our moving here. But I gained more than I gave up."

"I was hoping we'd get a whole new life's start. Not ruin our careers."

"I didn't marry you for your money or what you could give me."

"No, but having nice things help, don't they?" Lance tested cynically.

Kait wasn't about to answer. She knew her husband had something on his mind that needed to be released. "What did ya'll do today?"

"We all," Lance mocked, "listened to Scott change his mind five times about whether he was going to buy the Nashville paper or not. The guy is such a joke! How he ever became so successful, I'll never know. He can't make up his mind from one minute to the next. Pete Geary, I think you met him once or twice, negotiated the sale of the Nashville Messenger to Scott Silver for thirty-five million dollars. Even though the Excelsior Newspaper Group offered to pay forty million."

"What? That's ridiculous. Who in their right mind would do that? Why would they leave millions on the table like that?"

"Geary convinced them Silver was a better operator and cared more about the newspaper tradition than Excelsior. Geary lied through his teeth." Lance shrugged a shoulder. "Scott signed the deal to buy the Messenger and has his usual buyer's remorse. Every day since the closing, Scott's been in and out of Pete's office, asking whether or not it was the right investment. Pete came to me yesterday and asked me to go over the deal and research it all, you know, do my former job. I mean Burt Tyson's job; so sneaky Pete can calm Scott down and out of his way."

"Now be nice, Lance." Kait could see that Lance's emotions were escalating.

"Very funny, ha, ha. I don't have a lot to be pleasant about . . ."

"Oh, get off the 'Oh poor Lance' bit!" Kait raised her voice.

When he looked into her eyes, something akin to anger was within them. He was about to concede by changing the subject until his mother's voice resounded.

"What's going on down there?" she yelled. "You two fighting?"

"No Mom, of course not. We're opening the mail loudly. Stop being so nosy."

"Oh, by the way, Federal Express delivered an envelope this morning." Kait was hoping to table talk of work for the night. Nevertheless, a FedEx was usually important. Kait handed it off and gave him some space.

Lance looked at the postmark and return address was from Buffalo Niagara International Airport.

"So, whachya thinks in the FedEx?"

"I don't know, Dear, but we're fixin' to find out!" Lance had to poke fun at Kait's colloquialisms, then in conspiracy theory fashion he said, "Maybe John caught wind his partner really screwed up and decided to show Scott, who has the bigger purse strings and not only brings me back, I'm reinstated as the chairman of the board, along with full pension benefits." Lance joked; half wishing it was true. "The first thing I'm going to do doing is hire you, Mrs. McKnight, to be my sexy assistant, and together we will fire those bozos for ruining our post honeymoon."

To THE LAUGHTER OF HIS WIFE, he quickly ripped open the package and then the envelope with his name written on it. His eyebrows narrowed, and confusion showed in his face. "This is really strange," he said after reading the short note inside. "It's from Bobby Scaletti. The note makes no sense."

"Bobby Scaletti?"

"Huh?" Lance said with an absent mind. "Yeah, the crazy Italian, who took us to dinner in San Antonio a few months back."

"I know that, silly. Hey, over here, look at me. What did Mr. Scaletti send? Doesn't look like much."

"Not sure, Babe, makes no sense to me. Bobby Scaletti was Scott's first Chief Financial Officer. The last several years he's been Scott's personal financial adviser. Still lives and works out of Buffalo. Flies to Chicago every so often to cook Scott's books," Lance explained.

"What? Bobby Scaletti? A crook? We had dinner with a crook? He seemed so . . ."

"Whoa, Kait, slow down, Mama Mia! Nothing cryptic here; it's just everything about this makes no sense. Why didn't Bobby Scaletti say something when he was in Chicago last week? Or better yet, call me?"

"That's the second time you said it didn't make sense, but not telling me what you read, Lance. What does it say?" Kait was demanding to know, word-for-word.

Experience had proven there was no point in trying to hide anything from Kait. When his bride had her curiosity up, she wouldn't stop

53

pestering until satisfied. "He says he realizes that I'm in a tough position, so he wanted to help out. Apparently, I'll be sent to the Union to fill in for the investigative reporter who left." That's just like Silver, he thought for a few seconds. Scott's paying me to do nothing and thinks he's being cheated, even though he fired me.

Lance continued and read the rest out loud, "There's a Silver Bullet which will pass through the gateway with the keys to success. Then he wishes me good luck. That's it." Lance concluded.

"Wha . . . I mean, what do you think it means? Sounds so corny, don't ya think?"

"I don't know, babe. I don't know what he's talking about at all." Lance raised his voice an octave higher than his arms.

"Okay, don't get so testy,"

"Sorry. Well, I'm not even going to think about it right now. Hearing from Bobby has given me an appetite for Italian. Let's go out to eat tonight. We'll go to La Bella's."

"You don't have to ask me twice."

"Come on, Mom, we're going for pasta," Lance called. "You mean spaghetti? I wonder where did your younger generation get all these fancy schmancy words for everyday foods? When I was your age, we called it spaghetti, ravioli, manicotti," she informed her son. The words came loudly from somewhere on the second floor.

"Okay," Lance yelled back. "Do you want to come eat spaghetti with us if you can somehow find your way to the staircase?"

"You don't have to ask me twice."

Lance looked at Kait with a grin, shook his head, then mumbled something about echoes as he heard his mother coming down to the foyer.

Lance awoke early the next morning with absolutely no desire to get up. Although it was only Tuesday, it was the morning after he was fired, and would have preferred to stay in bed for another twelve hours with a pillow pressed tightly over his head to avoid the penetration of any light. Lance wanted to cocoon himself inside the blanket and hide from the outside world forever. This was the only way he could be safe, protected! He knew this feeling. It was depression and he hated it, but he couldn't seem to stop it.

After his divorce two years earlier, Jill took Devon back to Chicago rather than stay in San Antonio. Lance slowly fell into a deep, dark depression, convinced that he would never see his ten-year-old again. Eventually, he became so distraught that he felt there was nothing to live for and even contemplated suicide. Of course, none of his fears came to pass, but at the time he was convinced they were real and there was no one who could have told him any different.

Lance had flown Devon in once a month and had her six weeks in the summer, every Easter school break and every other Thanksgiving and Christmas. However, in the early days after the divorce, he never would have believed it possible.

Now he was blessed with her living close by in Chicago. There's always something to be thankful for he guessed.

Even so, Lance remembered how his depression had started out back then and was afraid it was happening all over again now. His ego and self-respect had taken a major blow with the news that his services were no longer needed by FEI. He felt himself slipping back. He became lethargic, sleeping thirteen to fourteen hours a day, using everything he had, physically and emotionally, to perform the simplest tasks like getting himself out of bed in the morning or driving to the office. He managed to get by thus far fighting off depression determined to snap out of it.

The last thing he wanted was to have this to affect his relationship with Kait while thinking it may have already started to do so.

As he lay in bed, trying to force himself out of it and dress for work, he reflected on the note he'd received from Scaletti the night before. Its contents had intrigued him, and this acted as a catalyst for Lance to arise and face the day. He showered, shaved, and dressed for the office.

When Lance came out of the master bath into the bedroom suite, Kait was sitting up in the bed, sipping her coffee and staring at the TV which she had turned on to her habitual waker-upper, Good Morning America.

Lance had found out very early in the

marriage that Kait, who normally had a hard time keeping quiet, rarely spoke in the morning. She could not wake up, much less function, without her coffee and TV. He was sure that, although the set was on, Kait wasn't going to register one word of the dialogue, not yet at least.

Normally, when he wasn't depressed, Lance was Kait's opposite in the morning. He would get up at 4:30 A.M., make the coffee, read the morning paper and work on something he had brought home from the office, respond to e-mails or slog through personal paperwork before it was time to get prepared for work. He was one of those people who hopped out of bed, ready to go, after only three or four hours sleep. Neither Lance nor Kait could understand the other's morning routine yet. So, the mornings didn't necessarily lend themselves to very much discussion.

This Wednesday morning was different. Lance spoke first. "Good Morning, babe," he said.

"Good morning," Kait croaked back. "You awake yet?"

"Not quite,"

"Well, I'm off for the office. It should promise to be an interesting day. If Bobby has it pegged right, I should be getting a call from Butch Logan with, at least, a temporary job offer," Lance said.

"I wish it was for a newspaper in San

Antonio. I'm homesick already," Kait whined.

"I'll tell you," Lance responded, "it's doubtful we'll be getting back to San Antonio anytime soon, but we'll visit often. I promise. In fact, if what Bobby predicted in his note comes true, we won't have to worry about conserving cash as much anymore. The heat will be off to find a job as quickly as I thought, and we'll be able to take a trip to San Antonio next month. How's that sound?"

"Wonderful!" Kait responded enthusiastically. The conversation, especially the part of visiting San Antonio, was beginning to wake her up. "You almost sound semi-excited about this 'temporary' job offer. Would you want to make it permanent?" Kait asked.

INDEED, LANCE'S BLUE FUNK had lifted significantly since he had gotten up. The prospect of doing some productive work, rather than spending the day writing letters and making phone calls to find just that, certainly appealed to him.

"I don't think I could make it permanent not working for Scott. I can't stand the guy. So why should I work for him and help make him be successful?" Lance now sounded irritated again.

"Please don't work yourself all up about it, Mr. Success," Kait shot back.

"I just thought I'd ask." Lance reflected upon the note received from Bobby the night before and realized that he had been taking some of his latent anger for Scott out on Kait. He certainly didn't mean to, but every time he thought about the guy, it just pissed him off. "I didn't mean to take it out on you," Lance said half laughing.

"Then why are you snickering?" Kait asked.

"Because I'm not myself, I need a snicker," Lance teased. "I was smiling out loud at you. The way you always seem to get me back on course." He leaned down and kissed her passionately. "I love you, Kait."

Kait pulled him close, pressing herself to him, kissed him and began to remove his tie.

By the time Lance left the house, he was approaching a late arrival to work. It was a good idea they decided he should take Kait's BMW to get to the office as fast as possible.

The day was perfect for taking an otherwise harassing drive to the city. He unlocked the front stays that held the rag top in place, pressed the electronic top release and waited the few seconds it took for the top to fall into place behind the back seat. He pulled out of the driveway and began the trek to the office. It was a simple reversal of the route he took home last night. By the time he made it to the freeway, he was ready to resume his reveries and, thus, artificially abbreviate his drive.

Lance couldn't figure out Bobby's note. The rapport between them was good. The note was strange. Was Bobby trying to tell him something? If so, what? And why didn't he just call? Gateway key to success? 'Silver Bullet,' what could that possibly mean? Lance pondered as he maneuvered through the typical backup on the Congress expressway. Truckers and commuters take turns to enter the Loop under the old Post Office building. He snapped to and began to concentrate on the traffic and streets to negotiate his way to FEI's new offices on Lake Shore. He was glad to be stripped of his duties, last Friday. There was no way he could think of anything other than the FedEx's cryptic contents, specifically sent to him. Lance pulled into his assigned parking slot they let him keep.

Lance McKnight sat in his car for ten minutes calming from his frustrating drive through the Loop. He put the rag top back up, locked the car, came through the lobby of the building and took the elevators to the fourth floor. Late again, Lance thought. His secretary and a few members of the corporate staff made some sarcastic comments about his being a short timer, which he ignored. He didn't want to appear as if in a rush, but he wanted to get to his office.

When Lance checked his desk, his anxiety doubled.

There was a message from Butch Logan. It came in at 9:03 A.M. Lance looked at his watch. It was now a quarter to eleven. For a moment, he reprimanded himself for not getting here earlier, but thought about Kait, and decided quickly his tardiness was well worth it. He picked up the phone and dialed Butch.

The phone rang two and a half times before Butch's familiar voice responded, "Logan here."

"Butch, Lance McKnight," Lance said, trying not to sound too excited or over-confident. He didn't want any- one to know he had been tipped off by Bobby.

"Lance, how are you?"

"I've been better," Lance replied. What's up?"

"I was going to call you late yesterday, but I didn't have a chance. Did you hear about Bobby Scaletti?"

Lance paused for only a second then asked, "What about Scaletti? Did Silver fire him too?"

"No," Butch replied in a somber voice, he's dead." Butch was never one to mince his words, even in the worst of circumstances.

"What?" He couldn't believe his ears! Bobby? Dead? Lance regained his composure as quickly as he could. "What the hell happened?"

"Well," Butch continued, "apparently from some freak explosion at the Buffalo Airport."

"When?"

"Late Saturday night,"

"That's unreal."

"Yeah, Bobby was just in my office Friday. Ironically, our conversation centered around you, Lance. We talked about a position here at the Chicago Union. Would you come by my office, around noon?"

"Sure, see you then." Normally, Lance would have asked why, but since he may already know, didn't. First, he called Kait.

"Hello?"

"Hi Babe, it me, listen, can you go get the FedEx package from my desk?

"Sure, why?"

"I need you to check the postmark on the envelope and tell me when the thing was sent out of New York. I'll hold thanks."

"One moment, sir." Kait giggled and put the phone down. "It was posted last Saturday." Kait looked closer to be sure. "Why does it matter when it was sent? What's going on Lance?"

"I don't know if anything is. It's just all so weird. I've got to get over to the Union for a meeting with Butch Logan. He called about a job offer. I'm running behind now, so I'll give you a call later and fill you in. Thanks, Babe." Lance hung up the phone. He hoped he hadn't sounded too abrupt, but he didn't want to worry Kait.

One thing was cleared up, the FedEx had been sent from the airport. This whole thing is getting somewhat scary Lance thought, hoping he was making more out of it than he should.

For Kait, the problem was that nothing sounded very simple. She wasn't sure it was over with. There were big holes in this piece of Swiss that only led to more concerns. Lance emptied his mind to concentrate on what the offer could be. He left the office, got into Kait's BMW and drove non-stop to the Union Building. Soon thereafter Lance popped his head into

Butch's office. Butch was wrapping up a phone call but waved Lance in with a nod. Butch replaced the receiver and walked around the desk, hand outstretched to greet Lance.

"I can't say it's been a long time, but it's good to see you anyway. How have you been?" Butch asked.

"Not great," Lance replied. "Frankly, I've been de- pressed, but I'm fighting it."

"If there's one thing I know about Lance McKnight, he's a fighter. Maybe I can help with this battle, eh Tiger?" Tiger was an affectionate nickname for Lance, Butch started in San Antonio to describe his scrapping and tenacious nature.

Lance, however, always felt as if he was back in little league, about to get up to bat with bases loaded, two outs and the coach telling him to "go get 'em, Tiger."

"Well, let's get to this. See, our investigative reporter, Skaggs, wasn't willing to work for Scott Silver. Now he's an ex-reporter of the Chicago Union. Hell, I don't blame him. The only reason I'm sticking around is to give Silver a little more grief. If I can do that, I can retire a happy man. At any rate, I'd like you to fill in for Skaggs."

BUTCH, I LIKE WORKING WITH you, and I do respect your tenure in the industry, but I got a real problem working for Silver. And, it has to be pretty obvious he has a problem working with me. I mean, he did have Burt Tyson fire me! What the hell makes you think he'd want me here?"

"Because I told him he did," Butch insisted. "Scott may be a lot of things, but he's not dumb. He knows you're one of the best in the business and I just reminded him. Silver knows he needs the best to make the Union work. Since Skaggs bailed, he needs you. No Lance, I need you."

"It sounds like we both just paid our dues to the mutual admiration society. I appreciate your comments, Butch, but back up for one second. What do you mean by 'fill in'?"

"Scott would only agree to bring you here for Skaggs's position, until we can replace him and understands that could take a long time to find someone that needs no training. I don't want that to be our understanding and if we play it right, you'll continue to 'fill in' for Skaggs for as long as you wish. Scott likes me, and he wants me here. So, worst case scenario, I'll threaten to resign or retire if you have to go."

"Butch, all of that is well and good, but I don't know if I could work around the guy. I mean I have absolutely no respect for him. In fact, I have come to despise him! I probably feel stronger than Skaggs did about not working for him at this point," Lance pointed all of this out rather quickly, working himself up more and more with each sentence. "Besides, why should I want to help fill his bank account?"

"Calm down, Lance, this guy isn't worth that kind of energy. I know how you feel. I told him you hated his guts. I told him I hated his guts. He doesn't want to see your face, and I'm sure you'd like to avoid him like the plague. So, we can all live together like one big happy family that stays away from each other. As for why you would want him to succeed; I'm sure you don't. I do know you well enough to know that you give a shit about the quality of work in the industry. Put Silver aside. Ignore him!" Butch knew that might be a stretch and looked squarely into Lances eyes and in his most convincing tone, "The way I figure it, he'll ignore you, and you will ignore him, which means, he'll mostly ignore me. You and I will run the Union the way we want. Like I said, one big happy family!"

"Butch, I love your logic!" Lance said smiling slyly. "There's one flaw. You know, I know, and I venture to say Scott knows, that you'll retire soon. Frankly, I sure can't understand why you even came to Chicago. What hap- pens when you decide to leave?"

"It wouldn't put you in any different position than you are right now," Butch said. "It would just mean that you'd delay working somewhere else for a while. And, for your information, I came to Chicago for a couple of reasons. First and foremost, my desire to increase my nest egg for a couple of years. Secondly, I love to give Scott crap. And, bringing you over here is the best kind of 'stick it to him' I can think of. What do you say?"

Lance reflected for about three seconds, although to Butch, it seemed more like a minute.

Finally, Lance said, "I only have three conditions. One, keep Scott away from me. Two, you let me know well in advance when you're preparing to resign and three, I want to attend Bobby Scaletti's funeral, on the company's dime."

"Why go to the funeral? I didn't know you and Bobby were that close," Butch responded.

"I don't know why, Butch, maybe out of respect?" "Whatever you want, Lance."

3
Storming The Gateways

SCOTT SILVER WAS ALONE in his office, surrounded by the artifacts of the past that furnished the lavish room.

The drapes were pulled and a small, but strong, fire burned in the fireplace. But for that, and the green banker's lamp on his oval desk, the room was dark. In fact, the greenish glow seemed to make parts of the room even darker. Scott liked it that way. It helped him think - meditate.

Killing Bobby Scaletti was regrettable. Scaletti did well for him and may have been loyal, but only to a point and he was sure Scaletti was up to something. Scott convinced himself he had done the right thing. Now, the only other people who knew how the money was being spent were in as deep and had too much to gain to talk. The glow of the bank light shed its eerie green tint. Scott was almost in the clear. For the next few minutes he re-examined the luck that befell him.

Aaron Carver, a newly hired reporter in Silver's South Florida paper, had been anonymously tipped off about an illegal gun smuggling ring. This was the kind of exposé that would easily become a career shaping investigative series. Jeffrey Bayer, the paper's managing editor decided to run it by corporate, first and was surprised Scott Silver, the man himself, was the one to call him back with approval.

Carver's first piece named Hafez Fakhouri as the presumed head of a ruthless arms dealing organization exporting massive amounts of destructive weapons, specializing in chemical and biological warfare. Aaron's second was about Fakhouri's alleged automatic weapons and explosives sales in the United States. Soon after the second story was published Aaron Carver disappeared.

Scott Silver acted on what he thought was a brilliant idea to make easy money by blackmailing Fakhouri. Scott flew to Miami and drove a rental car to Fakhouri's Beach house. Fakhouri thought he was there to discuss the missing reporter. Silver was only there to offer protection. "What makes you think I need protection, seddik?" Hafez emphasized the Arabic word for my friend. "And if I did, what makes you think you could protect me?"

"I can give you the power of the press, seddik, I do own forty-two newspapers across the country and have access to many more through media relationships. Don't forget you were nearly exposed by the papers, my newspapers. It could easily happen again. As I see it, I have already protected your organization. Who do you think killed the investigation into my reporter's death? I could have just plastered you all over front pages from California to New York and back. I could utilize that same media to divert attention or misdirect."

FAKHOURI'S INITIAL REACTION was one of anger, but he considered the offer carefully. This could be to his advantage in several ways. Cutting Silver in would be beneficial. With minimal negotiations, Hafez and Scott worked out the terms with conditions. Both were satisfied with the financial arrangement. They exchanged their contact information and shook hands to seal the deal.

Scott got busy right away and created his own news agency wire service. A public service wire exclusively for terrorist threats and illegal arms dealing to be used by newspapers across the country. The new, FEI Wire Service would please the editors at several national, regional, and local newspapers, and make Scott look like a champion of justice against terrorism.

Jeff Bayer was instructed to coordinate the new wire service and did so having no idea who he was working with, just that his contact was transmitting the information from a storefront in Miami. Bayer didn't know it was Hafez Fakhouri's people. Bayer uploaded the tips with relevant details. Once retrieved and re-written to article format; Jeff posted the transcripts to the news service, and from there handed it off to the desk editor to edit the text for typesetting functions.

One keystroke sent it over the Internet to newsrooms across the country. News desk editors would process the story. Reporters and editors would review the facts or related files and contact local authorities, including the feds, if necessary. Every paper would do what it took to turn the feed into their own exclusive front page news.

The idea was to feed information obtained from Hafez to FEI Wire to eliminate some of Hafez's competition, add validity to the wire service and keep the focus of the authorities' off of Hafez's organization. Many of the newspapers owned would generate exclusive front page news articles and rake in the revenue.

After careful contemplation, Silver's next objective was to cultivate a relationship with Clinton Excelsior, Esq., owner of Excelsior Newspapers. Excelsior and he bashed heads in bidding wars over newspapers on the auction block while developing a mutual respect for one another. In the process Scott and Clinton came to understand each other professionally; both were strong competitors and their personalities alike. When Silver told him he'd never have to lose a bid against him, again, that they could work together without merging corporations, he took the bait and the two newspaper executives came to an arrangement.

A deal was contrived to increase Silvers profits. Clinton Excelsior owned and operated sixty-four newspapers across the country and twelve throughout Canada. Even though he owned more newspapers, FEI's circulation numbers were greater. Clinton's papers may have small circulation numbers but were strategic in their locations. Excelsior Newspapers were in suburban metro areas and considered monopolies to local news outlets. Yet, the metro papers watched them closely because the smaller dailies could have a profound effect on their markets.

Thinking about it now, the only conflict they've had was when he asked Pete Geary to negotiate the sale of the Nashville Messenger to the Excelsior Corporation.

Instead, Geary convinced the Messenger to sell to FEI, although Clinton and Scott had an agreement in place for Clinton's company to be the buyer. Geary had screwed it up on purpose. It was later discovered he used to work for Excelsior and was disgruntled so he seized upon this opportunity to stick it to them.

The mess was straightened out and the paper was sold to Clinton. Silver made a note in the back of his mind to watch Pete Geary closely.

The 'pièce de résistance' to Scott Silver's plan was an afterthought out of necessity, Louisiana Senator, Andre Gaston. A relatively unknown, mild mannered elected official, trying to fulfill the duties of his office, and the promises he made to get there, but was making little progress since his wife, Suzanne, died of Leukemia. Scott remembered how that all abruptly changed when the news broke announcing the horrific explosion of a US passenger airplane at the Intercontinental Airport, in Houston, Texas.

There were no survivors. Like magic, FEI's papers were all over it, and his wire service fed the newsrooms with exclusive inside information leaking names of the dead and other details withheld. He and Fakhouri were well aware they furnished the weapons used by the extremists and knew Senator Gaston's daughter was one of the hostage fatalities before he did. Controlling the content of the FEI wire service enabled them to subtly direct all suspicion toward rival arms dealers and away from their operation.

Andre Gaston became a household name across the nation. The public sympathized with the awful tragedy that befell Andre this time because he didn't fold; he threw his entire being into his work. The press ate it up. Gaston even scored a prime time interview on one of the national broadcasting networks. The host wanted to talk about his wife, Suzanne's passing and the horrible and graphic details of his daughter, Marie's abduction and consequent death. Not about the radicalized committing acts of violent jihad, on American soil; like the extremists that murdered his Marie and many other innocent lives. He used his time on air as a platform to give notice he would push hard for a deeper investigation into the Houston terrorist cell behind the airport bombing; including the suppliers of the explosives and automatic weapons used in the massacre.

Scott Silver only paid attention to the biographical interview playing in the background when he heard the end of Senator Andre Gaston promise, ". . . and a vigorous investigation into the suppliers of the weapons used in the terrorist attack against the Houston Airport."

Scott grew very alarmed, almost to the point of sheer panic. As quickly, he calmed himself, sensing there was an opportunity on the horizon. The way to stop Senator Gaston from pursuing illegal arms trafficking which may lead to him, was to derail the senator with something much bigger. He would need the cooperation of Hafez Fakhouri and would also require another business arrangement with Clinton Excelsior. His new mission would also require Clinton's influence and deep pockets. However it made no sense to Scott to make changes to anything now in place until he dealt with Gaston. Silver lost little time in arranging an interview with the senator, saying that the Chicago Union was quite interested in publishing a follow up piece about the senator's television interview. He also guaranteed coverage in all of the papers under their umbrella providing a nationwide audience.

Scott always admired the political arena; a path that lead to the ultimate power in his mind, the Oval Office; the president's office. Scott Silver had the intense desire, but zero public appeal and couldn't put ten words together in the fashion required for public speaking. The only public office Silver's attitude, short temper and crude manner was suitable for was dog catcher, if he wasn't asked to drop out of the race. Long ago, Scott abandoned all hope for the valuable seat in Washington D.C., until now. Scott recalled their conversation as if it happened yesterday.

"I've listened to your speeches lately and your ideas for progress and stability make a lot of sense to me. I believe in the process and role the government is supposed to have and want to do my part to support candidates that share the same goals for our country that I do. You're one of those candidates, Senator Gaston." Scott was proud the words came out right.

"I'm flattered," Andre said, "but, I'm not a candidate. I already have a seat in the senate. I don't think I'll have a problem with re-election in two years. Frankly, I don't see how an expose' in local papers or nationwide can be of any assistance." The senator stood and was about to politely usher Scott out the door.

"With all due respect, Senator Gaston, I wasn't talking about a human interest story."

"I don't understand. What were you talking about?" Andre sounded irritated.

"The presidency." Scott replied flatly.

"The presidency? What do you mean?"

"The presidency of the United States!"

"You must be out of your mind! Who put you up to this?"

"This is no joke. I really believe you should be the next president of the United States and I am willing to do everything I can to make that happen."

"What? Me? The president?" Andre was more than flabbergasted, he was stunned. His mouth hung open in disbelieve. After a few seconds Senator Gaston regained his composure. "Mr. Silver, I'm flattered, really, but this was to be my last term in the senate. I couldn't accept your contributions anyway. Isn't it a conflict of interest if the media supports any one candidate, publicly, as you seem to be suggesting in this case?" Andre inquired with suspicion.

Scott was prepared to answer this question, knowing the delicate matter would have to be addressed. Silver had thought it all out knowing the answer given may determine whether the senator agreed to explore such a thing or not. "Senator, the media supports specific candidates every day in this country. Just take a look at our editorial pages. We endorse candidates for offices from city clerk to the presidency and, believe me, owners often get involved in those endorsements. I am also proposing support in a proactive way. I have accumulated a great deal of business relationships that can be essential to a campaign. As your campaign manager, I'd have everything we'd need to win, at my disposal. Your current campaign manager would be better served helping the right candidate fill your empty senate seat."

Both men knew decisions of this magnitude weren't made hastily. Senator Gaston would examine all of the pros and cons and then contact him at his Chicago office. They didn't know it yet, but Silver was confident Senator Gaston, Clinton Excelsior and he were to become the three most powerful men in the world! Packaged and sold by the freedom and power of the press. Thank God for the First Amendment, thought Scott.

Of course, neither Excelsior or Senator Gaston had a clue about his association and dealings with Hafez Fakhouri. Nor did they realize they would legally be as culpable.

Scott Silver's mind came back to his dimly lit office. The fire was nearly out. Scott wouldn't take any risks; his Silver Bullet accounts were essential. With Scaletti out of the way, he would have to transfer the funds himself and hire a new reporter to cover the copy published in order to generate capital.

Scott's motivation was the power this money

would buy him. Power he would share with a select few.

If everything went exactly according to plan, it was only a matter of time before he could become one of the most powerful men in the United States. That appealed to Scott. He may not be recognized as powerful but would be one of the few in a position to influence policy, from many fronts. Control was his power. The ill gotten money bought the venues and control of the media's effective tools. Now, he was the only one that would have the passwords to the protected accounts to transfer funds.

With that realization, Scott Silver turned off the desk light and whispered, "All's well that ends well."

4
The Cost of Transition

KAIT, FOR THE SECOND TIME in as many days, was awake and alert as she sat up in bed quizzing Lance.

"Well, today's your first day on your new job! Are you excited about it?" She asked.

"I'll be happy to have something to do. I think it's better than a sharp stick in the eye," Lance replied cynically.

"Why doesn't anything satisfy you? You should be happy you have someone like Butch Logan around who appreciates you," Kait scolded Lance.

"Butch is doing me a real favor, but it was Scaletti who set it in motion," Lance said defensively, "and the problem is, I'm still working for Silver and he doesn't want me around. That's hard to take. What bothers me even more right now, is Bobby's untimely, no, unusual death," Lance continued. "I liked him. And after getting that FedEx, I'm not so sure it was accidental.

Maybe I've read too much Sherlock Holmes, but something just doesn't sit right."

"I think it's all coincidence and you should spend your time worrying about your new job, not something you can do nothing about."

"I don't trust coincidences my dear Watson! So, what do you make of the 'Silver bullet through the gateway and keys to success' reference?"

"I don't know. The 'Silver bullet' sounds like something out of an old werewolf movie," Kait joked, "but I'm sure it isn't as mysterious as it sounds."

"Maybe you're right but I know it's some kind of clue, but why? It makes zero sense. I should investigate this as I would a hot lead. Never mind, I'll go to the police, maybe they'll look into it."

"Go to the Police? and tell them what? That you want them to find the gateway to the keys to success? Really Lance?"

"Okay, we'll let it be, for now. Will you come with me to his funeral?"

"I really didn't know Bobby. Funerals make me uncomfortable."

"I know," Lance said, "but I thought we'd spend the night and go to Niagara Falls before we come back. You said you've never been, here's your chance, Babe"

"Wakes in the wake of a wake?"

The truth of the matter was that Lance still wasn't quite convinced that the note and the accident weren't connected, but Kait was right. It sounded silly at this point. While in Buffalo, however, maybe he'd sniff around. Kait was also right about concentrating on his job.

After kissing her good-bye, he headed off to the Chicago Union, for his first day at the number two newspaper in Chicago and may already have a story to investigate. On the way into the Loop he couldn't stop his bombarding thoughts. He went back and forth from his new job to Scaletti's death and from Silver to the note from Bobby. Did anything tie together? Did any of it make any sense? He couldn't. He wasn't sure what to think, but decided that, somehow, he'd get to the bottom of all of it.

The Chicago Union was an old, elegant building. Not as lavish as Silver's private office but was more practical and conveyed the same timeless style. As Lance waited impatiently for the elevators in the lobby he took in the huge circle to his left with its ornate arches and frescoed dome.

The room was a cross between an Italian renaissance cathedral and an early 19th century government building. From the outside one could see the dome; its pinnacle reaching three stories high. One may see a structure that looks out of place next to sleek, glass and steel. Somehow the relic belonged; was as much of a part of Chicago, as Wrigley Field.

The elevator door opened, and Lance pushed Butch's floor. My floor now, he thought. Two females walked in and pushed the button for the advertising floor. Lance only knew what was on each floor because of the tours he had taken in the due diligence process right before the purchase of the paper was consummated.

The information helped. At least he wouldn't have to go groping around, looking for executives through a maze of unfamiliar halls.

Once on his floor, Lance walked briskly to Butch's office. His secretary was not there, it was too early. But, if he knew Butch, Butch would be there with a cup of coffee wishing he had a cigarette and reading the Union or the competition. Butch didn't let him down. He was halfway through the paper when Lance walked in the office.

"Hey," Lance greeted.

"Hi, Tiger," Butch replied as Lance cringed. Somehow Lance knew that was coming but wasn't quite sure how to prevent it.

"You ready to rock and roll?" Butch asked.

"Ready, Freddy," Lance quipped back.

"I thought I'd give you the office around the corner. That way you'll be in the back and away from Silver. I'd hate to have you two guys meet in a dark hall some night," Butch ribbed.

"Butch, I know I've got to work with Scott to some extent, so don't make special accommodations for me. I'll live through whatever he can dish out," Lance said.

"Nevertheless, they're moving the furniture while we go to lunch," Butch said. "Besides, I always thought Tyson had a nicer office with a better view."

"He did," laughed Lance. "That's the real reason I didn't want special accommodations."

"Let's get you started. You're not going to have the luxury of settling in. We have got a big story of our own involving our newspaper unions. Four out of five of our contracts are open, and negotiations are slowing down. It couldn't be worse timing. In my opinion, one of the reasons Silver was able to make this deal is because those contracts were coming up and old ownership didn't have the stomach to fight the unions anymore. We're going to have a tough time reporting the story without perceived bias."

"Well, you are right, Butch. In fact, that's one of the reasons I was against the purchase. But, Silver felt he could break 'em," Lance explained.

"I think he's wrong. These guys aren't going to roll over and play dead. They'll fight harder because of Silver's attitude and reputation for union busting. We won't roll over and play dead either. We can't fight a labor war for the next few years and expect to turn this place around. I want you to consult during the editorial negotiations." Butch would rely on Lance's experience and reason.

"Shouldn't you consult with our boss?"

"No. Your philosophy is a lot softer."

"Thanks. But don't paint me as your White Knight, just yet."

Butch chuckled. "I'll send the contracts to your office so you can look them over. When you're done, give me a buzz and we'll set up a time to meet."

"Is Mike Marenski heading up the negotiations at the table?"

"Yes. Stop by his office and take a hard glance at his proposal."

"Then my first order of business is to get caught up with M squared, and we'll get things all squared away!" Lance stood and headed toward the door.

"And by the way McKnight, I'm the White Knight!"

Mike Marenski earned the nickname "M squared" in part for his initials and more so for an obsession for the letter M, four of them to be exact; his wife Mary, two preteens, Marla and Matt and another little miracle on the way. Mike was always enthusiastic and happy. He was constantly talking his way out of situations with his sense of humor and fair play. He wasn't sure how he ended up in Human Resources.

MARENSKI WAS NOW the Chicago Union's new human resources director. He also left San Antonio when the paper sold. Mike and he agreed on almost everything; except their differing opinion of Scott Silver. Marenski thought Silver was a good businessman with a couple of quarks

"Give the guy a break. Nobody's perfect," Mike had once said.

"Yeah, especially Silver. He's on the opposite end of the spectrum," Lance countered.

"You've got blinders on," Mike said, "if he was that bad, he wouldn't have been able to put so many deals together. Give it a rest!"

"All right, Mike. Have it your way, but mark my words, someday I'll say 'I told you so'," Lance concluded.

Marenski had a four year degree in criminal justice and with that joined the military to work in military intelligence. When Lance pointed out that it wasn't the kind of resume he pictured for him, as jovial as he is, Mike agreed and told him that was why the military was hesitant to take him.

Lance entered Marenski's office without knocking. Mike was on the phone but offered a genuine grin at the site of Lance. Lance reciprocated. They both had a great deal of respect for each other, but more important; was the true friendship between them. Mike finished his call and hung up. He reached across the desk and extended his hand. Lance grabbed it with both hands and shook hard.

"M squared! It's great to see you! Sorry I haven't had a chance to come by since your move."

"Hey, can you believe it? We're back in the saddle again, and we're gonna have one hell of a ride. Butch filled me in on the consult. It's gonna be hot times in old Chicago now."

"You know, deep down, we both love this, but you seem to express it much better than I do. Okay, let's get me up to speed and we'll get these contracts prepared."

Lance and Mike took over three hours to review all the documents and minutes of meetings to familiarize Lance with everything to date. The biggest problem seemed to be the editorial contract—since they were asking for an outrageous wage increases in the face of the competitor's salary cut. The reporters were standing tough. Their main objective; to destroy Silver! The Union representing the press room, the Teamsters representing circulation and transportation and the other unions representing various trades in the plant had more or less reasonable demands.

Mike and Lance agreed they would have a much harder time getting a contact out of editorial. Which would prove to be really tough.

The two worked hard, breaking for a quick lunch in the Union's cafeteria. After Lance left Mike at the Human Resources office he headed back for his new office down the hall and around the corner. Butch was nowhere to be found.

Robert Talbot's company was the firm that FEI used for their computer and network systems. They gave him ad- equate space to work in every property as needed. Rob was really good. He was the "System Guru" Bobby Scaletti hired to update the computers in every office of all of FEI properties. Robert built a terrific network system and kept them current and operating properly. Every system came with fully backed up, hot swappable drives. On startup, every system he built displayed a welcome alert that scrolled horizontally across the center of the screen before the operating system loaded.

When McKnight reached his office, he saw the back of a familiar head crouching near the desk, fiddling with network cables. "Rob Talbot, is that you?"

The head turned around. "Hi, Lance, I'm just finishing setting up a computer in here for you." He went back to work, and a few minutes later turned to Lance, who was sitting on his couch reading the Union, and said, "She's all yours."

"Thanks a bunch, Rob! And please say 'Hi' to everyone for me on Lake Shore."

"You bet, Lance, and good luck here," and then waived goodbye. "Call me if you need anything."

Lance sat down at his desk and looked out his window to capture a stunning view of the Loop.

He turned in his chair to face the new computer monitor, then reached down to the tower and switched it on. When the screen displayed Talbot's welcome message he froze! The hair on the back of his neck stood on end as he read silently, Welcome to our gateway. "Gateway!" McKnight burst out loud. He looked around to see if anyone was in earshot. Suddenly, for the first time since coming into the office he thought of Scaletti's coded note. The 'Silver Bullet' to the Gateway of success. Of course! Gateway. Bobby had to be referring to his computer.

Rob Talbot had just returned to FEI headquarters from the Chicago Union when the phone in his IT closet rang.

"Yeah?"

"Rob? It's Lance McKnight."

"Problems already? My installations used to last at least a day," he chuckled.

"Nope, no. Nothing wrong, I was just wondering if everyone in the network uses the same computer system."

"Oh, yes. I'll also upgrade every one of the units as the industry demands. Why?"

"They look pretty new. When did you last upgrade?" McKnight held his breath and waited for an answer.

"The monitors and towers are relatively new, so I haven't had to perform any upgrades yet. You see, not too long ago, Mr. Scaletti wanted to replace every computer, so he gave me a purchase order to build a network system tailored to their needs and to replace the old system, which was a real dinosaur." Rob chuckled. "Why?"

"It's a really sharp set-up. The resolution is great, and it's so fast." Lance lied, he hadn't gotten that far yet, then redirected the subject by stating, "It's so sad about what happened to Bobby, isn't it?"

"Yeah, Butch told me when he called to order your office computer. It's awful," Rob agreed. "I didn't know him well, but he seemed like one of the good guys. He's the one that hired my company's services!"

"Yeah, he was one of the best. It won't be fun wrapping up some of his odds and ends. I'm supposed to finish up the editorial stuff for the Chicago Union deal he was working on." Lance lied again, "I also need to make sure there aren't any other projects left hanging."

"Anything else?" Rob inquired.

"No, thanks Rob." He hung up the phone.

I'm sure, thought Lance; Scaletti's computer was the gateway referred to in his note. And the "Silver Bullet" was sure to be the incriminating evidence in a folder or file on the hard drive. Lance wondered how to get to that machine and into those files. After all, Lance was still in the first day of his new position. Lance knew he wouldn't be satisfied until he found out what this was all about and would operate under his hunch that Scaletti's computer was the key to everything.

Lance walked slowly toward Butch's office, which he had to pass before he could turn down the hall toward the elevator. He tried not to look anxious, but he was apparently not too successful because when he poked his head into Butch's office, Butch immediately said, "What's wrong? You look like you saw a ghost!"

"Nothing's wrong. Actually yes, there is, I need to go to the old home office for a minute. I have a number of files I left behind that will help with my new position." Lance now wondered if that was the third or fourth lie? He was not keeping track.

"Go. I'll see you later," Butch said, "and while you're over there tell the jerks, we don't need them anymore. We got you over here now!"

Lance smiled, "And they're as happy as hell that you do! I'll be back before dark, Pa!" He got out of there before Butch had a chance to absorb what he called him and was on the elevator in record time.

L̲ANCE SHOT OVER to Lake Shore Drive. He ran into Rob Talbot at the vending machines on his way to the office Scaletti used to occupy. Talbot had a bag of chips and a Mountain Dew in his hands. "I'm ba-ack" Lance smiled.

"You've seen too many Steven King movies," Rob chuckled, went in his office and sat behind his desk to enjoy his snack.

Lance continued down the hall and entered the office. Not much here, he thought. There were a few tech books in an otherwise empty bookcase, and the rest of the room was sparingly furnished. The computer was still on the desk. The mini-blinds were closed, and except for the lack of dust; one would think the room hadn't been used in years. Lance looked down at the desktop computer and turned it on. The monitor flashed its eerie welcome; he was sure this machine was the gateway as it seemingly came to life until the password prompt popped onto the screen. Great, thought Lance, the darn thing was pass- word protected. Lance typed in 'Bobby' and hit return.

Nothing came up. Not even an incorrect password message. The screen just went blank, and the system shut itself down. Lance knew without the password; he would not be able to get in and couldn't risk attempting more than one more try or the system might lock for who knows how long. Now what? Lance searched his brain for an answer.

Rob Talbot came into the room. "So, finding everything okay, Lance?"

Lance jumped from being startled. "I was trying to get into this computer to access Bobby's folders. No one has any of his files here. I assumed he'd kept them on this computer." Lance made it up as he went along, "The only problem is, I don't have the password, and don't see it written anywhere."

"FEIpcII, I believe, yeah, that's it. When Mr. Scaletti's in Buffalo, this one's used as an extra archive for reference and important files; it's not networked to the others on the floor." Rob took a seat near the desk.

McKnight tapped away at the keys and the operating software began promptly. As casually as he could, he searched the directories, folders and sub-folders quickly and after a few minutes he decided to search the entire hard drive by typing in Scalett*.* and sat back putting his arms back behind his head and said, "Doing a system search for Bobby's files, may be a bit, huh?"

"You think?" Rob smiled, glad to see McKnight knew his way around a computer.

Twenty minutes had passed, and the multiple searches found nothing. Finding that odd he half said to himself, "I know he used this PC to store his files, and I really need to see the financial documents for the union deal we're negotiating."

"The files are probably hidden and are more than likely encrypted, Lance."

"Oh." McKnight's shoulders drooped with the thought, now what?

To Talbot, it looked like Lance was about to cry, and said, "Wait, that's not a problem. I have military grade forensic software, but you didn't hear that and don't want to know where it came from. Hopefully that will give us a pretty good picture of what's on the hard drive. Talbot was back and inserting a USB into an empty port. Rob typed a series of numbers and letters incredibly fast.

Along with unrecognizable characters there were also sections of readable text laced throughout some pages. Rob and Lance just looked at each other.

"I could take it to the shop and print out the data for you Lance. We'll shut her down and I'll just take the tower."

"Really? That sounds like a lot of extra work to put on you. I know what to look for, so could I view more pages for a while? Actually, I'd like to borrow your flash drive for a day or so. I should check some terminals at the Union."

"Sure, just don't forget to give it back when you're done. By the way, I only give someone my trust once."

"Thanks Rob, you are a life saver! Hey, by the way, have you seen 'Tyson the Terrible' today?

"He's out of town for the purchase of a newspaper in Arizona. Have a good night, McKnight!"

Lance sat for a moment and went over options in his head. He needed to pilfer through pages of information that may or may not be what he is looking for, wondering exactly what it was, he was looking for? The task in front of him would take a very long time. McKnight's spirits lifted after he figured out the only solution, even if the risk could be his grave.

McKnight took a quick route to his old office. It was locked. He asked Burt Tyson's secretary to open the door because he needed labor files. If there was any truth from that, it was that he could review some of the minutes of negotiations he had kept from San Antonio. They really might become helpful in Chicago's negotiations. More important was something else he desperately needed.

After selecting specific files McKnight placed them onto the desk, and then swiftly removed the cover to the computer tower after removing a few thumb screws.

Expediently, he removed the hard drive and slipped it into the stack of files and went back to Bobby's computer and swapped the hard drives.

Lance pocketed Scaletti's computer's hard drive, Rob's flash drive and left the building fast and as inconspicuous as he could. Forget about lying so much his pants could burst into flames at any moment, he just committed a few serious felonies. Lance was full of adrenaline, but glad to be back safely in his office. Lance looked at his watch. It was nearly 5:00 P.M. "Holy moly!" He yelped and hurried to Butch Logan's office.

"Hey, Tiger," Butch hollered from behind his desk. "That was a hell of a long few minutes."

Lance cringed again at the use of the nickname, but again decided not to say anything. "Yeah, but I discovered a useful approach to finalize your negotiations, that'll put the deal in good shape."

McKnight had never lied as much in his

entire life as he had in this one day; finding it increasingly necessary as the day progressed. However, it really wasn't as easy as the lies sounded. Something was bound to backfire. For now, Lance was content to change the subject. "How was your afternoon, Butch?" That sounded lame to him but was the only thing he could think of to say at the time.

"Boring," replied Butch. "I haven't talked to Silver all day, and I need to insult somebody!"

"Don't look at me, Butch. I still need your support and understanding," Lance fussed. "By the way, did you hear any more about Bobby or the funeral?" Lance inquired.

"Only that it's at St. Agnes' Catholic Church at 10:00 A.M., Friday morning," Butch replied. "If you're going, give my condolences. I never met any of his family, but as I said before I thought highly of Scaletti. The company's sending flowers and covering the expenses."

"Can I ask you something confidentially, Butch?"

"Go for it!"

"Doesn't it seem kind of strange the way Bobby died? Unusual even?"

"Well, I certainly wouldn't call it routine, but I'm not sure what you mean. The gas tank exploded. It happens all the time. Accidents happen, Lance"

"Yeah, they do, this just all seems so unlikely. And, where are the cops on all of this? You think they're sure it was accidental?"

"Hell, McKnight, how would I know what

the police think? All I do know, is there is no investigation. It was an accident."

"Well, I might snoop a little bit in Buffalo. I'm not so convinced!"

"What are you talking about, Lance? Why would any- one kill Bobby Scaletti?"

Lance could see further pressing Logan wasn't wise and better change his tune. "I don't even know what I'm saying, Butch. Forget I even said anything, really. I'm just paranoid, I guess, I don't even know where that came from. It was a tragic accident."

"Meanwhile, here's the summary notes and proposal terms I put together for the negotiations. I'm gonna head home pretty soon, so I'll see you tomorrow. Good luck."

Lance put the rest of his notes away. He saw a lone pink square of paper with bold black ink, skewered onto a spindle, a message from his wife. He would return her call on the way home. He checked to see if he still had Scaletti's hard drive and Talbot's USB drive. He would work on it more in the privacy of his home office.

Before he left the suites, Lance popped his head into Butch's office. "Hey, I'm sorry I freaked out about Bobby. I can't believe how crazy I sounded, thanks for straitening me out." He hoped what he said would stop Butch from passing along his tirade.

"Forget about it! And have a good evening!"

"Did you get my message today?" Kait asked.

"Yes ma'am! I didn't get it until I was leaving. I tried to call, but the line was busy. Sorry about that!" Lance gave his wife a quick kiss on the way to his den.

"What's going on with you Lance McKnight? I can tell something is up!"

"In a minute, Babe! I need to put some stuff away," Lance told her, "I'll tell you all about it, I promise."

She and Lance prepared dinner together as they talked more about his day of sin and felonious acts of corporate espionage; all in pursuit of the meaning of a mysterious note from a dead co-worker. The more Lance talked, the more Kait became flustered and concerned. She wasn't so excited about the trip to Buffalo, New York, anymore. "Kait, I was serious about Niagara Falls. So, pack your bags and get ready to shuffle off the minute I get home, Thursday night. Pack for the weekend and we will make another honeymoon of it."

"Alright, honey. I'll go, under duress," Kait finally added, "because I still think this is a bad idea"

After dinner, and much less discussion, Lance and Kait retired early, but Lance awoke in the middle of the night. Unable to drift back to sleep; he crept out of the bedroom and down the stairs to his den to try to see what he could find using the borrowed decryption program with the stolen hard drive.

A couple of hours viewing tokenized pages in the wee hours of the morning proved to be worth the blurred vision and droopy eyes when Lance came across a page with a hidden directory of encrypted files except one small text file: locksmith.txt. For the second or third time in 24 hours a shiver ran down his spine. He was actually afraid to open it, but double clicked it anyway.

When the document opened he saw an oddly named file; >uniondues.exe< and wondered for a minute what it could mean, but grateful to Guru Rob, for getting him this far. Now that he had what may be a file name, unhidden due to the forensic software running, a search should lead him to the hidden folder. In no time at all, he was staring at the executable file. The bad news now, was that the files were password protected.

Obviously, Bobby Scaletti went through a lot of trouble to make sure no one randomly came across the file or its purpose. It should all make sense if he can figure out the password.

He couldn't just sift through the pages for related files, the data was scrambled. He knew he hit the jack-pot. This had to be something very big. In his experience, hidden information, buried assets, and encrypted data only spelled one word: illegal.

He copied the entire unencrypted folder, then copied the uniondues.exe file to another clean USB drive and stashed them in a metal box inside another wooden box. He placed the wooden box into an open back shelving unit as to hide it in plain sight. Talbot's software was put back into the pocket of the jacket hanging on the coat rack.

Lance still needed to keep Scaletti's drive in his system, for just a little bit longer. He only knew of one person he would want to look at the system files and the only one in the company he trusted enough to ask for help, Mike Marenski. The difficult part was his relationship to the situation.

This will take some thought he decided, then looked at the clock and almost fell out of his chair; it was 6:30 A.M. By the time he finished straightening up his desk and splashing his face with cold water, he told himself it was not too early to call Mike Marenski and ask for his help. He needed Mike's advice and an independent witness to the contents of the file.

"Marenski residence," came a voice.

Lance knew it was one of the kids. "Is your dad there?" "May I tell him who is calling?"

"Yes, this is Lance McKnight, thank you." "Hello?"

"How did you teach your kids to be so polite over the phone, when you're so rude most of the time?" Lance always enjoyed teasing Mike.

"Actually, my wife taught them. They go through that routine so that I don't have to talk to anybody I don't want to. I guess they screwed up this time, but considering the early hour, how may I help you, Mr. McKnight?"

"Oh, you do have manners. Listen Mike, will

you swing by the house for a cup of coffee on your way to work."

"As long as breakfast is served with the coffee, I can be there say, an hour?"
"See you then."

Without waking Kait he shaved, brushed his teeth, showered, and dressed. In the kitchen, the coffee was brewing, bagels were warming in the oven and the table was set for three.

"It's a long story," he told Mike, as he led him straight to the den. Lance started with the receipt of the cryptic note from Bobby Scaletti and went through the afternoon of computer games and fabrications. Careful to omit details about the software Talbot entrusted to him or the copies he made. He didn't lie to Mike; he just didn't tell him that he sifted with software he shouldn't have had access to at home and not with the computers search engine on Scaletti's computer.

Mike leaned over Lance's shoulder as they watched the screen when Lance clicked executed the uniondues.exe file and another prompt requiring a password appeared. He turned his head to Lance and asked, "Lance, where is my coffee?"

"Right. Payment upfront."

Kait eased into the kitchen before 8:00 A.M., surprised to see her husband and Mike Marenski having coffee, and an empty lined college ledger and pen nestled between what looked to her like a Travel Lodge's Continental Breakfast. After their morning greetings, she leaned in and gave Lance a squeeze hug and kiss on the cheek, sat down next to him, and poured herself a cup and watched her beloved man at work.

"So, Mike, how many tries do you think we have to get the password right? My guess would be no more than three."

"Well, we'd better make them count."

Kait's head moved in a ping-pong fashion as she watched the two debate and write down possible pass- words. "Listen to you two! With your names and words and letters, numbers, uppercase, lowercase, blah, blah, blah," she mused, "any of those in the note?" Kait was pointing to the list.

"All of them!" They answered in unison.

"We had better get on it, or I'm going to be late for work."

"Even better, I'll call Logan and tell him I'm hauling you into HR this morning to finish your intake paper- work. He won't expect you until after lunch."

LANCE AND MIKE were seated in front of the computer monitor, about to try the third password written down.

Lance started to type then abruptly stopped, "Wait! No. Hang on a minute," he belted out as he pressed the back- space. "Bobby secured my job and sent me the message so that I would discover the file. He believed his life was in danger, and he wanted someone he trusted to follow through. I don't know if this was mob-related or not. One thing I know as fact; Bobby Scaletti wanted me to find the file and open it using a password easy to figure out." Without thinking, Lance's fingers typed 'silver bullet' and pressing the enter key.

The first window message read, Do you wish to proceed using defaults? Along with a choice of Yes or No. Lance selected yes. Another window opened that had individual line boxes displaying a partial number on the left and another on the right. The incomplete default numbers were grayed out and could not be altered, and the rest of the number fields had to be manually entered with the correct information. Additional sets of empty fields had many spaces with decimal points. Below, was a list of IP addresses to pair with choices of available routing paths. At the very bottom were user options to Abort, Review and Continue. Mike said to print the screen and abort.

Sitting in the kitchen again, Lance and Mike looked at the printed screen capture.

"I think we can agree the prompts were asking for bank account numbers and dollar amounts. The first two in each set, 09, look like bank routing numbers. Money transferring?"

"It looks that way," Mike agreed, "must go through a series of routers, presumably to other 'friendly' computers involved, and by friendly, I mean known. Once all the hand shaking is done, the transaction is complete."

"Say Mike, tell me how money-laundering works."

"Sure, Lance no problem. I took Money Laundering 101 in college and later joined the military and went to Afghanistan to hunt for buried money cashes." Mike was shaking his head in wonder, "What are you talking about, McKnight?"

"What are you both talking about?" Kait asked. "Money laundering, embezzlement." They both said and laughed.

"I don't think I like the sound of this. And, I don't really understand, either, Lance. Thanks for including me, but maybe you and Mike should work it out alone."

"Are you for real, Kait? Sit down, please. You are a part of this, too. I think Scaletti could have been shaving money from one or more Chicago Union accounts," Lance theorized, "then cleaned it and wired it off-shore to a bank somewhere to hide. We know he is good at hiding things."

"Sounds so conspiratorial." Kait excused herself promising a quick return.

"Why use a hidden program, if it was normal everyday banking? We don't know if he is working with anyone else. And with the different IP addresses, this could be worldwide!"

"Slow down, Sherlock! You're taking giant leaps here; from meatballs to mobsters!" Mike said. "Let's take a step back. This could be for routine wire transfers; businesses do it all the time. Maybe you're overly stressed from all the changes in your life, and recent losses nudged you off your game a bit! It could be you're over thinking this. Simple as that."

"I hear you Mike. I do. I don't particularly like being the 'chosen one', or believing Bobby was willing to commit a 3rd degree felony. I didn't think he was that crooked."

Kait came back into the kitchen, topped off their coffees, and started clearing the table. "I don't think you can be just a little crooked, Hun. I know I joke about this, but it's getting kinda scary," she said. "Maybe I shouldn't go to Buffalo for the funeral. Maybe you shouldn't go to Buffalo for the funeral," Kait concluded.

"Why not?" Lance asked. "Mike may be right, and I might be all wet, but either way; our going to the funeral isn't going to mean anything to anybody-except people paying their respects."

"We don't know what Bobby was involved with, or whoever else is involved. What if he was involved in something serious? What if who he was involved with knows we're involved."

"Kait," Lance said in a comforting yet stern voice, "no one can know we're involved. We don't even know if we're involved, what we are involved in, what our involvement might be in something we don't know how involved it is! Well, that did not make sense. The point is, only three people know about our involvement, Mike, you and I. So, what could possibly happen?"

"A long jail term for me if either of you uses the word 'involve' one more time in a sentence."

Lance and Kait turned their heads to face Mike. Kait broke the silent stares by excusing herself to leave it to the pros. She had gathering and packing to do for the trip. "I liked Bobby and don't care if he was a crook. Maybe I should just turn all this over to the police."

"And tell them what, Lance? It looks incriminating for Bobby and will not matter if it turns out the program was only a sophisticated way of recording a normal business transaction. The news agencies would latch onto an 'alleged money-laundering scheme,' and ride it to death. Most of all, you're forgetting our boss, Scott Silver; he and the Chicago Union would be dragged into the dirt along with Scaletti, do you want that for Bobby or his family?"

"Well, no. What do we do then Einstein?"

Mike had to think about this; Scott Silver could not be part of anything illegal. If Scaletti was stealing from the paper, he should find out so he could inform Scott Silver. Stretching a Human Resources title a bit. Aware of the tension between Silver and McKnight, he would have to proceed with caution. He could use McKnight's help as much as he needs his to clear things up. "Do you think you can get a look at the Unions bank account numbers? Someone in payroll could be helpful. I'll look into the telephone numbers. I know a guy who works for the phone company that still owes me a favor."

"I'll see what I can do when I get in; let's see its 10:30, so we had better wrap this up. Thanks for coming Mike." Lance quickly wrote out the numbers shown on the printed page, handing the copy to Marenski.

Once Mike was out the door, Lance darted back to the den. He used the forensic software to re-hide all the files, and made another copy of the entire hard drive, onto a spare Western Digital external drive. Lance put Rob's encryption software into the pocket of his sport coat with the stolen drive. He'd return the thumb drive to Rob after he re-swapped the hard drives.

Upon arriving to the Union, he stopped by Mike Marenski's office. He was in, but the receptionist wasn't at her desk, so he waltzed right in and anxiously asked, "Find anything out yet?"

"Lance, I just got here myself. What do you think I have, twenty-four-hour access to people who will give me private data? Get to work and relax, McKnight. It's going to take a few days. I will let you know as soon as I know. Trust me! I think maybe you should continue playing an investigative reporter. That's a fun game!"

Butch Logan was not in his office, so Lance didn't have to waste time on greetings and went about his business for the next thirty minutes, trying not to be too anxious. Butch was taking him to lunch. Since Butch loved to tell stories, he would provide distraction with a far-out tall tale. Lance needed to clear his mind, so he could come up with the best way to get someone in accounting to help, without raising suspicion.

Lunch concluded with a tour of the Chicago Union's operation. After shaking forty hands and engaging in a little chitchat with each manager, there were only a couple of hours left of the workday to get the information he needed.

ONCE IN THE accounting room, he went to the newest clerk and gave the usual, "doing a story" routine, but with a little twist; he'd put their name in the article as an expert witness as long as nothing was said to anyone until the article was published.

Lance took the notes he made from accounting and compared them to the printed screen capture he made attempting to match bank account numbers, but none of them matched the grayed partial numbers. Now he didn't know what to think and headed over to Marenski's office to share the bad news.

The receptionist said Mr. Marenski was in a meeting but will be through any minute. Lance paced back and forth in the outer office for ten minutes when Mike finally emerged, walking an employee out. Mike pulled Lance into the office, closing the door. "What the hell is wrong with you, Lance? The receptionist buzzed me twice to tell me you were pacing the place like a caged lion. You are supposed to be working editorial, and instead you are convincing everyone you are a fruitcake! Calm down!"

Although Mike was a mere five-foot seven inches tall, Lance never really realized it. He had a great deal of respect for Mike and viewed him as equal in physical and intellectual stature. As Lance looked down at Mike at that moment, he did not realize he was doing so.

"You're right, Mike, but this whole thing is beginning to really piss me off. None of the Chicago Union's bank accounts, or regular accounts they use to wire match the account numbers we found. And if the program was transferring funds using a phone from the paper, then the account numbers would match. The program was being used in the offices, so they should be in the billing. I'm stumped." Lance was frustrated. "Did you find out anything yet?" He asked hopefully.

"No. I got hold of his secretary. He is out of the office until tomorrow morning, but she promised me I would be the first call. Chill out, man! Maybe the bank account is at corporate and has no connection to the Union. Maybe it does not even have a connection to FEI. Maybe, you are jumping to outrageous conclusions!"

"I don't think so," Lance said flatly. "Somehow I sense I'm right."

"Well, you're often right," Mike conceded, "but let's take one step at a time. I will let you know what I found as soon as I can. And, in-between, you might at least try to convince some of our employees that you're a Professional Journalist."

"I'm going to Buffalo. Maybe I'll find something there, while I'm at Bobby's Funeral."

"Yeah, I'm sure his family is going to want to talk about his involvement in the money-laundering business. Good luck, pal," Mike replied.

"Well, we'll see," Lance said. Marenski just shook his head and waived him off.

Kait and Lance were on the 7:23 P.M. flight, from Chicago's O'Hare Airport to Buffalo, New York. Kait did not lose her apprehension.

"I know a funeral isn't your typical good time event, but once it's over you'll love the Falls," Lance promised.

"Are you sure we should be doing this? Everything that's happened screams crazy to me. Why do you have to do this anyway?"

"You mean 'We.' We're in this together. As I told you before, Bobby Scaletti essentially asked for my help by sending the FedEx. I doubt anything will come of this, there's nothing to worry about," Lance was getting good with shading the truth lately. "Kait, you'll be very helpful while I nose around. You'll be the most beautiful cover ever imagined."

The rest of the flight was uneventful. Kait

read while Lance dosed in and out of his thoughts about his wife. He thought of how lucky he was to catch Kait. She was smart and beautiful, inside and out. A bit shy at times but was no country bumpkin. Yeah, I'm a lucky man; he thought, as the captain announced the approach to Buffalo.

The next morning was a scramble to find the directions to the funeral from their hotel. After referring to numerous maps and asking several hotel employees, Lance and Kait drove the airport rental car to the church.

A number of people milling about the sidewalk close to the street were waiting for the arrival of the hearse. Lance and Kait parked the car and joined the small group. After a few moments, Lance decided to introduce himself and Kait to the nearest couple. "Hello, Lance McKnight," he said extending his hand to the older gray-haired man.

They shook, and the man spoke, "Tom Scaletti and my wife, Karen."

"This is my wife, Kait." Kait nodded.

"I can't tell you how sorry we are. I worked with Bobby in both Texas and Illinois."

"Bobby was my nephew. We loved him a lot, him and Maria," Tom explained as he looked and nodded toward Bobby Scaletti's widow, Maria.

Maria Scaletti was being cradled in the arms of another older woman, tears streaming from both their eyes. As they turned back toward Tom and his wife, a lanky nervous looking, man pushed his way up to Lance.

"Mr. McKnight, sorry to interrupt, my name is Claudio Falco. Excuse me Tom, but I really need to talk to Mr. McKnight," he said as he pulled the McKnight's away from the Scaletti's confusing both couples.

"Mr. McKnight,"

"Please, call me Lance," he said quickly, before Claudio could get in another word, "and this is my wife, Kait."

Claudio bowed in Kait's direction. "Lance, did you happen to get a FedEx from Mr. Scaletti recently?"

Lance stared at him for what seemed to be an eternity, while Kait gasped, wide-eyed Lance whispered, "Yes. How did you know about the FedEx?"

"I sent it from the Airport right after Bobby's accident."

Claudio had a mild shake as he talked.

"Well, then you can clear up the whole thing." Lance said feeling relieved for the first time in nearly a week.

Kait was still dumbstruck, trying to digest it all.

"I'm afraid I can't clear anything up," Claudio said. "In fact, I thought maybe you could. You were the addressee, of what I presumed to be very important content for Mr. Scaletti to have sent it as he did. I was his attorney for his personal trusts and will."

"Well, we were friendly to each other, and we worked for the same company, but only socialized on occasion. Why don't we swap stories?"

Claudio gave him his business card and said, "Give me your smallest bill."

Lance accepted the card and put it in his wallet; he saw a five-dollar bill and handed it over to Mr. Falco with a stunned look saying, "First time I ever paid for someone's business card."

"You didn't Mr. McKnight; you just retained me as your attorney for this matter."

Both shook hands and agreed to meet somewhere more appropriate to exchange their knowledge of events. By this time, the hearse had arrived, and pallbearers were moving the casket out of the church.

"You know Hun, the deeper we get the scarier it gets. Do we really have to go to the police? Can't we just go to Niagara Falls?" Kait begged.

"When we meet with Mr. Falco, he'll advise us."

The McKnights followed the funeral procession two and one-half miles to the cemetery. It had started out as a beautiful fall morning, but by the time, they reached the cemetery, it started to sprinkle, ever so slightly. By the time the ceremony at the grave site ended, rain was pouring. After the service, the priest had made the announcement that family and friends were welcome to the home of Mrs. Scaletti. Lance told Kait he wanted to go.

"Lance isn't it enough that we've come to the funeral? We didn't know anyone here."

"Yes, but I need to talk to Mrs. Scaletti. I have to."

"About what, Lance? The last thing that poor woman needs is you asking questions about why her husband died."

"I'm not going to ask questions like that, but she still may be able to help me," Lance insisted.

"How?"

"How am I supposed to know that now?"

THEY DROVE IN SILENCE as Lance worked his way to the Scaletti residence. The street lined with cars told Lance he found the Scaletti home.

They went in, mingled a bit, had some food and drink, waiting for an opportunity to approach Maria Scaletti.

"Excuse me, Mrs. Scaletti, my name is Lance McKnight, and this is my wife, Kait. Please accept our deepest condolences. I worked with Bobby at FEI."

"Yes, I recognize your name. How good of you both to come."

"We liked Bobby a great deal."

"Yes, thank you," A flicker of tears shown in her eyes. Kait reached for her hands and squeezed them tightly, silently letting her know that everything would be all right, eventually.

Lance hadn't noticed until that moment, Scott Silver didn't attend the funeral, burial, nor was he there now. Odd, very odd, thought Lance; Scaletti worked for Silver for a long time, and Lance knew Bobby was one of the few people who really cared about Scott Silver. All that aside, his absence gave Lance the opening he needed.

"Mr. Silver also wanted me to convey his sympathies, and to tell you not to worry about sending all his office effects and keys until you are able." Lance ignored Kait's tugging on the back of his jacket as a middle-aged woman came up and hugged Maria Scaletti.

Kait pulled Lance aside. "What are you doing? That poor woman has gone through enough today, and you're going to ask her about office property? What's this crap about Silver? You didn't even talk to him, did you?" Kait whispered sharply.

"Kait, calm down, I got this." Lance stepped back close to Mrs. Scaletti. "I'm sorry."

"It's all right," Bobby's widow said with tears in her eyes adding, "The world keeps going, doesn't it? Mr. Silver was so kind to send flowers and even provided the mortuary services. Come with me, please."

The three ducked down the hall away from the guests and turned into the second doorway on the left; their master bedroom. Maria Scaletti continued to the closet and removed a medium cardboard office box and handed it to Lance. "In this are my husband's home office FEI files, briefcase with paperwork and his office keys. The police said they didn't need any of Bobby's personal effects that survived." Maria explained.

"Thanks so much, Mrs. Scaletti," Lance said

sincerely and took the box from Maria.

Mrs. Scaletti began to cry softly as she handed over her husband's effects. Kait shot Lance fierce and threatening stares.

"I'm sorry," Lance whispered. "Thank you, again, Mrs. Scaletti."

Kait hugged her again on impulse, and they squeezed together for a time, after which the three went back into the living room filled with mourners, celebrating Bobby Scaletti's life. Lance and Kait blended in long enough not to be noticed leaving.

"Jackpot," he said, on the way to the rental car careful to put the box onto the back seat rather than in the trunk. Once inside the car, Kait started up again.

"Please, Kait," Lance said as he got into the car, "and one question at a time. I didn't lie to her to be untruthful; I wanted her to gain her confidence, so she would talk to me. It was an afterthought to mention files and office keys. I asked about them on a hunch, based on Silver's absence and Bobby's note to me, 'the keys to success' is the plural, more than one key. And, you're right. I was very unkind to deceive Bobby's wife; I feel awful."

Kait gave him another blazing gaze before asking Lance, "How could Scaletti's briefcase survive the fire? All that heat, should have destroyed everything, yah?"

"Normally, but Bobby had one of those

fireproof-brief cases. He said he needed it because he would often carry original documents, which are not that easily replaced. Presumably, his keys were in the case. We'll know what files are there and get a closer look at the keys in our hotel room."

"You better hope Silver never talks to Bobby's wife about those files and keys."

"You're right about that," Lance agreed, "but, I doubt he will. I have a feeling Silver will never talk to Maria Scaletti again. Not very considerate, in light of all the time Bobby invested in FEI and is given flowers and a funeral in return." Lance pulled into a half-empty strip center lot, pulled out his cell phone and started browsing.

"What are you doing now?" Kait asked.

"Getting the number for the police station."

"I like this less and less. Is this what investigative reporting is all about?" Kait asked.

"Pretty much, except usually not as fun as this" Lance hoped a little humor might ease his wife's tension. "We keep asking the questions and following leads until something turns up. Investigations can be gruesomely slow and un-informing sometimes, but you don't let go until you get the right answers that solve the puzzle."

"Oh, please Lance," Kait moaned. "Can't we just get out of here?"

"I promise we won't spend the night in Buffalo.

"I thought we would meet with Mr. Falco, before going to the police. Doesn't that make better sense? Getting the advice of your attorney?"

"If Scaletti was connected, how do we know we can trust Mr. Falco? He could have been 'sent' to find out what we know."

Kait just shook her head back and forth in resignation. Lance telephoned the police and got directions to the station. The detective who was assigned to the Scaletti investigation would see him. Lance was at the station within ten minutes. Kait chose to wait in the lobby while Lance met with the detective.

"Detective Sabre," the officer introduced himself while extending his hand to Lance.

"Lance McKnight. I thought I might be able to help you with the Scaletti case."

"Well, the case was officially closed."

"I have information that may change that status."

"Okay, sir, follow me, please." Detective Sabre showed him a chair to sit in and asked his secretary to hold his calls.

"Now, what is this about, Mr. McKnight, is it?"

"Yes sir. I'm the man, Claudio Falco, identified the night the of the Niagara International Airport explosion. One of the victims, Bobby Scaletti, addressed the letter Mr. Falco mentioned to me."

Detective Sabre scrolled through the report on his monitor. Sabre had little interest in it because he didn't think the explosion was anything but a tragic accident.

"We would have found you, Mr. McKnight, if the note Mr. Falco mentioned had any impact on our investigation, or if we considered it evidence."

"Don't you want to read it?" "Okay, I'll read it, let me see it."

"Well, I left the note at my home in Chicago, Illinois. My wife and I are here for Mr. Scaletti's funeral. I don't have it with me, but can tell you what is in it, word-for-word." Lance graduated to lying to police; the note was in his suitcase at the hotel.

"That would be 'hearsay', and I can't act on that," he said. I need the actual note. You can mail it in, with your contact information, and we'll schedule an appointment for a statement if necessary. If not, you're welcome to come back. He edged Lance toward the door saying, "Have a good day, Mr. McKnight."

"Wait a minute. What about the papers you found in Scaletti's fire proof briefcase?" Lance asked angrily.

"Everything we found was returned to his widow. Have a good day, Mr. McKnight." This time he pushed Lance through the door and closed it in his face.

5
Clandestine Banking

LANCE AND KAIT, WERE SILENT for ten minutes. To Kait, it seemed like hours. Lance's face was red as hell, his breathing heavy. He periodically beat his hands against the steering wheel. Kait knew better than to say anything. She sat quietly, letting him calm down. He finally spoke.

"I can't believe he's a detective. 'Mail it in and we'll call you for a statement.' The case is closed. Babe, you believe that? Closed! The police believe it was an accident! Sabre wouldn't let me tell him what Bobby wrote, either. He sure doesn't need the letter to start investigating." Lance fumes filled the car. "Oh, he'll get his letter and then some."

"Lance, let's go to the hotel, check out, meet with our new attorney, then drive to a nice place and spend the night near the Falls. Tomorrow morning we can take the earliest tour. Make a full day of it. Tonight, after we check in, we can freshen up, order room service and go through the box Mrs. Scaletti gave you, together. After all, we've come this far together and we should finish this, together, you and me. Together forever . . ."

"Yes, together. We're in this together. Together may be the only way to solve this. Come together, right now . . ."

"I'm glad Mike isn't in the back seat right now, he would have flipped out on us again."

"No, Kait. He would have shot us both in the back of our heads."

THE MEETING WITH Claudio Falco didn't last very long. They exchanged their stories in great detail, sure to answer each other's questions concisely without hesitation. This was one of the first conversations Lance had in recent times that he told the entire truth and didn't leave anything out, an attorney's dream client.

The last thing Mr. Falco said was that since Lance paid five dollars for his retainer, he'd continue to represent them 'pro bono publico' and if anyone, the police, or a private eye — anyone, wanted to talk to either of them about anything related to Mr. Scaletti, FEI or Mr. Silver, to contact him, for 'the good of the public', before giving an answer. And he turned full focus toward Lance and finished by telling him if the urge to go to the police is too much to resist, please, notify him, and he would accompany him, be it in Chicago or New York.

The twenty-five minute drive to Niagara from

Buffalo was uneventful. Lance and Kait were both lost in their own thoughts, so the trip was quiet.

Clean, fed and for the first time that day comfortable, the McKnight's removed the contents onto the spare, queen-sized bed. Manila file folders fanned across the pillows. None of the files were of any importance; back up files of projects Bobby worked on for FEI. The contents of the briefcase were strewn between them as they sorted through the papers and business tablets mixed in with writing or signing supplies.

"Yup! Jackpot! I recognize the main office entrance key!"

"Boy, I hope Silver never finds out. We can't be sure if anyone else attending knew Silver or not."

"Forget about it!" Lance smiled at Kait; she mustered a smile back. "Anyway, besides the corporate offices' floor key, I think this key is for Bobby's office; this key is to a file cabinet; this security key is to a strongbox maybe, leaves these little piggies to open; I don't know what? A safety deposit box?" Lance removed the ball beaded connector clasp with two, nondescript flat metal keys on it; same cut, but the teeth were ground on opposite sides of each other.

Kait picked up the key ring. The first one she studied, the security key, had a plastic head. The shaft was flat, narrow with no teeth and only one bevel ground into the center of the face. "Lance," she began, "we're taking this thing too far. What you should do is turn in the keys to someone at corporate and forget this whole thing. If you are so sure Silver won't contact Bobby's wife, then you can say she didn't know who to send them to and asked you to bring them for her. It's really none of our business!"

"Babe, how many times do I have to say, Scaletti made it my business. The police won't do anything with the FedEx without corroborating evidence, which we do not have. I promise, once we find out what is in the safety deposit box, we'll bring Mike up to speed, call Mr. Falco and turn it over as he advises."

Kait could tell Lance was cooking something up, and it was going to involve her. His voice changed ever so slightly, and his demeanor was shifting from aggressive toward charming. Kait's ears paid special attention when she heard him say "we" find out.

"But I need your help to get into the box," Lance pleaded. "A page inside the ledger had the account information and key holder names and signatures. It isn't FEI's bank box, or Scott Silvers, it's Bobby Scaletti's. You see, this signature card requires two signors and two keys. At first, I thought this was hopeless, then I remembered Bobby told me he used a secretary in administration, Becky Hansen, to sign as his witness sometimes; here is her name and signature. I looked in all pouches in the briefcase and bingo! So, what do you think?"

Lance tossed copies of Bobby and Becky's driver licenses down.

"I think I'm not Silver's secretary!" Kait began." "I think I have no business looking anything like her. I think I don't want to go to jail! I think I don't want you to go to jail! I think we should forget it!" Kait huffed. "That's what I think."

"But other than that, Kait, you think you'll do it?"

"I don't know, Lance."

"Look, they're not going to be paying a lot of attention anyway as long as we have the keys. The problem will come when they look at the IDs. I think we both look close enough alike, and with the right costumes, it might work."

"Costumes?"

"We'll dress the part, wigs, make-up the works. We'll shop for what we don't have. If all goes well, we'll take the late morning tour of the Falls, and be on our way back to Chicago."

"Alright, Hun, but I don't know why I'm gonna."

"Because you love me that much, or you've secretly wanted to be an investigative reporter like me?"

"If being an investigative reporter means lying and cheating to get the facts you need, even a little bit; I'm not sure I want to be one. Wearing a wig, extra makeup and using a fake accent will be fun."

By early evening, he was sure his wife knew what he did, about Ms. Becky Hansen. They both practiced the signatures as ideas bounced from one to another. Lance was trying to mimic Bobby's voice and mannerisms and Kait worked on Becky's.

The following morning they approached the counter marked for safety deposit boxes, and Lance rang the bell for service. An older, Grey haired woman with over-sized brown-rimmed glasses came out from the room behind the counter. Merriam, the Librarian, thought Lance.

"May I help you?" She asked.

"Ah, yes, Mrs. Frank," Lance replied after noticing her nameplate on the counter. "I'm here to get into my box."

The old woman looked up from her screen asking, "Your name?"

"Robert Scaletti, box 3771." He verified his address doing his best to sound like he was from the Bronx.

"Yes," Mrs. Frank said, "here you are, and your second signatures' name?"

"Rebeca Hansen." Kait did as Lance had, believing her Jersey gal accent was authentic. "May I have your IDs please?"

Bonnie and Clyde McKnight efficiently dug out the driver's licenses and set them onto the counter.

Mrs. Frank stared back at them, giving them her own contemplating look. Finally, she said, "Key's please? And I'll need to have you sign here and again here."

Lance and Kait scribbled forgeries they had practiced, and both held their breath after they finished.

"Okay let's get you into your box Mr. Scaletti." Lance and Kait looked at each other with inaudible sighs of relief as they entered the vault. Ms. Frank told them to press the buzzer when they were finished and left.

They toted the heavy box to a table inside a private booth. Lance held Kait and said, "You were marvelous darling!" and kissed her lips gently.

"You were so smooth, Mr. McKnight."

"Thank you, my Dear! We'll take it all and get out of here."

"Good, we shouldn't be here anyway. I want less and less to do with this, and I don't want you to have any more to do with it either," she finished as she opened the door, stepped out and pressed the buzzer. Lance followed her half-humped over from carrying the box alone.

"Let me help you with that," offered Mrs. Frank, while shooting a disapproving look at Kait. The older woman finished sliding it into place, and they locked it. Lance put his key into his pocket, thanked Mrs. Frank, and opened the door to the lobby for Ms. Hansen and left the bank.

Since it was only 9:30 a.m., they decided to go back to their room and see what secrets the safety deposit box could bring to light. Both had their separate reasons for being disturbed by everything, even each other at times, but they also knew it was only because they were both scared. By the time they were safely in their room, they were in tears, from laughter. They had the most fun they have had recently.

"Let's see if there's anything interesting in here."

"What should we look for?" Kait asked.

"Something very informative and incriminating?"

Both began sifting through the copies of financial statements from different holdings with their annual financial reports and related tax returns attached. When finished flipping through most of the papers, he turned to Kait, who seemed very perplexed.

"There's nothing here, just financial statements and tax returns."

Although confused, he explained, "We have these in the office. Why would he go to the trouble of locking this stuff up in a safety deposit box?"

"I hope you're not asking me. I haven't a clue. Here Lance, look through this folder while I finish reading this handwritten list."

Lance shuffled pages until he saw a familiar document. Once reviewed closely, he located the corresponding tax return attached to the financial statement. He put the documents down and stared at the wall, deep in thought. "These aren't right," he said loudly, not necessary directed at Kait.

"What do you mean?" Kait asked.

"They're not right! The financial statements for San Antonio aren't right! The loss figures reported are right, but the revenues and expenses are way high, millions too high!"

"How would you know that?"

"I was involved in the due diligence process when the deals were closed. I remember the numbers. I learned about business finances during some investigations that involve companies. I'm not sure," Lance, said, again more to himself than to Kait, "but the revenue reported is highly exaggerated and is covered up with inflated and fictitious expenses. We do know Bobby was creative with Silver's financial records."

"We don't know anything, Hun, but this sounds like a job for the IRS."

"Probably not, unless the IRS did a full audit and the likelihood is slim when you're reporting losses. The IRS may audit by random means but won't waste much time unless there are red flags. And I'd bet, that much of this paperwork is a perfect trail of evidence for the IRS."

"Detective McKnight . . . earth to Detective McKnight, I think you ought to leave this up to the experts, Lance; This stuff is really serious. If Bobby Scaletti can be dead because of it, so can you or me. I'm done playing Bobby and Becky and McKnight and McKnight. Look, Hun, look at this. Does this look familiar to you?"

His lovely bride who looked very different with the wig and heavy makeup, was not joking in the least. The paper she was handing him was the one she was distracted with earlier. He could not believe his eyes. The numbers looked like the batch of routing numbers in the transfer software in the union dues file. This is it! This whole enterprise is *Silver Bullet*.

The Falls lie on the border between Ontario Canada and New York State, but the most spectacular views are of Horseshoe Falls on the Canadian side. That's where Kait and Lance were.

"Have you ever seen anything so phenomenal?" Lance yelled over the rushing of the Falls as, he, and Kait held tight to the rail overlooking the miracle.

"It's marvelous, so forceful!" Kait hollered back.

Kait was right, thought Lance. The sheer power of the thundering water and the cool mist of the spray covering his whole body as he watched was the most invigorating experience he could imagine. It was also one of the most frightening.

When he was three years old, his parents had taken him and his older brother to the Falls. He could still remember a stranger who had lifted his brother up to get a better look and in so doing, held him out over the rail.

That was when Lance developed a fear of

height. Convinced looking far down into that foggy abyss caused it.

"The great thing about Niagara Falls," Lance began on their way back to the Buffalo airport, "is that it only takes about fifteen minutes to thoroughly enjoy it! I always love going and I always love leaving."

"I thought it was wonderful. That's what my momma would call a lot of 'fallen' weather."

"What's 'fallen' weather?"

"You know, rain, snow, sleet. Anything that falls," Lance laughed.

"Well, I guess she's right. That would be a lot of 'fallen' water, but only if you're at the bottom, I guess."

They enjoyed the ride back, talking about the Falls, New York, but nothing about Bobby Scaletti, his keys and the doctored documents.

Abdul Baten, a smarmy ex-navy seal was a munitions and demolition expert; blowing things up was his forte. After a dishonorable discharge, Baten became an independent contractor for hire. Abdul was six feet tall with pasted back, jet-black hair and physique like a young Muhammad Ali. He was well-spoken and had a quick tongue. Abdul Americanized himself by using the name Abe; Abe Baten. Hafez Fakhouri referred Abe to Silver, telling him Baten was reliable, but unforgiving. Silver waited impatiently as the phone rang four times before it was picked up.

"Yeah!"

"I am not impressed with your recent assignment in Buffalo. Too many loose ends. Lucky for you, Abe, the case was closed. Now I need you on another matter—to act as personal assistant to a Louisiana senator who will run for the presidency. He will believe you are his bodyguard. What you really are is an agent in my employ, keeping an eye on him. It will take all the finesse and diplomacy you have, and you will be on him 'round the clock'."

"Sorry Mr. Silver I don't do that kind of work. I'm no one's Nancy, I prefer to keep my distance from political circles. I'm a behind-the-scenes guy."

"You'll do it because you owe me."

"You're forgetting all Senators have their own secret service agents. How am I going to get around that?"

"I've got it covered. You just be packed and ready to fly there when I need you to."

The next item on Scott's agenda was to regain control of 'Silver Bullet'. He needed to get Scaletti's computer over to his office, so he could manage Silver Bullet himself and called Robert Talbot. "Talbot, this is Scott Silver. I need you to bring the archive terminal over here and set it up."

"No sweat, Mr. Silver. You want me to set it

up in Mr. McKnight's office?"

That reply threw him off, and he hesitated. Then Scott asked Rob, "Why would I want it set up in his office?"

It was Rob's turn to pause. "Well . . . ah, um, I'm sorry Mr. Silver, it's just that Lance was here and needed a little help getting some files he thought may be needed that he believed was on the system Mr. Scaletti used when he was in Chicago. And since Scaletti has, ah, left us . . ."

Silver cut in warning, "From now on Talbot, you check with me before you let anyone near computers that are not in their own office. Now get that computer set up in 'MY' office—pronto!"

After hearing a meek "Yes sir," Scott slammed the receiver down and wondered, *what did McKnight want with files on that computer?* I should have said, "NO!" to Butch when he asked to keep McKnight on, he reckoned.

Silver's mind raced with fury and decided Butch may know something about what is going on. Scott marched out of his office and into Butch's, who was on the phone as Scott stomped to within two feet of his desk.

"Excuse me, I think I am about to have an emergency. I'll call you back," Butch said. "So, what's the emergency Alex?"

"I'm not in any mood for your crap right now Butch.
What was McKnight doing at corporate?"

Whoa, I don't have the slightest idea what you are talking about. You mind calming down and explaining yourself?"

"I don't need to explain myself!"

"You're right you're inexplicable, so what exactly is your problem?" Butch jibed.

"Your boy McKnight is the problem. He has been over at corporate screwing around with Scaletti's files. What do you know about that?" Scott screamed.

"I know nothing. I see nothing. Lance was there to get files that belonged to him, from his old office which he believed may be helpful. Lance did not need anything from Bobby's files. Who fed you that nonsense? I also asked him to consult with Marenski on the negotiations. He may have wanted to know the union's position since the last meeting. Anyway, that's all I can think of."

"Well, keep that snoop away from everything, from here on out, and further away from me. If he needs any information regarding these negotiations or anything else, he can go through Marenski or you." Silver stomped out with the same intensity.

Back in his office, Scott Silver was finally able to get a hold of himself. Maybe that is all he was looking for, although he would keep a sharp eye upon him.

Silver Bullet was too essential in the grand

scheme of his future and would be protected at all cost.

6
UNION NEGOTIATIONS

LANCE TRIED STROLLING casually into the office the morning after his return from Buffalo, but felt as if he was fooling no one. His immediate objective was to talk to Mark Marenski about what he found on his trip, but he knew he had to go to his office, which meant he would not be able to avoid Butch. Sure enough, as he passed Logan's office he heard, "Hey Tiger." Another cringe.

"Hey Butch. What's been happening since I've been gone. Am I still employed?"

"Barely." He noted Lance's eyebrows raised in surprise. "Silver came in here on the warpath wanting to know what you were doing over at corporate looking through Bobby's computer files. I obviously didn't know, but I told him you may have been doing some research on the editorial union. I think he bought it. So, Lance, exactly what were you doing?"

"Well you got it absolutely right," Lance lied. "So, why was he was ticked?"

"Ticked? That is an understatement. Anyway, you are to go through Marenski or me if you need anything regarding negotiations or anything relating to anything. In addition, do not go anywhere near Scott. Out of sight out of mind."

"No worries there."

"So how did it go in Buffalo?" Butch asked.

"Bobby's funeral was a bit surreal. It was a long day. We didn't know anyone there but were able to give our and the company's condolences. The family really appreciated the company's contribution." Lance was not prepared to discuss anything else of the trip with Butch yet. Lance couldn't be sure what was going on, who was involved or how deep it went, but he knew someone in the company was up to no good.

"Well, I'm glad we were represented anyway. I just can't believe Scott didn't go with all the history he had with Bobby, but so be it."

"Yeah, well, I need to go over to see Marenski for a while, so I'll check in with you later." Lance got ready to cringe again but was relieved when Butch said, "Yeah, later."

Lance went to his office, dropped his things on his desk, and sat for a few minutes thinking.

Robert Talbot didn't burn him completely, singed maybe. And more than likely, unavoidable, as Rob could have said much more.

Lance made a mental note to send him a bottle of a fine wine with a sampler cracker and cheese basket. Lance knew the two were the only ones who knew about the encrypted version of the hidden software file. Then, he realized, the only detail he didn't tell Falco about was about Talbot's security software. At that moment, he decided to refer to the program file, uniondues, by the password used to open it, Silver Bullet. All copies of the locksmith files and all of Scaletti's other files were hidden in his den.

MIKE MARENSKI'S RECEPTION room was empty. Mike was in conference with an employee, with the door ajar so Lance thumbed through the newspaper as he waited for Mike to finish.

"How'd it go?" Mike asked, as he welcomed him into his office.

"M squared! You won't believe ten words of it." Lance shut the office door and proceeded to tell Mike almost everything, he and Kait accomplished in Buffalo. "Now I'm sure, serious money is being washed through FEI accounts, and transferred off shore. The way all the pieces fit together, we may still have miscalculated a couple of things, and a couple of pieces are not in place, but what is evident, suggests that Bobby Scaletti was only willing to go so far with FEI books." Lance was careful to keep his voice quiet and level. "Somewhere along the line, Bobby figured out that 'Silver Bullet,' that's what I'm calling the union dues program, is far more than just a tax evasion account or money-laundering account. Mike, I'm certain it is why he prepared all the clues that were positioned to domino, if, no, not if, he knew it was only a matter of when, something happened to him, and he intended to expose Scott Silver and his Silver Bullet. I'm not sure what we do next."

"What do you mean we Ace? I'm sure as heck not going to put on a wig or lipstick and boots."

"Hey, what about your guy at the phone company? Hear anything yet?"

"When I hear something you'll hear something."

"So, don't you think something has to be done about any of this? Don't we have to try to figure out what's going on? Obviously, it's illegal. We are key employees in this company, for now at least, well you are. I don't like the idea of working for a person that's fraudulent, especially when the guy is the head of a Media Company as large as FEI. My reputation isn't for sale, Mike. Who knows, maybe we could be drawn into this mess somehow and end up facing some kind of prison sentence. You've heard of RICO, right? It's not just for the Mafia anymore! That'd make a great slogan, and I'd laugh if I wasn't so mad."

"Chill out, Lance! Of course, we need to do something. I just do not know what. Nevertheless, on the surface I agree, it certainly involves money laundering. Have you discussed this with anyone else, like Butch?"

"Well no! I would hate to think Butch may be involved. I can't fathom that. But who knows. I thought I'd discuss this mess with you before I did anything."

"Yeah, best to keep the circle tight. What do you think you'll do next? If you're planning to look at the file again, stop. Silver had Talbot move the system to his office. Rob also said it wouldn't matter anyway because it was mostly archives, and all the sensitive files on the hard drive were encrypted."

"Butch told Silver I was researching files for negotiations. Maybe he bought that, but he'll watch me like a hawk. Who knows what he plans to do? I know he'll do something for sure."

"Well, you can probably bet on that," Mike agreed. "Speaking about negotiations, the editorial union is ready to get started and that may just help play into the story about your research."

"When are they supposed to start?"

"I told them I'd call them today since you were out of town. They said that was fine, but they wanted to start as soon as possible, maybe even have an initial meeting later this afternoon. What do you think?"

Lance sighed, "Well it's not like I have a lot to do at the moment, seeing as I just got grounded by dad. I can't really do any investigative reporting on the laundering without him or Scott wondering where I'm spending my time. Are you sure, I'm allowed to be in the meetings? I'm only 'consult' remember?"

Mike laughed. "I cleared it with Scott and Butch; you're sitting in. As far as your 'Bullet' project, we'll just sit on it for a day or so, make it look like its business as usual, I'll call you and let you know what the union wants to do."

Mike Marenski phoned Jarvis James Houston, the international rep for the editorial union. A meeting was set up for early that afternoon held in the conference room of FEI. Mike and Lance were waiting in the conference room adjacent to Marenski's office when Marenski's secretary ushered Jarvis Houston and his delegation of union representatives into the room. The group filed in as if ready to announce a guilty verdict to the court. Lance could not help but smile. He and Mike stood up.

Mike whispered quietly to McKnight, "What are you grinning about?"

"Fate" Lance whispered back as he extended his hand to the man he knew as J.J. Houston. "How have you been J.J.?" Lance asked while shaking his hand. "It's been a long time."

They shook hands vigorously as Jarvis Huston looked at Lance with a question mark. Then his jaw dropped as he managed to say, "I nearly didn't recognize you. Because I got laughed out after the negotiations I had with you. Man! I never thought we would meet up again. What brings you to Chicago, Lance?" Jarvis wondered, still too surprised to close his mouth.

"Oh, the same thing that brought you here. We just took different paths," Lance philosophized smiling inward and outward bowing slightly toward Mike, "Well let's get started then."

"I want to hear the story that made you two high-tail it out of Cali?" Mike insisted.

Houston and McKnight exchanged smiles before Jarvis said, "Let's see if Lance can tell a story as well as he investigates them—go for it Lance!"

"When I was in Oakland an organizational attempt led to an election for a representative for editorial personnel. The union won the right to represent them. My lawyer and I represented the company at the bargaining table, and we negotiated in good faith for sixteen months, but we were unable to reach an agreement on most of the issues. The union decided to call in help; Mr. Jarvis James Houston, the regional rep with staff in tow. Anyway, J.J. had his team of three; I had mine. Management was at one end of the conference room table, staffers at the other. We were trying to negotiate acceptable terms. We talked for maybe twenty-five minutes when we all became aware of a strange smell. The scent of burning weed. Pot! We all recognized it at the same time. At the end of the table, they were passing around a joint. They must have assumed they were invisible or were bored. I never really heard."

"None of them had jobs the next day," J.J. shifted toward Mike and admitted, "Consequently; I had to have the union withdraw as the editorial bargaining agent for those negotiations."

"And we lived happily ever after," Lance finished for Houston with a smile.

Marenski was laughing uncontrollably, and the union reps showed no response as if they were cardboard cutouts.

"Just goes to show you that you should really find out who's at the table before you start dealing," directing his comments to the rest of the union reps he added, "But, that's all water under the bridge," turning toward Mike, he politely said, "Let's get started. I understand that you guys have some objection to the staffing proposal we put forth under old management."

Mike tilted his head and said, "Lance?"

"Absolutely," Lance replied seriously. "We do have a big problem with the mandatory staffing period. We do not intend to allow that in our newsroom." Lance struggled to keep a straight face as Mike continued chuckling over the marijuana story.

Lance's statement set the tone for the rest of the day. Although each side listened patiently to the other sides arguments, nothing was accomplished. The atmosphere had deteriorated throughout the afternoon, so they called it quits about six o'clock.

The next day they were right back at it. Both sides held their positions on the issues, and little was accomplished. Lance and Mike did not stay to recap the session, as was their practice of old. They were both beat and decided to head directly home.

THE TRAFFIC WAS LIGHT. Lance made it home in half the usual time. He pulled the car into the driveway, checked the mail, and went inside through the garage.

When he got to the kitchen, he stopped dead. Kait was on her knees in the middle of the kitchen floor sobbing uncontrollably. Lance rushed to her and put his arms around her in an attempt to comfort her.

Squeezing her gently and rubbing her back softly, he whispered, "What's wrong Hon, what happened?"

Kait could not talk. She continued sobbing, heaving without the ability to get anything recognizable out of her mouth.

Lance kept holding her, comforting her, and trying to calm her down enough so she could tell him the problem. She was finally able to say, "In the back," and gasped wiping tears and pointing to the back yard.

"Stay here Babe. I'll go see," he whispered. Lance grimaced at the scene and looked away, holding his hand to his mouth. He wanted to vomit, but all he could manage were a couple of dry heaves. Regaining composure, he turned back to see his

Cocker Spaniel, Rusty, laying stiff on the brick patio pavers dead, choked with the heavy flexible wire around his neck. "Bastards," he whispered bitterly as he made his way back into the house.

Kait was still on the floor. Lance helped her up and held her. "Let's go to the living room. I'll get us waters. Do you want an aspirin?"

"Why would anyone do that?" Kait asked between sobs. "How could anyone do that?" Kait accepted the water and headache pills.

"People are cruel, Babe. They do things like this to create fear or just for kicks because they're sick in the head. Killing a human or animal for any reason other than self-defense is wrong."

"I know we have to tell Devon. She'll never trust me again! I'm sorry I let Rusty play outside alone."

"No, Kait, please don't, don't think that. It's not your fault at all. I'll handle everything." Lance held her in his arms and kissed her forehead.

"I think I'll take a long hot shower, maybe a little nap."

While his wife tried to rinse away the horrific image, Lance put thought into what he would tell his daughter. Suddenly, it occurred to him; maybe random pranksters weren't responsible. Someone from the negotiations may have decided to play hardball. How would anyone know that the dog was really his daughter's? Devon will be devastated, heartbroken.

The first thing to do was call Marenski, to see if he was okay, hopefully nothing happened over there.

"I can't believe it," Mike replied after hearing about the dog. "These fellows are serious, but I didn't think they were vicious."

"Well you might be wrong about that Mike." Lance then vowed, "I'll tell you what, I'm not standing for it. These card carrying thugs aren't going near my family again!"

"Why didn't they hit me? Why only you?"

"Maybe they want you to sweat it out. Think about what else could happen; expecting some concessions at the table."

"Listen, McKnight, I think you need to call the police. Get this on record. Let them know about the negotiations and let them follow where it leads. Don't push them too much. They hate that."

"I know that," Lance agreed. "I quickly found that out in Buffalo."

"Meanwhile, I think I'll give the family a little vacation.

Off to the local Holiday Inn for a change of scenery." "Yeah, see you in the morning."

"It may take a couple of days though," hedged the lead officer. "We're dealing with a different jurisdiction. We'll radio for Animal Control to come, or do you plan to get a permit to bury the dog?"

"We'll do the latter, thank you."

Hastily, it crossed Lance's mind to ask how the police departments own affiliation with the union affect their investigation, but his anger wasn't going to control his mouth. They had been very kind and respectful of the situation. As they got back into their squad car, Lance rummaged around the garage for the supplies he needed to prepare poor Rusty for burial.

Lance carefully swaddled Rusty completely in cloth, after that in plastic. Gently, he placed Rusty into a cooler and the cooler inside the chest freezer.

"The only reason I need to talk to Butch, is to let him know he'll have one less union official to deal with around here, Mike."

"Calm down and let's talk to Butch."

Lance was so upset he needed to wait for his heart to slow down before he could get up and sat panting until he was calm enough to resume. Finally, he and Mike rose in unison. Lance held back to allow Mike to lead the way to Butch Logan's office.

Butch was writing away on a yellow legal pad with his signature, "number 2" pencil. Butch would rather go to his grave without ever learning anything about a personal computer when they replaced all the typewriter's decades ago. Of course, that didn't deter him from making sure his secretary knew how to negotiate her way through the Internet, but Butch held true to using Neanderthal tools for journalistic endeavors.

"You got a few seconds?" Mike asked as they burst into the office hoping to avoid any other kind of interruption.

"I guess I don't have a choice," Butch observed. "The two of you together somehow tells me we're about to talk about labor, and I love to trade strategies with you guys on labor issues. How are we doing with the editorial talks anyway?"

That was like a toreador waving a red flag at a bull. Lance closed the office door, wasting no time launching into his recollection of the disturbing events. "Can you believe this? They were outside my house! Kait was in tears, took forever to calm her down! My daughter's dog?"

"Whoa. Whoa, whoa," Butch hollered, raising his hand.

"This is serious. I know."

Lance jumped out of his seat blurting, "Ya think?"

"McKnight!" Mike shot him a glare.

"Butch, Lance is convinced it's union motivated and on the face of things, he may be right. He wants to file an unfair labor practice claim. The police went to their house, processed the scene and took his statement last night. I believe it would be inappropriate to do anything with the National Labor Relations

Board at this point, but Lance disagrees." Mike shot another look at Lance that told him to keep quiet. "You're our leader. What say you?"

Butch didn't answer for a few seconds and when he spoke he simply looked at Lance and said, "I'm sorry. Sometimes this business really stinks. Is Kait okay?" Lance nodded soberly. Butch turned to Mike. "I don't think you can do anything until we get the police report. They may not turn anything up which might complicate things, but I think you at least have to wait for that."

"And what if the police can't come up with anything?" "Let's wait until that happens, Lance. I will document this conversation. Mike, When's the next session?" "In two hours," Mike replied.

"Oh, great!" Butch turned to Lance and began, "I think the best thing to do right now is to act normal. Go back to the table, be firm, but pleasant. Don't give them a hint that anything happened. I know you're pissed. I know you want to rip their eyes out and I'd probably feel the same way. We do not have proof of their guilt and there is too much to lose, if they are innocent. Do you think you can pull that off?"

"Hell, I don't know Butch. This thing has got me so upset—not so much for myself but for Kait. She's ready to pack for San Antonio. She may have already started. I'm fortunate my mother's there. I'm glad she's consoling her, or I might return to an empty house,"

"Sounds like a plan," Mike looked from Butch to Lance and back again.

"Yeah, go get 'em Tiger," Butch said to McKnight with enthusiasm.

Lance got up and walked to the door, following Mike out. Before exiting, he turned around and scowled as he said, "Please don't call me Tiger. I really hate that."

"Okay," Butch said somewhat surprised as he backed up in his chair. "No problem Laddie."

McKnight walked out wondering which nickname was worse; questioning having said anything.

Mike and Lance were at the bargaining table early, discussing the open items they needed to address and the strategy they hoped to employ for the session.

Jarvis Houston and his team came streaming into the room all at once—their usual practice. Mike thought they did this to convey a sense of strength and unity.

Once seated, Mike began to explain where he thought they were when the last session ended. Houston listened patiently until Mike finished.

"We understand your position on the manning issue but let me make it clear that this is not something the union is willing to give up. We believe strongly in this and intend to maintain our position anyway we can."

"Do your ways include intimidation? Trespassing? A little cruelty perhaps?" Lance spoke out in an unexpected, low roar . . . edging closer to Houston's face with each question, as Mike pulled on Lance's arm frantically.

Jarvis Houston reared back in his seat. The entire other side of the table was staring at Lance, their mouths open, unable to speak. "What the . . . ? Back off! Do not play me, Lance McKnight."

Mike pushed Lance out the door, holding up his free hands asking the union team to calm down and have some patience.

Once outside, Mike just stared at Lance in disgust. "So much for the 'act like nothing happened' strategy,"

"I'm sorry," Lance apologized. "I don't know what came over me."

"Well, you screwed up. It may have even cost us our hand in the negotiations! Way to go Ace. You might as well go back to your office. No, go home! That's an order. We are obviously not going to get anywhere today. I'll see what I can do to troubleshoot your damage. You better pray I'm successful."

"I'm sorry, Mike. I lost my cool."

"Ya think, Sherlock? There better not be a next time, Now, get going. I'll give you a head start, but I can't guarantee they won't be right behind you."

Mike reentered the negotiation room. He walked to the table shaking his head, sat down, interlocked his fingers, placed his hands out on the table and said, "Gentleman, all I can do is offer my sincere apologies and regret for my associate. Not to excuse his behavior, Mr. McKnight has suffered difficult challenges lately, and he just flew off the handle."

"That's an understatement," Jarvis replied, somewhat calmed down from the incident, yet still hot. "What was McKnight's problem with me?"

"If you would be willing to recognize this session as canceled, I'd be glad to talk about it, off the record," Marenski proposed.

Houston stayed, but sent the rest of the team back to work—instructing them to keep the incident among themselves.

Once they were gone, Marenski explained what had happened to the McKnight's, that he was still emotionally exhausted and not thinking clearly. When Mike finished, he watched Jarvis Houston, awaiting a response. Mike was expecting a confession or at least an acknowledgement of understanding Lance's behavior.

"Why accuse us? We did nothing. We have a bad reputation in this town for slowdowns and strike threats, but we would never push that hard. We draw a line and don't cross it. I thought you knew us better. We're not thugs."

"Hey, Jarvis, no one believes you did it. That's why I'm here right now, apologizing and explaining his actions. I am not excusing them. He was sent home, and I can take him out of future sessions."

"I do have control over my membership. This

couldn't happen without my knowledge or approval, which would never have been given."

"But it did happen," Mike insisted.

"I have no doubt that it did, but I'm telling you no one from our union was responsible. I understand why Lance went crazy, but I am telling you again, editorial is not responsible. I've been in the negotiations, and I think I have a good understanding on what has occurred to date. I do not pretend to know the intensity of feelings on either side of the table, but I will tell you right now, the entire union negotiating team will be willing to submit to polygraphing tests."

"Spoken like a true negotiator," Mike replied. "No Jarvis that will not be necessary." Mike picked up the phone and dialed Lance.

"McKnight," came the stressed greeting. "I thought I told you to go home? You're screwing up the negotiations with your maniacal behavior, now go home!"

Less than a minute later, Lance with his tie drawn down from his collar and his hair a mess, was at Mike's office doorway.

"I needed to rest my brain a bit," he said flopping down on the chair in front of Mike's desk.

"At least you're halfway intelligent! While you were 'resting your brain', I was smoothing things over. They were really upset."

Mike held up his hand to keep Lance from responding, "Please listen before you open your mouth. They agreed to take polygraphs. The entire committee, which is not necessary, because I am convinced they are telling the truth, they did not do it. And, If these guys didn't do it, then it was neighborhood hoods, if not, who? Who would want to scare you off or lead you in a different direction? Who might want you off your game? When you look at the bigger picture, it does not add up. I think someone else is responsible."

"Looks like your Criminal Justice degree is paying off. Do they pay you by the day plus expenses? I didn't even stop to think it could have been someone else. I was so confused. I'm clearer now. I would consider it may have something to do with 'Silver Bullet,' if I thought it was relevant. But, I'd been taken care of in a more direct way; like shooting me, running me off the road, or just beating me into a coma as a warning."

"Look, you messed around with Scaletti's computer, let's hope no one knows you borrowed the hard drive for a few hours. You accepted the box from his wife, then unlawfully entered his safety deposit box. Lance, Is there anything you haven't told me? Anyway, it may also be a way to distract you," Mike theorized.

"Well, maybe we should take all of this to the police. Tell them about the negotiations and the alleged money laundering, and let the proper authorities sort the whole thing out. Let the experts take it from here. If you're right about 'Silver Bullet' and Scaletti acting under duress, we need to nail down better proof before we take anything to the authorities," Mike insisted. "I would sure like to have some hard evidence—enough to put the right people away before we expose ourselves. Then, I'm all for letting the cat out of the bag,"

"Mike, this scares me. Where do we go? I think I got fake financial records and information about a program that moves money around, but I need to know where it's coming from and where it's going. I need to sleep on it, and I need to get home to my wife. We'll catch up in the morning."

Before Lance left, he decided to check in at home first, to check in with his mother. "Thanks for looking after her, mom. She really loves you; you know."

"Well, I really love her too!" "I'm on my way."

7
Press The Pause Button

ON HIS WAY HOME, Lance spent the entire drive reviewing all that he had uncovered. He also rehearsed the story he would tell his wife and mother. He wasn't about to frighten Kait to San Antonio and didn't want to worry his mother either. He decided to cast the blame on a satanic cult or gang initiation. Lance wondered if it would wash.

After pulling into the drive, he checked the mailbox, glad it was empty and hurried up the front walk and in through the door to enter the house.

"Hello," he called from the foyer. "Hello," he called again as he strolled toward the master bedroom.

"We're in here," came the reply from his mother.

"Is Kait actually awake?" Lance asked as he walked into the room. Kait was sitting up on the bed with her hands around her knees, which were pulled up close to her body.

"Yes, I'm awake but I'd truly like to sleep some more. I wish I could sleep forever so I wouldn't have to remember. Why do people do the things they do? Things like this don't happen in San Antonio! I want to go back"

Lance responded with kindness and understanding. Slowly and deliberately, he said, "Kait, please listen and don't get angry with this, but they do things like that in San Antonio every day. You just haven't had to hear about it. Evil people are everywhere, unfortunately. However, the police believe it was a gang initiation. There have been similar random attacks in three gated communities. As for going back to San Antonio to live, it can't happen now, but we can go for a weekend."

JANICE MCKNIGHT NOTICED the smile across Kait's face. "That's the first smile you've had all day. It suits you, honey."

Lance picked up on that. "You know Rusty was special to me, but even more so to Devon. I haven't had the heart to tell her what happened yet. She's the one who picked him out. She loved seeing him when she came to visit in San Antonio. Now that we're in Chicago . . . well, It's going to be harder on her than any of us. I'm trying not to think about it right now. So, what should we have for dinner?"

"I'm not too hungry," Kait protested softly.

"You will be after you get cleaned up and out

of here," Lance promised. "You've been cooped up in the house all day long. The fresh air will do you good," he coaxed.

Kait gave in and with the help of her mother-in-law; they were dressed for the evening.

Lance poured himself a wine and was sipping on a glass of Pinot Noir in the den while waiting for the two Mrs. McKnights. Finishing the glass, he went back toward the bedroom to give the women a nudge.

They were just coming out. Lance felt good and hoped the evening would prove to be a relaxing way to avoid thoughts of the many recent woes faced.

Another Italian dinner, a lot of small talk about their family, museums in the city, and concerts in Grant Park helped lighten the evening.

When they returned, Janice said her good-byes to both with hugs and kisses.

Lance and Kait retired early. Kait fell asleep quickly, even with all the sleep she had during the day. A definite sign of depression, Lance thought as he recalled what seemed to be endless days of wanting nothing but sleep. And sleep he got, but not without one of his dreams, which he often had when facing a conundrum. Lance dreamed wildly about a crazy Italian with a mask like the Lone Ranger. The Lone Italian was forcing banks to hand over their money to Tonto, who looked surprisingly like Scott Silver. The ranger communicated with his victims and cohorts via Skype. Everyone was dressed in pinstripe suits and armed with machine guns. The Lone Italian would be eating pasta as he watched the money roll into his bank. When Lance finally woke, he tried his hardest to put the dream out of his mind.

Mike Marenski was in the office cafeteria making a pot of coffee. Lance McKnight took his briefcase into his office and returned to catch the second cup of freshly brewed coffee. The two acknowledged each other and went to Marenski's office.

"I don't know what to say to you. I still feel awful," Lance lied, again with cause, "Listen, I'm sorry for any problems. I'll clear it all up."

"I don't know what to say to you, McKnight. I do not understand how you can believe the bad things that have happened to you excuse your behavior. You had better get a hold of yourself, Ace. If everyone that observed stands true to their word, and says nothing, you will probably be able to keep your job. Until further notice we will just put yesterday behind us both."

"What about Silver Bullet?"

"Everything we have is circumstantial and only proves that Bobby Scaletti has copies of what appears to be tax evasion and laundering documents, but nothing is the original paperwork. Anyone could forge the invoices and returns. There is no proof they are actual copies of real transactions, Lance. There will be no more B & E or any felonious activity. It's pretty natural for a guy to take over his dead assistant's business materials and equipment in an effort to find out what kind of shape he's in."

"For a bloody Criminal Justice graduate, you sure aren't very suspicious."

"Oh, I'm suspicious all right, Lance. Any missteps and Bobby Scaletti would go down for all of it, because all the "evidence" you think we have, points to Scaletti, so far. I thought you wanted justice for a friend and co-worker?" Mike was starting to think it was possible Scott Silver was the sole owner of the Silver Bullet account, and paid Scaletti well, until something happened to spook Scaletti into collecting evidence to turn Scott in, but he turned up dead.

"Well, then I'll get the evidence. Somehow I'll get the evidence." Walking out of the room, he noticed Mike, shaking his head.

Lance spent the majority of the day putting out fires in the newsroom. It was amazing to him, once he thought about it after the fact, that no matter what other problems he may have outside his routine, he could always discard them once he was immersed into his work. He loved this part of his job. It held that intrigue and sense of urgency that allowed him to get lost in its depths for hours; hours that seemed like minutes and wiped his mind totally clean of other worries.

But, today was somewhat different. Today, although he went about his responsibilities with the same professional acumen he always did, for some reason, the latest series of challenges in his life didn't bring depression; it felt energizing. Curiosity, anger, and rage had taken over. There were so many unanswered questions that Lance had no time to think about depression.

When Lance got home that night, Kait was in a much better state. Thanks, in most part to his mother, who came over again to spend the majority of the afternoon showing more, old family photos to Kait.

"I didn't know you were such a fat little kid," Kait mused to Lance after he had kissed her hello twice.

"I wasn't fat. I was a little chunky," Lance explained defensively.

"You were fat," Kait insisted. "Wasn't he Janice?"

"I'm taking the fifth. I always told him, Kait, he was pleasantly plump, but all toddlers are a little pudgy at a certain age, you'll see, won't she, Lance?" Janice looked at Lance wide-eyed.

"You'll be the first to know, right, Babe?"

"Sure, Hun, first call," and turned to her mother in law, "we promise."

"Well, I thought since the week is almost over, you and mom could have a quiet, early night of dinner and binge a few episodes of a series. Mom, would you mind spend- ing the night. You guys could have a pajama night, unless you are sick of being here, I'd understand."

Kait looked a little dismayed. "I don't feel like cooking and will not let your mom cook for us. She should relax; she's mothered us well these last days. It's our turn to care for her, Hun. So you'll need to make us some dinner before you leave." She looked at him with a straight face. "Please?"

"Sure, I'll just do like you—snap my fingers and voilà! Dinner is served." Everyone laughed with him. "Surly I'll be able to make something we can eat. Kait, you and Mom get the TV trays set up and find something to watch."

Kait turned on the gas fireplace and stocked the spare chair with more pillows and blankets while Janice set the TV trays with additional napkins, an ice bucket, a bottle of wine chilling in it and three glasses. Finally, she got cozy inside a blanket on a comfortable recliner, while Kait sat on the couch scrolling through the series guide and let her mind wander. No one said a word while they ate whatever it was they were served. Janice winked at Kait, and Kait made a mental note not to ask Lance to cook on his own, again.

Kait McKnight always felt Lances weekends should be reserved for the two of them. It was a time to shake off the world and everyone should respect that. Kait was not selfish with her husband's time when it came to Janice or her step-daughter, Devon. As odd as it may be, her mother-in-law and she had a warm relationship. Devon was nearly a teenager, smart and witty like her father, and sometimes fairly stubborn—like her mother. Devon was scheduled for a three-day visit. A quick trip to Texas would be a good way to occupy her time with them.

DEVON WAS USUALLY POLITE and respectful of people in general. She loved music and books as much as her father did. Devon was what most kids her age would call a nerd, lessening the possibility of getting in with the wrong crowds. Kait and Lance were proud of how Devon was developing, but also knew Lance regretted not having enough time with her. His work schedule presented a difficulty in balancing the time he had to spend with her.

Saturday morning Lance and Kait secured their home, packed the car, and drove over to Jill's to pick up Devon, who will be stoked to fly out of town for a couple of days. Lance practically had to pay Jill to let him take her to Texas.
Sometimes she was so difficult to deal with. He asked her not to tell their daughter; he wanted to surprise Devon.

"Hi Kait! I didn't know you were coming with. Mom just said dad and I were going to Texas for a couple of days. We're still going dad, right?"

"We're all going."

"Oh, good. I wanted Kait to come too. Is Nana watching Rusty?"

Lance sighed deeply. He looked at Devon

while trying to decide whether he should tell her now. He didn't have much choice. How was he to explain Rusty's absence? "Rusty's dead," he blurted out, feeling sorry he had that instant.

Devon looked at her father with tears streaming down her cheeks.

"It was an accident, Sweets," he lied.

Still crying, Devon asked in a whimper, "Will we be able to get another puppy?"

"I don't know sweetie. We'll see."

When Devon finally got over Rusty's death she wiped her eyes and asked Kait, "Aren't you excited to go to San Antonio, too?"

"I am. We will have as much fun as there is to have. Did you pack yourself, or did your mom pack for you?"

"You're silly Kait. I'm old enough to pack for myself." Devon really loved Kait, although she still couldn't quite understand why her parents divorced or why her mother and father weren't friends but accepted how everything turned out.

The McKnight's were seated, buckled in and ready for takeoff. Kait and Devon talked about what they could do.

Lance finally felt like he could carve out a piece of time to think about everything, and everyone. He closed his eyes and leaned against the window, only pretending to sleep, although he was deep in thought. The problem in Lance's mind was he had all the evidence needed. He had all the proof the District Attorney would need—documentation the courts would accept as evidence to hand down a tight conviction.

The problem was how the evidence was obtained. It was one of the reasons he didn't tell M Squared about the copies he made of everything; that he didn't care if Scott had blocked the access to the computer with Scaletti's files on it; that whole bit was a charade.

The other reason Lance withheld information from Mike was because he still wasn't sure what side he was on, completely. He and Mike were good friends with mutual regard and a difference in opinion about Silver. Yes, if Scott Silver is guilty, Mike Marenski would not destroy evidence or obstruct justice.

Why was it that every time he asked Mike about the telephone company guy, he appeared shifty? Suddenly he became aware of why Mike seemed sketchy; Mike knew he was withholding something big. Lance would ferret it all out next week. For the rest of the weekend, it was going to be all about the McKnight's.

Monday Morning brought thoughts of Silver Bullet along with concern about a seat at the negotiation table with J.J. and the union reps. Sounded like a oldies pop group, he mused. Kait would bring Devon home after breakfast. He felt a twinge of guilt as he walked into her room and looked down at her sleeping. He saw himself in her. She looked more like him than like Jill. Dominant genes, Lance thought.

The light Auburn hair and puppy-dog eyes made her look remarkably like the photos of him that Janice had organized in a family album she had given Lance one Christmas. The resemblance was striking. Lance woke her. "Hey princess," he said softly. "I love you."

" I love you too Daddy," she said sleepily.

"Kait's going to take you to your mom's since I have to go into the office. I'll talk to your mother about you coming for Thanksgiving. Maybe we can go to the Omni." "Okay, Daddy," Devon yawned, "I love you," she said again.

Lance kissed her, gave her a big hug, made a little burp noise quietly in her ear then said, "Nana loves you too." He left the room feeling guiltier than when he entered. He hated the good-bye part of her visits.

Arriving at the Chicago Union, Lance verified neither Scott nor Butch was in yet, and then burst into Mike Marenski's office. "Let's get to it," he blurted out as Mike shot him a disgusted look. Lance hadn't noticed the young woman who was sitting across from Mike looking distraught. "Oh, sorry Miss—Mike, I'm sorry for the interruption." Lance left the door slightly open and went to his office.

Ten minutes later, Mike entered Lance's office with as much ado as he could muster. Lance was taken aback; his mouth stayed open for the first few seconds until he saw Mike's smile.

"Sorry about that," Lance apologized, "I feel like we're really close to solving this thing."

"We'll see," Mike said skeptically, "but, not now. We need to go talk to the editorial union. Mike thought for a moment before adding, "This may be a mistake, but I'm going to give you one more shot at the table. The first thing you'll do is give a heartfelt apology to everyone for your foolery. You better keep your flippin' cool today."

8
WHO'S WATCHING WHO

ABDUL BATEN HEADED to Louisiana right after leaving Illinois. Unfamiliar with New Orleans, he did not know what season of the year was pleasant, but was sure it wasn't fall. It hadn't stopped raining since his arrival and he felt cooped up in the insidious mini-mansion, miles from Bourbon Street; in his opinion the only place Louisiana had to offer. So far this part of the Bayou wasn't a welcoming place.

Baten reacted in much the same manner toward Andre Gaston. After unpacking his suitcase, Abe made a call to Silver. "Why do I have to keep vigil over this old, yuppie Cajun? If you need him watched, hire a Pinkerton. You presented this very differently to me. I won't play bodyguard for this French whiff."

Baten wasn't a glorified babysitter. In fact, most

people wouldn't want to be alone with him under any circumstance. Abe Baten was an evil man. This voyeur job was not going to interest him. He was still a little sore at Silver over the assignment in Buffalo, New York. How Silver viewed it didn't matter. Abe had some scruples. He felt better when his mark was deserved; like most of Hafez Fakhouri's competitors and a few others, he's come to know.

At the moment Abe must play ball. Being nobody's fool, he knew when he wasn't appreciated. The Gaston household, the senator's aides and staffers made no secret of it. Abe had been with Senator Gaston nearly every waking moment and they barely exchanged names. Abe called Scott with an update saying, "How am I supposed to do my job when the senator disregards my presence? And his campaign manager, James Hillerman, is even worse than Gaston. Oh, he's a smooth talking, slick con artist with a hundred and one tricks up his sleeve. Every time I get close to Gaston, he gets in-between us. It doesn't matter where we are or how close together we are; James drives a wedge between us. If the senator is sitting at the head of the table, and I'm next to him, Hillerman picks up a chair and squeezes in-between the two of us. I'm starting to feel like a leper."

SILVER TOLD ABE to suck it up, do what he was told and abruptly hung up on him. So Abe made a game out of it to cut the boredom. Finding ways to position himself in a way that Hillerman couldn't displace him, which drove Hillerman crazy.

Amazing to Abe, Mr. Gaston was positioning himself to become president of the United States. Mr. Silver failed to mention that, and Abe sensed Mr. Silver had his greedy hands all over it and figured out what the people in the Big Easy thought of their Senator's run for the oval.

Prior to now, he had no use for newspapers, rarely listened to news, and didn't watch television. The only current events important to him were related to Fakhouri's business. After living in this place with every media outlet staring you in the face, and reporters calling for interviews or comments, it became evident to Abe that Senator Andre Gaston was a popular man. He hated to admit James Hillerman was quite effective in managing the press. Still, he hated taking orders from Scott Silver.

Next, Abe called Hafez Fakhouri. "Give Silver someone else for this job. This isn't working out."

"Relax and enjoy New Orleans."

"Hafez? Hafez, you there?" Abe was more than a little perturbed Fakhouri also hung up on him!

A few days later, Scott Silver called him back. "I'm coming for a little visit."

"Great. We have a lot to talk about."

"We do."

Scott Silver perfected the ability to appear to have class when, in fact, he had none. He indulged in all the trap- pings befitting a wealthy CEO. The private jet was an eight passenger Bombardier Learjet 35A.

Silver used the aircraft like the family car, although it was almost never full of passengers. He hated company, hated people in general, really. Pilots were on 24 hour call, rarely having to layover in destinations for more than one night. He also used the Lear to wield as a perk for business associates; more for the impression made, than an act of kindness. The jet was at Midway airport being fueled and checked for a trip to New Orleans.

Butch was a little irritated with Scott. He was going to leave him holding the bag as usual by flying to some reception in Louisiana! To top that, he took one of the Chicago Union's security guard off watch to drive him to the airstrip in the company sedan. It played havoc with scheduling. Invariably, Butch would have to find someone to fill in for the missing guard and usually Scott gave such little notice that Butch couldn't get another one to cover in time.

Therefore, he'd have to pull someone from one of the departments that could spare a body, for an hour or so. The redeeming value was Scott Silver leaving town for a while.

A white stretch limo FEI NO 1, pulled into the

corporate terminal at Midway airport and parked. "Here you go, Mr. Silver," the guard said as he pulled up within ten feet of the jet.

"Thanks. Now hurry up!" Scott mumbled, wiggling his way out of the car—breathing as if he had just finished a marathon. He stood, impatiently tapping a foot on top of the pavement waiting for the driver to return.

The chauffeur rolled his luggage to the stairs, then handed them off to attendees to carry aboard.

"Tell Logan I said to put 'round the clock watch on our floor."

"Yes, sir."

The pilot and copilot watched everyone board from the hangar. Even from their view, both noticed Mr. Silver was in a pitiful mood as normal, a reason they usually waited for him to huff his way up the air stairs and was seated comfortably before they were crossing the tarmac. The pilots came out of the hangar five minutes later; the time it would take Mr. Scott Silver to calm himself and start reviewing newspapers, as was his ritual. They climbed aboard and took their seats inside the cockpit, nodding to their boss on the way, afraid to say anything for fear of reprisal.

The pilot called Scott on the telephone intercom to ask for their destination. He radioed the tower, and the copilot raced back inside to file the flight plan. After he closed the clamshell style door, and buckled in, the ground crew taxied the craft out to the runway to await their turn for take off.

"We're just about ready, Mr. Silver," he yelled over the roar of the two Honeywell 2-2B engines. "Make yourself comfortable, we'll be above Toronto in two hours. Skies are clear."

He closed his eyes tightly and envisioned "Alex Scott Silver, Clinton Alvin Excelsior, Esq., Advisors to President Andre Gaston" splashed across newspapers, magazines, and blog posts nationwide. All put there by him, with the help of the freedoms and power of the press. Scott felt almost invincible as his mind raced. Adrenaline pumped with the thoughts of the things he could accomplish with the power, control, but mostly the adoration he would soon acquire. There were still a few hurdles to trample over. He would have to smooth the way with the senator and Hillerman, once Abdul was put in check.

Clinton Excelsior's headquarters was located in the capital of the province of Ontario Canada. Therefore, additional logistics were necessary to maneuver through conducting business in two separate governments.

Although their business arrangement in newspapers extended to another in politics, that was the extent of the knowledge of each other's business or personal lives.

The arms dealing stories the Excelsior ran, were pulled from the FEI Wire Service Silver set up. Clinton Excelsior believed as everyone else, that all transcripts had been thoroughly vetted and the information exclusive—selling record numbers. Both parties made real profits on both sides of the border. Clinton naturally assumed Scott's monetary contribution in the political arena came from those earnings.

Now, Scott Silver was on his way to Toronto to pick him up. The two were to have a couple of discussions on their way to Louisiana for a meeting with a US Presidential hopeful.

Clinton stood to make a lot of money from the access and inside information from the American Politician.

Two hours after take-off the jet landed on the corporate strip of Toronto's International airport. It taxied slowly to a halt; the copilot opened the door allowing a Customs Inspector to board the plane. He greeted the pilots and Silver cheerfully. Both pilots responded with a smile, but Scott simply stared at the government agent thinking rude thoughts. The Agent made a perfunctory sweep of the plane asked the pilots their business in Canada and left.

M OMENTS LATER, MR. EXCELSIOR boarded.

He ducked as he came through the jet's door to enter the main cabin. Scott stood up, smiling for the first time since leaving the limo in Chicago.

Clinton smiled as well, and they greeted each other warmly.

"Gentlemen, please take your seats and secure your restraints for departure," the pilot announced this while standing in the doorway of the cockpit. "Can we get you something to drink first?" Both men refused politely.

After takeoff, Scott and Clinton chatted about the many newspaper industry changes time and technology brought. Both owners agreed newspaper profits could be maintained in spite of online papers having subscribers. Some were paper customers who canceled delivery for electronic access.

Exclusive associated content and entertaining articles were getting tougher and tougher to obtain. Both moguls agreed that the fastest way to squeeze out profit was through squeezing out costs.

"Scott, do you really think it wise to introduce me to the senator at this point?" Clinton asked in his refined, executive form. He was a third-generation newspaper owner, raised in the most proper circles of Toronto.

"Absolutely Clinton! As Senator Gaston's Presidential Campaign Manager, it is up to me to become the liaison between the senator and campaign donors. Since you are solely representing our combined assets, which is like giving the campaign as many blank checks needed, it's perfectly acceptable to be able to meet and dine with the candidate. We need to make sure he knows he can't do it without our help. Before he realizes it, Gaston will be in this thing up to his neck."

"What does he know?"

"If you are asking if Gaston, or anyone else knows about our business association; the answer is no. The senator only knows that I lobbied hard for your money. I've sent a man to New Orleans as full time live in security for Gaston, and as a watch dog for us. His former campaign manager, James Hillerman, is now a top Aide. Our guy,, Abe Baten, and Hillerman are 'The Clash of the Titans,' making things a bit difficult because of their indifference toward one another. The situation is getting tense, and I thought a little intervention might straighten things out. Your presence is strictly for intimidation by way of purse strings."

"What if Gaston decides to drop out?" Clinton had to wonder because he too, had been following the flow of increasing interest in Senator Gaston, and responses to his political platform. In his latest television interview, Gaston mentioned announcing a change to his campaign in the coming days.

"He won't. Trust me," Scott smiled widely, while mixing two scotch and waters. The remainder of the flight they spent sifting through the stack of newspapers.

Scott called Senator Gaston to tell the senator what hotel suite he'd be in and agreed on a time to meet there.

Once on the ground in New Orleans, the pilots checked in the plane and headed off to their hotel. Scott reserved two suites in the lower French Quarter near the river. An hour later, the senator arrived with Hillerman and Abe.

"Come in gentlemen!" Scott greeted them at the door. He scrutinized them as they filed in the room. Senator Andre Gaston looked distinguished as he did when they first met, followed by an impeccably clothed James Hillerman and Abe Baten, dressed like a door attendant at a Los Angeles nightclub. "A melting pot if I ever saw one," Scott said rather plainly.

"It never ceases to amaze me, Mr. Silver," the senator began, "what a dichotomy you are. You can come on with so much polish and finesse one minute and turn into a street urchin the next."

"I detect a hint of irritation, Andre. I do, but we're not here to discuss my dual personality. Let's skip all your psychoanalysis and get right to business." Scott proceeded to introduce everyone seated in the parlor of the hotel suite and took charge. "I guess the first order of business is to discuss the problems we seem to have between Mr. Baten and Mr. Hillerman. I'm of the understanding, that Mr. Hillerman isn't very cooperative in allowing Mr. Baten to fulfill his duties," Scott shot one of his piercing glances at Hillerman.

"And what are Abe's duties?" James Hillerman asked angrily. His ire grew when his question wasn't answered.

"Mr. Silver, surely you're aware that I am Senator Gaston's longtime advisor and campaign manager."

Scott shot up from his chair surprisingly speedy, when considering his obesity. "Listen to me," he screamed. "You're a face and that's all. Perhaps the senator has not been candid with you. You're not advising anyone. You give Abe what he needs to get his job done, got it?" Scott had crossed the room and was shouting at James, a foot away from his face.

James backed against the sofa, horrified by Silver's outburst. Baten was propped against the wall wearing a smug smile. Excelsior, stunned and not impressed, was too fearful to intervene. Addressing it another time would be prudent.

"Andre!" James protested his head whipping toward the senator. Andre simply shrugged and held his head down sadly. James regained his composure on the couch. Silver backed up and plopped down, still seething. "I don't know what's going on here, but you can count me out. There is a long road ahead of you, Andre, a couple of years. I think you can win, but if you have 'these kind' of people on your team, I won't participate."

"Who needs you?" It took a while for Scott Silver to know when to shut up, when mad.

"Just a minute," Clinton interrupted. "We're obviously a bit heated here. Perhaps we could discuss this more calmly. Mr. Hillerman, the 'kinds of people' you refer to are the people that have managed to get the senator to where he is now—the most popular candidate in the race. If it were not for our media houses, Senator Gaston would be as obscure as he was before the terrorist attack in Houston and retiring from his seat at the senate. I mean no disrespect toward the senator, but that is the reality of it all. Now, can we proceed in a gentlemanly manner?"

"Mr. Excelsior, the only thing I see you have going for you over Silver is that you have a few more manners, and a better vocabulary than he does." James Hillerman swiftly gathered his effects and walked toward the door saying, "Good-bye Andre. I hope you clearly understand whom you are bedding!"

Abe Baten flashed Hillerman a parting smirk along with a rigid salute.

"Was that necessary? You better start acting like you've had an education," Senator Gaston said to Abe after the door closed.

"You're absolutely right," replied Scott heatedly.

"We did not agree to go that far with James, Scott. He's been my ally and friend for a long, long time and deserves to walk this path with me. I thought we were keeping him on as the front man; that you would only manage the campaign funding and public relations in newspapers. I also didn't think James needed to meet you, Mr. Excelsior, but I am very pleased to make your acquaintance and looking forward to sharing a traditional Cajun meal tonight, to thank you for your gracious benefaction."

Clinton Excelsior acknowledged the senator with an aristocratic bow of the head, then said to Scott, "You were supposed to be behind the scenes. Everything was going as planned until you sent Omar Epps Corleone!"

"Well, Clinton, I went that far. Senator go get Mr. Hillerman back in here. Make sure he knows to keep his smart mouth shut. If he decides to stay on, he had better play as a team member and keep his nose out of areas that do not concern him. We can work together and with his stratagems, but if we come to an impasse, I have the final say. Since Abe said the media are like putty in his hands, he'll continue as 'campaign manager' and spokesperson under my direction."

It took everything Andre could muster to agree to Scott's demands. He wanted to tell him to shove it, that the whole thing was over, but could not, for two reasons. First, he believed that if he were successfully elected the presidency, there would be a few policies he could change that would better serve and protect the lives of every American. Secondly, he needed Silver's connections to the money needed for campaign financing. That would give him the same advantage to win as an established politician.

HILLERMAN WOULD HAVE his back. Hopefully he'll be able to convince James to stay with the campaign. When considering all the power that the office of a presidency lent, there had to be a way to send Scott Silver packing on his own accord.

"Well, I think you've made your position clear to us all, Scott. I've made dinner reservations for the five of us at 8:00 P.M., in this hotel's restaurant. Mr. Excelsior, good day. I will see what I can do about Mr. Hillerman. If he joins us for dinner you'll know he's on board." Andre crossed the room, stopping in front of Abe. "Are you coming?" His tone was brisk.

"I'm right behind you senator, after I talk to Mr. Silver. Scott, you, me," Abe's finger pointed to Scott, then unto himself, "this, were done here. You square things with Hafez. I'm leaving the Gaston's, tomorrow."

Scott Silver stood with his mouth open, as if to speak, but was mute.

Abe shook his head and grabbed the doorknob. "See you at dinner." Abe said facetiously and left.

Scott looked at Clinton and smiled. "All's well that ends well," he said.

"Did it end well?" Clinton did not think it ended well at all.

"Well, it's probably not over, but I think we can safely say it's under control," Scott replied still smiling.

"Let's hope so."

After the best Cajun cuisine either ever ate, Scott and Clinton spent the rest of the evening in the suite talking casually about what issues may become important during the campaign. They also discussed potential candidates for the vice-presidency. Something they felt may become important when the time comes, since the candidate would need to be someone with influence and someone, they could influence. They decided picking a V.P. was not so dire. It was Scott's opinion; the vice president did not carry the kind of power to interfere either way.

Meanwhile, although late, the senator convinced James Hillerman to come to his estate and hear him out. It took a lot of talking to get him to agree. Abe had no problem staying in his quarters, giving Gaston and Hillerman all the privacy they wanted.

Abe took the opportunity to spend his alone time packing his suitcases. As far as he was concerned, it was his final night on duty.

"I'm sorry I didn't tell you about Scott Silver or our arrangement. I was blinded by the prospect of making it to the Oval Office. When I heard him say, 'a campaign fully funded, free print advertising on Sunday and Wednesday in newspapers across the United States,' I did not think twice, James. I hastily accepted the offer."

"What is the extent of your relationship?" "I don't understand what you mean?"

"In return for his 'generosity' what have you promised him once you are elected?" James was visibly upset.

"I really don't recall promising anything."

"To me, Scott Silver sounded as if he believed he was running the show, with plans to run the country, through you!" James was visibly torn. "Andre, how could you let this happen? Why would you accept the presidency under those conditions? You would be a puppet. I can see the headlines now, Pinocchio for president!"

"Look, I thought if I could become president, I could really shape America's future now, for the generations of tomorrow. I will budget for programs that help us adapt to the technologies of the future to benefit the lives of all. I will work hard for a safer place for everyone. And in Maria's memory, I'll fund nationwide support programs for survivors of those lost in terrorist attacks on American soil."

"Where does Mr. Excelsior fit into all of this?"

"Actually, I didn't know who the benefactor was until introductions were made by Mr. Silver this afternoon. I had no idea Scott was bringing him. Unfortunate as it may be, no Silver, no financing. Excelsior owns several US corporations that can generate the large donation checks. We hold rallies in the cities of those companies, and it all looks like the donations correspond with the rallies, I think . . . I know now, how irrational my actions were. At the time, I convinced myself that I would not have to spend time writing speeches that will generate donations. I could skip that step, and deliver my message, with no worries or barriers. All I had to do was agree. Believe it or not James, Scott can be very convincing."

"'I'd call it threatening, not convincing!" He exclaimed. "Scott has another side that I now see, like Jekyll and Hyde."

"You've made a deal with the devil, Andre. I

think you need to cancel the contract."

"I can't. Silver knows I know it, and now, you know it. He is right in that he made all this happen. He controls a lot of print media, and he can probably make it disappear just as quickly. Worse yet, he can probably make many other unpleasant things happen. For one thing, where would I ever get the money to reimburse what we have spent to date? Worse than that, Scott Silver set me up to commit campaign fraud. How many years in jail is that? What would happen to my family, or you for that matter? No, I think I should proceed and in the meantime, try to figure a way to get out from under all of this."

"You're probably right. I just wish you were not in this position. Okay! We are in this position. I will stick by you, not only for you, but to nail Silver somehow. That guy is dangerous. Whatever happened to the press keeping the politicians honest? Oh, look, here I am now, talking to one of the conspirators. You cannot do this Andre. Not the way Silver wants it to come down. Not for Suzann's or Marie's sake! It's all wrong," James beckoned.

"Let's try to make it right," said Andre sincerely.

"Well, then start with Mr. Baten. Can we take charge of our own security detail? This guy, Abe, frightens me. There is something sinister about him, and honestly, Abe's is not the right image we want to project for our campaign. People are uncomfortable around him."

"I'll see what I can do. We have to regain

control, and that is a good place to start. Thank-you, James."

Early the next morning, Scott and Clinton met with the pilots for breakfast at the airport before boarding. They worked out their flight plan, which called for dropping Scott off in Chicago and then going onto Toronto. On the way home, Scott used his private air phone to reach Butch Logan at the Chicago Union.

"Did you get the message from the guard yesterday?"

"Your Majesty?"

"Butch, I'm not in the mood."

"I put extra security on as told."

"Cancel it. I will see you in a couple hours. I'll be back in the office before the publisher's meeting tonight."

"Why don't you take the rest of the day off? We really won't miss you." All Butch heard was the phone hanging up with a loud click. "It must have been something I said." Butch mumbled nonchalantly as he put the receiver down.

Scott dialed New Orleans after hanging up on Butch. He was finally able to convince the servant who answered the phone, he wanted to talk to Abe not Andre. Moments later, Baten answered.

"I'm sending the plane for you at ten this morning. Be on it."

"I'm already booked on a flight to Miami."
"Cancel it! You'll be met at the airfield."

"He's in a jewel of a mood today, laddie," Butch told Lance after talking to Scott. Butch's phone started to ring again. "Hold on, Lance. Butch here." A few seconds later was a loud "Shoot!" Butch slammed the phone down. "He's back. Just when I was shaking his call, he shows up in the flesh. Wish me luck. He wants to see me right away. Are my shoes polished?"

LANCE SMILED, AND left the room with Butch, turning in the opposite direction, toward his office. *Thank God, I don't have a meeting with Silver*, he thought. Nobody even noticed he had tampered with the computers, or that he procured financial records, he had no business seeking. *Was it that easy?* Lance wondered, then asked himself, "Have I just been lucky so far?" He quickly realized, even the luckiest person's luck runs out.

Butch took his usual position in front of Scott's desk. "What's up boss?" He asked. He debated whether to start with his typical wise crack but decided against it. His sixth sense told him that Scott's mood had not improved since his earlier phone call, and for once, Butch decided to play it straight—at least for starters.

Scott was busily editing something and did not

bother acknowledging Butch until he was through. He tossed the finished piece of paper into his out basket, loathing Butch. "You're lucky I like you, Logan," he said finally, although regretting his choice of words. Butch was going to give a smart-ass retort. He just knew it!

"I wouldn't call that luck." Butch replied with his most sincere expression.

Scott shook his head and tugged at his sleeves. There was something about Butch that always made him tug at his sleeves. He looked at Butch more seriously, if that was possible. "I've been thinking, we should probably ask McKnight to attend the publisher's meeting tonight. I want to put the Chicago Union's best foot forward. These guys should know that Chicago is going to end up being our flagship, so they should get to know the players."

"Did we join a rugby team?"

"Can't we get through one conversation without all the shtick?" Scott complained.

"No," said Butch nonchalantly, checking out his finger nails.

Scott pretended poorly to ignore him. "This meeting is not going to be so pleasant. I am tired of hearing all the crying about our investments in all the losing markets at the expense of the moneymakers. I want no more second guessing from these people and no more excuses about their inability to provide operating profit because their resources are washing down the drain in places like Chicago. These bastards ought to be able to stand on their own two feet, and if they can't we'll find somebody that can!" Scott threatened.

"Shouldn't you save the speech for tonight, Scott?"

"Look, wise guy, just make sure you and McKnight do a good job of representing how important the Union is to this organization, and how we're going to win the war while still bringing in an operating profit. Tell them you will be glad to help them in every way you can. Offer them editorial support or advice if they want it. Make 'em feel good that the Union is part of the organization."

"In other words, you want me to lie? Just kidding, I know you're not in the mood." Butch knew Scott was never in the mood. "We'll take care of it and make you proud. Will there be anything else?"

"Get out of here!"

"Love those four little words," Butch said on his way out, knowing how much Scott hated it when he did not have the last word. Butch went back to Lance's office.

Lance was working on the contract language for their editorial negotiations when Butch plopped down onto the secretarial extension next to his PC. Looking up to Butch Lance asked, "Good meeting?"

"Weird meeting, for a guy who said, he didn't want to see you around; he sure talks a lot about you."

Here it comes, thought Lance. "What'd he say?" Lance was sure Scott's only interest with him related only to his interest in the computer terminal. Lance wasn't about to involve Butch, determined to keep whatever else he dug up between himself and what he shared, would be with Marenski and Mr. Falco.

"He wants you at the FEI publisher's meeting tonight. We're supposed to carry the 'Chicago Union Flag' into battle. Tell them how we're winning the war and making a good operating profit doing it," Butch explained.

"You mean we're supposed to lie?" That should be easy since he had a lot of practice lying lately.

"Hey, that's what I told him," Butch laughed, "great minds think alike!"

The two executives spent the next half hour outlining their presentation, avoiding any exact numbers since most of them would be contrary to their orations. Butch was pleased with the planned deception. Sure, that Scott would be happy with the misinformation.

"You know," Butch said as he was leaving, "this could lead to a whole new, different relationship between you and Scott," he surmised.

"I've got to admit that Scott insisting I take a seat at a quarterly meeting, is opposite of what I expected from him. In truth, the only way it would be better is if Scott tumbles over the edge of a cliff,"

"Now, now, McKnight, don't be so cynical.

Where on earth do you get that stuff? Certainly not from me." Butch smiled slyly and left.

Lance picked up the phone to call Kait, dreading the conversation. Normally, Kait was a very rational and understanding individual. She was loving, loyal, and would do almost anything for Lance, but she did have one flaw, if you called it a flaw. Kait didn't like surprises. When it came to spur of the moment changes in his routine, she became irritated. Kait's reactions were not extreme; her position was distinct. On the other hand, Kait had a prior experience that lent itself to negativity.

Early in their relationship, Lance would call her to tell her he had to stay late, or he had a dinner engagement with an advertiser or supplier. Lance chalked up her being terse and silent to moodiness.

In time, Kait shared the details about her first husband. Kait told Lance that shortly after getting married, her husband started staying late, or had to take a client out to dinner. It was only one or two nights a week, then three or four, and occasionally a weekend of golf. Kait found out that often, he was not at his appointed meetings; he was in various bars, drinking and carousing. She heard rumors of his escapades all over town. Their marriage ended when Kait came home early from a visit to Dallas and found her husband in bed with another woman.

Lance was never unfaithful to his wife, and

believed Kait knew that, but because of the residue baggage from her first marriage, she was suspicious when unplanned delays came about. Reluctantly, he called with his news.

"Hello?"

"Hi, Kait, what's going on?"

"Okay, what's happening Lance? I can tell from your tone you have a specific need to talk about something."

"I can't just call to see how you are doing?" Lance said defensively.

"Sure, you can, but that's not why you're calling, is it?"

"Okay. You're right. Let me get right to the point. Scott wants me to attend FEI's publisher's dinner tonight. He wants to show off the Chicago Union. Butch and I have been nominated."

"Of course," was all that Kait said. There was a long pause.

"Kait? Come on now. You make it sound like I'm deserting you or something,"

"No, Hun. I just wish you could come home. Why do you have to go? I thought you were being phased out?"

"I don't want to go. It's mandatory. As long as I keep getting a check, I have to comply. If I had my druthers, I'd come home."

"If it makes you feel any better, we're not going out for dinner. The food is being catered to our boardroom."

"It's just that all this cloak-and-dagger stuff with

Bobby, poor little Rusty, and all. I don't want to be alone."

"Then call my mom. She'll be happy to come over; I'm sure," Lance said firmly. "If I didn't have to attend tonight, I wouldn't, Kait. I'll be home after the meeting adjourns."

"Sure, I'll see you when you get here."

As usual, Lance ended up feeling guilty, as if he were being compared to her ex-husband. Lance wanted to call her back but thought they would both end up feeling worse.

The meeting would be a nice work related transition for him. Lance hoped to see some of the publishers he knew and liked. Most of them worked for Scott, but some were independent of him.

9
THE PUBLISHER'S HOT PARTY

MCKNIGHT REVIEWED ALL of his notes for the meeting, polishing his words with a little more detail. When finished, he called Mike Marenski's office. Mike already left. He thought about calling him at home, but decided against it because he didn't really have anything specific to talk to him about.

Maybe he just felt like he needed some male bonding or something. It was a little after 6:00 P.M., and he decided to go over to the boardroom. Although the meeting did not officially start until 7:00 P.M., publishers would be trickling in after they checked into their hotels.

After all, they really didn't have anything else to do, at least not until the dinner was over. He was right. There were several publishers milling around the room, forming small groups, and chatting. The largest group gathered around

Butch, listening, and laughing intensely.

He always kept them in stitches, and the thing was Lance thought his anecdotes had lessons in them. Real life, down to earth stuff. Like Aesop's fables, although funnier and stranger than science fiction.

Lance made his way around the room, stopping by the make-shift bar to pour himself a vodka and diet tonic water, and circled the room. Shaking hands with each publisher he encountered, to his surprise, they were genuinely glad to see him. Later, he found out why.

APPARENTLY, 'TYSON THE TERRIBLE' was a huge understatement. Publishers found Burt Tyson impossible to deal with, and they missed how it was when he was at FEI. The conversation made him feel humbled. By the time he spent two minutes in Butch's clique, his negative mood was beaten.

Scott came into the room only minutes before seven o'clock, and every group grew quiet, every group except Butch's. After glancing up at Silver and shrugging his shoulders, he went right on with his storytelling. Silver said nothing and when Lance looked toward him, Silver's black holes bore right through him. All that Lance could read in Silver's expression was hatred and the promise of revenge.

A chill swept over him and the only way he could shake it was to turn back toward Butch and rejoin the fray. Still, the hairs on the back of his neck were standing on end, and he could feel Scott's demonic optical organs penetrating his back.

This time Scott really scared him. Not once had he felt comfortable with Silver. Scott Silver truly frightened him.

It was that moment that Lance realized he was capable of every evil imaginable.

Behind Silver's baby face with conflicting onyx eyes was a demon. Lance did everything he could to avoid any eye contact with him and shake the feeling of dread.

Scott Silver's voice broke in, "Let's all sit down and get started. We have a lot to cover and I, for one, don't want to be here all night."

There was little discussion when seats filled around the long, cherry wood conference table set for dining. Many of them acknowledged Scott with a nod, handshake, or plastic smile, but within a minute, they were all silent.

Scott Silver sat down at the head of the table, tugged at his sleeves ferociously, and then folded his hands. He looked around the table in disgust, shaking his head. "Each one of you came to me at the beginning of the year with a goal. You promised me advertising revenue would be up an average of three percent. You promised me, circulation would be up by four. You also promised, operating profits would be up more than ten percent. You promised me you would cut costs; do whatever it took to meet those goals. I've been patient."

Silver's hands were shaking, every ounce of exposed flesh was crimson. "I've been understanding and worked with you in every way I know how. But now, I'm pissed!" Silver uncoupled a hand and sent one crashing down onto the top of the table. Silverware clinked, water glasses spilled, and China rattled.

No one dared to look at Scott Silver. They all had their heads down, staring at the plate in front of them, like whipped puppy dogs waiting for their master to tell them; it was okay to move. Scott continued pounding the table. "Not one of you has met your goals. There isn't a publisher at this table that has made budget yet!" Silver screamed loudly, barely controlled.

"Including, the publisher of the Chicago Union!" Butch piped in, referring to Scott's budget numbers. Normally, this would have resulted in a roar of laughter, but not tonight. The only one who even giggled was Lance, and that was probably out of fear. The rest of the table sat motionless, their eyes staring at the table.

"Butch! This isn't humorous!" He roared. "No more jokes!" Scott began pounding the table again, glaring with the same intense stare. Butch just shrugged and smiled politely.

"Each one of you will submit a plan that will bring you back to your budget showing the operating profit that you said you would achieve by the end of the year. You have two days. This time, if you do not achieve them, FEI will have a number of new publisher's next quarter. Are there any questions?" No one made a sound. "Good! I'm glad we understand each other, now. Dinner is served,"

It was thirty minutes into dinner before

anyone dared to comment or question. Butch Logan started it all by banging a table knife against the water carafe. Butch went on to suggest the group skip dessert and ask for a credit, to reduce costs. Luckily, for Logan, Silver did not hear him. He was busily shoveling his second plate of food into his mouth. By the end of dinner, even Scott was civil.

Butch politely drew everyone's attention and he, and Lance made their presentation. Butch wrapped up their presentation by inviting the publishers on a tour of the plant. Lance was never happier to have anything finally over with in his life.

"We should just be starting up the state press now," he announced. "So, let's go down and see how the big boys do it," he said laughingly. Turning to Lance, he said softly, "Come on. Let's impress the hell out of these guys."

"Butch, I really have to go home," Lance replied. "Kait's upset with the short notice and a bit on the edge about everything."

"Okay. I'll cover for ya, laddie! See you in the morning," Butch patted him on the shoulder.

"Thanks Butch," Lance turning for the door glanced at Scott, in the back corner conversing in a group, and Lance thanked his lucky stars his back was toward the exit and bolted out of the room, into the elevator, down to the parking lot, and into his car.

A chilling fear came over him as he drove out of the lot, staying with Lance all the way home. He didn't know if it was fear of Scott, Kait's reprisal, or fear for his life.

Earlier in the day, Abe received a call from Scott Silver minutes after he arrived at the hotel. Although he did not know what he was to do for him in Chicago. Abe was sure another impulsive order was about to be issued.

As agreed, they met for drinks in the lobby bar after he refreshed from the flight. He didn't care, one way or the other, about the McKnight's. The rub was these kinds of jobs were for armatures. Abe had grown tired of the petty gigs Silver forced onto him since Buffalo. He was into the kind of ops that required genius and meticulous planning, a little mystique, danger, intrigue.

The wife was the only one that was supposed to be home. Silver said he would keep Mr. McKnight in town until 10:00 P.M., giving him the rest of the day to get what gear he would need, take a little nap have a bite to eat, and then get to it.

It would be an easy in and out having the advantage of remembering the layout of the neighborhood and the property. After he completed the job, he would go to the airport where the jet with his luggage stowed aboard, would be waiting to take him to Miami, Florida.

Kait decided not to impose on Janice; she had helped them so much lately and should be allowed some time to herself for a change. Lance would be home when he got there. The more she pondered it, the more she knew how silly she'd been. Lance just started the job, and even if it was temporary, she needed to support him in the things he had to do for that job.

Kait made a salad, and by the time she was finished with it, she realized it was dark, pitch black; the clouds covered any evidence of the moon. It sure got dark early these days. Under the cover of clouds, was there a moon? She couldn't tell. Well, she couldn't worry all night about the dark, or the moon, or even Lance. She decided to read. Taking the recent National Geographic, Kait sat at the kitchen bar flipping through the pages.

Fifteen minutes later, she got up for something to drink. She poured herself a cup of milk, grabbed a few cookies from the cupboard and went back to finish reading an article about the Mayan Indians.

Kait then decided to take a shower and perhaps watch TV in bed for a while. Once the water was hot enough, she eased her body in and let the running water soak her for quite some time before she even thought of using the soap. One thing Kait enjoyed was taking long, steaming showers.

Abe was lying in wait, hiding under a bush behind the McKnight residence. He was content to be alone and in the dark. In fact, the cover of darkness and clouds blocking the moon made his job easier. He had a perfect vantage point and waited patiently, as he watched a woman inside moving about.

Abe was waiting for her to settle in any room. Up, down it did not matter; she just needed to stay put. He would be able to tell by the lights turning off and on because none of the windows' curtains, drapes or blinds were closed. He sat there for a while, before lights went off and on a few times until they were all off, except for the strobe like a glow from a television, and the usual night lighting people use to deter thieves. Every movement ceased. Abe gave it another ten minutes.

Baten opened up his duffel bag and dug out a home modified thermos crafted into a bomb and threw the cylindric explosive into the room where his target was. The thermos crashed through the glass like a rocket and burst into flames climbing and engulfing the room.

Lance cut the usual hour commute down to a twenty-two minute drive, thanks to the lack of rush hour. Still fearful of something, he screeched into the driveway and jumped out of the car. Something was wrong. Something smelled. Smoke! He saw a faint glow coming from inside their house. He fumbled for his keys at the front door, pounding, hoping someone would answer. The keys were in the car. He rushed back to the car, yanked the keys out of the ignition, and tripped back to the door. Finally, the lock turned and he flung the door open.

"Kait!" Lance screamed as he rushed into the

family room. He looked frantically throughout their house. Lance raced to their bedroom and saw the blaze roaring along the ceiling and walls. The closer he got to the door, the thicker the smoke. He could hardly breathe.

Flames spewed everywhere. He heard Kait screaming hysterically. In a panic, Lance rushed back down the hall, into the guest bathroom, wetting towels and hand towels then ran back to their master bathroom where Kait was, covering all but his eyes.

Her pajamas were drenched from backing herself into the shower, frantically splashing water in an effort to keep the flames out. Lance grabbed the towels off of the rack, tossed them to Kait, and told her to get them wet and wrap one around her like a shawl and one over her head like a ghost. He left the towel on his head but took the one wrapped around his shoulders—holding it out like a Matador against the flames. He swung around and opened the shower door. He went in, still holding the towel out in order to shelter Kait.

She stood frozen. Lance stepped in and lifted her out through the flames, out of the master suite, and safely outside. Holding her tightly, Lance looked for injuries. The fire singed Kait's hair a little. The whole ordeal shook her up, but she did not look burned. "Are you all right, Kait?"

Kait looked at him for a moment, tears welling in her eyes. "Oh, Lance," was all that she could get out before she started sobbing uncontrollably. Lance held her tighter. He looked at the flames eating their beautiful home right through the roof.

Lance's jaw clenched. "Silver!" he said. Kait did not hear him. In that moment, he had no doubt that Scott Silver was behind all of this. "Kait!" Lance yelled over the crackle of the flames. "Honey? Come on, we have to get to the neighbors!"

Kait was still crying, and Lance carried her to the yard's side gate. As he walked, he looked down in amazement at his clothing. They were steaming against the cooler air.. His burnt pants smoldered, and his hands were bleeding. Lance could barely open the gate. He dredged across the lawn to the neighbor's front door, somehow managing to ring their doorbell, before leaning against the porch wall.

"My God, what has happened?" A distraught woman in her early fifties cried out. "What's going on, Joan?" A deep voice came from further inside the house.

"We need to use your phone to call the police and fire department!" Lance cried without introducing himself. They had not really met yet, although they had seen each other in passing.

"Come in, come in. We're the Shelbys, your neighbors. "I'm Joan, and my husband, Ralph. Ralph! Call 911, Hurry!" Escorting them in, she said, "I'll get you blankets, sheets and a pillow so you can put her on the couch," and ran down the hall to her bedroom. Seconds later, she came out with everything and a fresh terrycloth robe.

Lance tried to put Kait down onto the sofa, but

she only held him tighter. "It's all right, Kait, we're safe now. The firemen and police are on their way. You're sopping wet. Please let me put this robe on you. She looked at herself in horror as Lance laid her down.

"Let me get you some dry clothes," Joan offered over Lance's shoulder.

"Thank-you. Not just yet," Kait muttered. Joan looked at Lance quizzically.

"I think she just needs to rest a minute. Dry clothes would be great, thanks."
"Of course," Joan agreed.

"What happened over there?" Ralph asked as he came from the kitchen where he'd placed the calls. "Do you need a drink or something?"

"No, thanks," Lance replied. "We appreciate your help. Someone set the house on fire with Kait in it. We almost didn't make it out. Another minute or so . . . well, let's just say we were lucky."
Again, Lance thought to himself

"Look at your hands. We need to clean them up. I have some things in the guest bathroom that may help. I can fix you up temporarily." Then she told Ralph to get a pair of sweats for him.

"Thanks," Lance mumbled. "The pain is just starting to register. Amazing how fear and panic can shut everything else out."

They both went into the bathroom. Lance could hear the sirens in the distance but could not budge an inch.

Joan handed Lance a class of water and ibuprofen. He sat on the toilet seat while she cleaned and dressed his wounds. Joan wrapped Lance's hands tighter than Mummy's hands, and was now clutching an ice pack, but they felt better.

Ralph sat in the corner, sipping on a drink and staring in disbelief at all that was happening.

"Now, young lady, let me help you to the bedroom. We will find something to your liking in there. Maybe you would like a hot shower," Joan suggested.

Kait shook her head to say no. "I think I just had one," she said very softly, yet sincerely. Kait followed Joan into the bedroom.

Ralph told Lance to sit down. "Relax. Oh! I guess that is somewhat stupid. It is hard to relax when your house is burning down. So, tell me . . . what happened?"

"I'll make a deal with you, Ralph. If you'll let me use your house to talk to the police; you'll get the whole story. And I won't have to tell it twice."

"Okay, want a drink yet?"

"No thanks, I'd better wait. I think I'll go over and see if the firemen are there yet." Lance was exhausted, but he knew he would have to keep going for several more hours. He stopped at the door. "Tell my wife where I am, will you? And give her a drink, Kait needs one a lot more than either of us," he told Ralph. Lance left and walked back across the lawn. There were two fire trucks in front of his house. A ladder was propped against the side of the house supporting a firefighter flushing water from a large hose down into the master bedroom. Two more in the back of the house were working their way through the house, and another was still hosing down the roof. It was only then that Lance realized he was going to have to find a place to stay, not only tonight, for quite a while.

He studied the scene to discern which one of them was in charge and approached someone he believed was issuing all the commands and said, "I'm Lance McKnight. This is, was my house. I called the police, and they are on the way. My wife and I are at the neighbor's house, next door." Lance pointed to the right. "My wife and I will be there for questioning." Lance went back to the neighbors, knowing they were not likely to say much. Their mission was to extinguish the fire. When the fire was out, and considered cold, fire investigations would take over from there. All depended on the evidence gathered.

Kait returned to the living room dressed in the wildest animal print jumper, that he didn't think Joan would even be caught dead wearing and decided Ralph probably gave it to her. Joan removed the damp sheets from the couch and helped Kait get comfortable, leaving the pillow and blanket to wrap in.

"How are you, Kait?" Lance grasped her hands gently into his damaged hands as he sat down next to her.

"I'm okay, but I'm still very scared. Did somebody just try to kill me?"

"I don't know, maybe, but it won't happen again," Lance vowed. "I won't let it."

"Lance," Kait asked sadly, "why didn't you tell me the newspaper business was so dangerous?" She did not say it to be funny, Kait was quite serious. Somehow it struck Lance as humorous, and he laughed. Then Kait started giggling. Lance was rubbing off on her, possibly his was mother, too.

"Babe, it's not dangerous. I am!" Lance said before he kissed her.

The doorbell rang. Ralph got up to answer it. He must want to hear the story pretty badly, thought Lance. Two police officers were there to take statements. Ralph led them into the living room where Lance and Kait waited.

The officers were the same two that handled the dog incident. "Mr. McKnight, so far, we've come up empty, and are closing your dog's file," said the heavyset, balding officer.

"Yeah, must be why I haven't heard anything." "Sir, can you tell us what happened here tonight?"

Lance gave a detailed statement, starting from the minute he turned down his street. Then he let them know, tomorrow he would bring his wife to the precinct to give her account, but she was in no condition to give a statement now.

"We're going to have to rope your place off. Give me a number where we can reach you."

The police took the Shelby's statements. Lance found out during the questioning, they had nothing to offer other than what happened after they answered their door. They had no direct knowledge of the fire until then, they told the police.

As the officials were leaving, Lance walked them to the door and asked, "Should I get a permit and buy a gun?"

"I don't think that is necessary, Mr. McKnight. Please be careful who you tell where you are staying, and do not take unnecessary risks. Most important of all, leave the investigation to us. I understand you are an investigative reporter. Consider it a conflict of interest; you are too close to be objective, and likely to miss pertinent clues. Buying a gun is only going to get you in trouble," warned the officer.

"Or save our lives."

The police officer shook his head. "Or cause someone to shoot you first. Believe me, Mr. McKnight, unless you are certified and know how to use a handgun, you should not own one. Please go to the emergency room and get yourselves checked out. You both appear to suffer from smoke inhalation. Your wife looks to be in shock; you may be in shock. Leave the investigating to the department. We'll all do our best to get the answers for you to proceed."

"No offense," countered Lance, "your ability to solve this is questionable based on our prior experience." Lance walked them to the door.

They left without a response.

Lance discarded the advice from the police as he did his bandages in order to take a shower. He would keep an eye on Kait, and if she did not improve, he would take her to the hospital. His hands felt a lot better, and the wrappings encumbered him. He put on the jogging suit Ralph gave to him to wear, then called his mother. Rather than alarm her over the phone, he told her they had a flood from their new washing machine and asked if they could come over and spend the night. Of course, she said, 'yes.'

Lance and Kait drove in silence to Janice McKnight's house, Kait leaning against Lance all the way there, whimpering and quivering over the night's events.

Janice McKnight lived in Western Springs, Illinois, less than ten miles away. She'd lived in the same house for over thirty years, raising her children, sharing the joys and sorrows of life within the same walls for longer than Lance could remember. Janice was always there for him and his brothers. She stood by her children through their terrible teens, weddings, divorces, and every obstacle faced. Always the Rock of Gibraltar, Janice McKnight held her family together even during her own divorce which came after twenty years of marriage.

Lance always turned to his mother during a crisis, and this time, he was more scared than he ever remembered being. His mom was aging, and he was afraid any undue stress might not be the best prescription for her health. However, her age did not slow down her mental capacity, evidenced by her insight the following morning.

Lance could not sleep. He tossed and turned all night, never waking Kait, who was out like a light the minute she hit the bed. He got up about five o'clock, wrapped a blanket around himself and went into the kitchen to make coffee. He found the Chicago Union out on the lawn and perused it, barely able to concentrate.

Something woke his mother, whether it was the smell of the coffee or Lances rambling in and out of the house. Janice joined Lance at the kitchen table.

"One thing about getting old," his mother told him, "your days are a lot longer. You don't sleep as much." She looked at her son lovingly then asked, "What's really going on, Lance?"

"What do you mean?"

"I could tell from your tone and, later, from how Kait looked, that there was a lot more to it than a flooded washing machine. Did I fail to mention the faint odor of smoke? What happened, son?"

Lance sighed. "I was going to tell you. I just wanted to wait for the right time," Lance told her. "I guess this is the right time, so here goes; we had a terrible fire last night! A quarter of the house is gone. Kait nearly died, and I al- most wasn't able to get her out." He did not know what else he could tell her—never really knew how to tell her anything life threatening, except straight out. He always wished he was better at cushioning blows.

"My Goodness! Why didn't you tell me, or ask for my help?" Janice McKnight questioned, now grabbing hold of her son's hands. "Oh,

Sweetheart, look at your poor hands," she said with generous concern and sorrow.

"I didn't want you to worry. Mom, a lot more is going on. I have no idea how to begin to tell you everything that has recently happened to us."

Janice put her arms around her son, and held him for a moment before saying, "Tell me what's wrong, Honey." She let go, patted his shoulder and sat at the table with him.

Lance explained. He told her of the entire incident, much in the same detail as he had told the police the 'night before. He also decided it best to omit any of his suspicions about Scott Silver. "I've got to go to the office this morning to let Butch Logan know what's going on," he concluded.

"Dressed like that? Don't you think you should at least comb your hair and wipe your shoes?" Janice enjoyed the sight of her son looking himself over and said, "All the stuff you left behind is boxed up or still hanging in your closet. Surely you'll find something more suitable"

It WAS 10:45 A.M. BEFORE Lance left his mother's house. He would be later getting to work because he had one stop along the way. He took interstate I-55 into the city which would dump him onto Lake Shore Drive, to the Cicero exit. Lance continued down Cicero Avenue until he found what he was searching for.

The storefront windows and doors had fixed,

stylish security bars. Upon opening the door, a buzzer went off. Simultaneously, his motion started an audio video recording system filling small monitors scattered around the shop. He walked up to the clerk at the counter. After a lengthy discussion about the right gun for him, Lance picked out a weapon. The clerk told him, he'd have to fill out the forms and wait for the licensing, before he could take the weapon. Lance put his key chain onto the glass display case, and with a few taps said, "Never mind."

Lance drove down Cicero Avenue to take the freeway into the city. Parked at the Union, he sat in his car trying to figure out who he could get a gun from. He waved at the security guard and headed straight for Butch's office.

Butch was eating lunch at his desk. "Where have you been?" He demanded, choking on his sandwich. He drank some ice water, staring at Lance with disapproval. "You might at least call when you decide to take a half day off," Butch scolded. "I have been trying to raise you all morning. What's the story?

"You want my story? Here it is . . . ," Lance told Butch what happened the night before; the third rendition of attempted murder and arson, which varied little from each other. Again, Lance didn't disclose the suspicions he had about their boss.

When Lance finished, Butch looked at him for

several minutes, frozen in awe. "For one of the first times in my life, I don't know what to say. It is a miracle Kait is still alive. We've got to stop these guys," Butch was referring to the editorial union. "I knew the Chicago unions were tough, but I didn't think they were murderers! As of now, negotiations are off. I am going to talk to Houston, and then file an unfair labor charge this afternoon. They don't know what rough is yet." Butch calmed down slightly. "What are you doing here? You could have called, and you should be home with Kait," he reprimanded.

"Right now, there's no home. Kait's still at my mother's sleeping soundly, I hope. I will go home in a while. I have a couple of things to check on here." Lance got up to leave.

"Lance. I am sorry. I am sorry I got you into this. I had no idea. I will make it up to you. I promise, hear me?" "If you really want to help me, get me a firearm and bullets to protect my family, Butch."

Lance did not wait for a response and headed for Mike Marenski's office. Mike was on a telephone call, but Lance didn't let that hasten him to take a seat. Mike nodded a smile to him and continued his conversation. Mike did not finish before Lance said excitedly, "We've got to put a stop to all of this right now!"

"Hold on," Mike said. "How about telling me about the fire Butch is ranting about."

"It sounds like Butch already did. I don't want to go through the whole story again."

"Lance this is serious! You and I know that it was not, and never was the union! A good man was murdered; somebody tried to scare you, now it appears your family is also in danger. The next step is to kill you—over Silver Bullet. We both have a good idea of whom. We need to cool it for a while," Mike insisted.

"Cool it? Somebody tries to kill my wife and scare the life out of me; which they did successfully, I admit, and you want me to cool it?" Lance stared at him in disbelief.

"I just want us to stay alive. That's all!" Mike yelled back.

"Look here Mike, I've got to figure out how our FEI Wire Service in Miami fits into this whole thing. We can be sure Silver uses burner phones to communicate with all of his co-conspirators. You know, if Bobby was in this with him, don't you think Silver would have gone to his funeral? Don't you think Bobby, would have had a pile of money in assets or savings?"

"I agree. We do have to keep an open mind. Lance, you are too closely connected to do so. Take some time away from this. I've decided to have my contact discontinue; it is too risky now, and way beyond favors."

"Mike, don't you have a criminal justice, or military intelligence friend you could call?"

"Lance, right now I am Human Resource Director, Mike Marenski"

"I know, but listen," Lance said waving his

hands as if clearing air, "we're really outside of the human resources realm at this point, and we need to get to the bottom of this before we don't have any resources at all."

By the time he finally reached his mom's, it took every bit of energy to get into the house. The smell of her home cooking was welcoming to Lance.

His mother was humming a familiar tune until he walked in. "Keep as quiet as you can. Kait's still sleeping. It must be how she copes, huh? I eat, she sleeps. Sleep is medicinal!" Janice turned around further noting, "I like that outfit."

"Thanks. Is it giving you a flashback? It should, you probably bought it for me. Mom, I don't think I can wait to eat, I am too bushed. I'm going to heal with Kait."

He went into the bedroom they were staying in and watched Kait for a minute. Her breathing was slow and heavy. She looked so rested lying there asleep. Lance believed most people slept peacefully, and some of them sure changed when they awoke. Lance took off his jacket and shoes to lie on the bed next to Kait. Quickly, he fell asleep. Soon, he too, was breathing peacefully and sleeping soundly.

10
THE TEXAS TWO STEP

AT MID-AFTERNOON, Abe Baten phoned Scott Silver. He had accomplished his charge, maybe in a different manner than expected, but Abe went about it with a level head—unlike the irrational request from a deranged mind. He knew exactly what to accomplish quite well, in his opinion. Although, others may see things differently. Scott Silver's hot line rang twice before he answered it.

"Yeah," Scott said curtly, wondering who was ringing him on the hidden phone. Three or four people had the number and were to use it only in case of an emergency. "What the hell are you talking about?" You did not do what I paid you to do! You made a mess of the house all right, but McKnight's wife is alive and well. I just finished talking to Butch Logan. He told me Lance pulled her out of the house." Silver was beside himself with rage as he spat into the phone.

Abe was silent a minute. He had plenty to say to Mr. Silver, but remained silent instead, preparing for his verbal attack. After several seconds, he said, "Perhaps in time, you'll see it was all for the best. McKnight's wife won't stay around Chicago after this, and McKnight will back off to protect his family. Because of the change, the police have nothing to investigate. The fire investigation will concentrate on arsonists. I did you a favor, Mr. Silver."

"Don't try to rationalize your disobedience!

"Wait a minute! I didn't screw up; that's on you. I saved you from yourself."

"You're supposed to get the job done. Whatever it takes!"

"I did!"

"I obviously made a mistake when I gave the job to you."

"Listen to me Mr. Silver! I won't tolerate any more of your disrespect." Abe disconnected the call.

SCOTT WAS STILL trembling as he put down the phone. Too many things had gone wrong, and really needed something to go right for a change. He picked up the crimson cell phone and called Clinton Excelsior.

Clinton always made him feel better because Clinton was so insightful, did not give him a hard time, and agreed with almost anything Scott said or proposed. Scott knew how to manipulate people and situations. Silver thought Clinton was a dupe, along for the ride. Having nothing to offer other than money.

Scott believed Clinton Excelsior was only

courting this relationship for the financial gains. Every time Clinton nodded his head to whatever Silver was peddling; Silver had no idea he was savoring thoughts about yachts, the South Pacific, and the coming weekend.

Clinton had been successful beyond the family fortune because he surrounded himself with the right people to ensure success. He was like Silver in the way he ran the newspapers, but less demonstrative and generally let his managers and department heads make the decisions, rarely intervening. Clinton hated confrontations of any kind with anyone. He could indulge himself because he had a staff of people to be the heavy for him.

Scott called Clinton. They talked for an hour. Clinton, as anticipated, agreed with the schedule he proposed for the wire service feeds, and would run the campaign pieces, calming Scott down immensely.

Of course, the reasons he was agitated had nothing to do with the newspaper business, or the presidential race advertising. He was worried for the first time about his dominoes falling one after the other, solely due to Lance McKnight. Nevertheless, Scott felt better because of the fireside chat with Clinton—until the red phone rang.

"I told you not to call me on this line unless it was an emergency, no! I don't accept your apology for hanging up on me and if you ever . . . what do you want?" Scott was fuming as he waited to hear Baten's response.

"Mr. Silver, your phone manners are quite crass. Perhaps if you would tone them down a bit, Abe would not take such offense to the conversations he has with you, nor would I." Hafez Fakhouri's voice was smooth, yet threatening.

"Hafez, good to hear from you," he lied in an effort to help Hafez forget about his crude manner. Hafez was about the only individual Scott did not push as hard, partly because of the millions Hafez meant to him, but most of all he was afraid of the arms dealer. Whatever the combination, it worked in Hafez's favor. Scott could tell Hafez was not happy now.

"We have an issue to resolve, Scott. I have talked to Abdul, and as you may know, he is very unhappy. We've had a lengthy conversation. In short, Abdul makes a number of valid points that would be wise to take into consideration. You must realize, when I agreed to let you use Abdul's service, it was to help you protect our mutual interests. You seem to think he is your personal 'fixer'. I think we need to set new ground rules. You will come to me when you need his help in the future for the duration of our arrangement. Secondly, when Abdul is on your clock, I expect you to treat him like a professional, which he is. You know, Mr. Silver; you may be successful based on the newspaper empire you created, but you're likely to come crashing down unless you are wise to surround yourself with people you can trust to have your back. You will only earn that unwavering loyalty through respect and forethought," Hafez warned.

"Is this from the Dean of the School of Arms Dealing Management?" Scott replied without thinking; certain Abe must have gone crying to Fakhouri.

"Mr. Silver," Hafez said interrupting him, "your sarcasm will not take you very far with me. I am deadly serious about these matters, and your attitude is regrettable. My concerns are how your affairs directly affect mine, which extends to the anonymity of my involvement. I am told Mr. McKnight may have uncovered your part in our operation. With the forensic software the government has, I may now, need protection from you. Mr. McKnight is your responsibility to deal with. Take care of it Scott, or I will take care of all of it." Hafez's comments were sincerely stated and their meanings unmistakable.

"Just who do you . . ."

A click echoed into silence followed by a dial tone. He was furious. Hafez Fakhouri hung up on him! Once he stashed his hot line, he clenched a hand into a fist and slammed it to the desktop. Instead of hitting the surface, he managed to thrust his hand onto a pen. He screamed something undesirable as he shook his hand in an effort to alleviate the pain. Silver did not wait long to retrieve the phone again. He began to place a call to New Orleans. After the fourth digit, he realized Abe was not there, he was in Miami. Scott decided to complete the call and speak with the Senator. He needed to lay into someone. It was very rare that anyone had the balls to talk to Scott the way Abe and Fakhouri had. When it happened, Scott wanted to reciprocate, not necessarily with the same individual, but he just wanted to get even. Gaston would do.

"Why did you let James Hillerman run Abe off?" Scott demanded angrily.

"What? Mr. Baten hasn't even been here since you summoned him to Chicago. He told us he was returning to Miami when he left Chicago. You should know this. After all, you're the one that sent your plane for him."

"Mister Baten? Since when did Abe gain your respect?"

"Since we discovered we had something in common!"

"And what's that?"

"Our mutual disdain for your behavior Mr. Silver."

"You wouldn't be anywhere without me Gaston! Don't forget who you are talking to!"

"We've had this discussion before Mr. Silver. Right now, Jim Hillerman and I feel we could raise enough money for my campaign without your help and are now contemplating doing so. Our arrangement is over, and I will speak with Mr. Excelsior and work out a re-payment schedule with him, since he is the benefactor. Mr. Silver, you are fired! And you are no longer connected to my campaign."

Scott was so livid he did not notice; the

Senator had disconnected the call when he yelled, "You think you can raise enough press and media support? I doubt it! I can ruin you, and I will unless it's understood by you 'who's in command' here, senator!" Scott believed he'd had his turn hanging up on someone and stowed his little red burner phone. Now, he was even more upset and blamed his empty victory on Lance McKnight.

Scott picked up the office phone and rang Butch. "Get in here. I need to talk to you!"

Once Butch walked in and sat down in front of his boss, Scott said, "Let's not screw around today I'm in a bad mood."

"Me too!" Butch replied with some understanding. "I had to come in here."

"Butch," Scott blurted out without acknowledging the comment, "McKnight has to go."

Butch jumped up out of the chair, leaned across the desk, and halted less than a foot from his boss's ruddy face. "What are you talking about Scott? McKnight has been through a number of obstacles working for you, and the awful tragedies the McKnight's have had since they moved here for the job you keep canning him from. The day after he loses his house, you want to fire him, again. How many times is that, this month, Scott? This makes zero sense." Butch threw his hands up.

Yeah, well, maybe all those bad things happened to him because he's not doing his job." Scott yelled, trying to sound convincing. "Look at it this way, Butch. I am doing FEI a favor, and McKnight a bigger favor. He leaves. We settle with the unions, and they do not end up killing him, because McKnight is gone. Everybody wins!"

"At least there is some logic there. What are you going to give him?" Butch inquired.

"What do you mean?"

"How much are you going to give Lance for severance pay?"

"Not a penny. It is not an early retirement. He is being fired!"

"You're going to give him a check for a year of his wages, to include a lump sum as an annual bonus and profit sharing dividends based on last year's numbers; all in a certified check. Troy in accounting can add it up and arrange it with the bank. They can messenger the check over here. I'll be back for it," Butch said storming out.

Scott was screaming as Butch left, but it was doubtful Butch heard anything. He was too angry to hear a word.

Butch went straight to his office, opened his briefcase, grabbed a legal pad and pen, then scribbled out a draft of his letter of resignation. Then, he had his secretary type it up and print two copies. While he waited, he called Lance at his mother's house. Janice McKnight answered. Butch explained who he was and asked to speak with Lance.

"Mr. Logan, he and Kait are asleep right now. Could I take a message?" Janice offered with a quiet voice.

"No, I really need to talk to him. What if I come by and take you all out to dinner tonight? It has been a hard, couple of days for everyone. Maybe some diversion would be good," Butch suggested.

"Well, I don't know what the kids will want to do when they wake up. It has been a terrible time. I'm not sure, how long they will sleep, and it's best not to wake them. They might not be in any better spirits."

"I agree with you completely Mrs. McKnight. I would not be in any mood for socializing either, under the same circumstances. However, I really do need to talk to Lance, and it would be a pleasure to meet you as well. Lance has spoken so highly of you. I'll come now, if you'll give me your address."

Asking for the address made Janet suspicious. For all she knew, the person on the other end of the line was an- other murderer. She hesitated for a few seconds, "Just hold on a minute Mr. Logan . . . I think I heard Lance."

Janice lied, but she did not know what else to do. She put down the phone and went to wake up Lance. Lance picked up the extension as Janice went back to hang up the receiver in the kitchen. But, before hanging up the extension,

Janice listened to the two men talking for a bit.

"Sorry 'bout my Mom. She's just developed a case of the willies like the rest of us,"

"I understand. Lance, I need to see you right now. What's your mother's address?" Butch wrote the address down and stuffed it into his shirt pocket.

Butch felt certain, by now, Silver had Lance's severance check ready to deliver. He had his resignation signed and sealed. On his way to the boss's office, Butch noticed his mood had lightened.

Scott Silver handed the envelope to him. Silver did not expect to get an envelope in return, and a puzzled face stayed with him as Butch Logan left the building.

Lance thought it best to wake Kait and warn her, Butch Logan was on his way over. After their talk, everyone would go out for dinner together. Everyone was up and dressed and awaiting the sound of the doorbell.

Janice and Kait were in the living room watching an early evening game show, blurting out letters, words and phrases.

As Lance escorted Butch to his Mother's kitchen, they stopped by the living room, and he introduced her. Butch bowed and pretended to tip a hat to her and smiled like Lance had never seen him smile. Butch and his mom's eyes and smiles locked briefly.

Now seated at the table, Butch hesitated for a moment. Then decided to tell Lance straight out.

"Lance, you're fired, effective immediately!"

It was Lance's turn to hesitate and then came a laugh. "Ha, ha, real funny, what's up Butch?"

"No, really, Lance, you're fired, as of this moment, here, right now, and here is your parting gift, your severance check. Oh, by the way, I also turned in my resignation."

"Why did you do that?"

"Because I can't stand how Silver treats people. It pisses me off more than having to watch him roll in, in the morning," Butch chortled lightly.

"You shouldn't have quit on my account, Butch. There's nothing that could have saved my relationship with him."

"Don't flatter yourself, Ti . . . laddie. I did it for the rest of the poor stiffs in the place," Butch joked.

"If you wanted to do something for them, you would have stayed. Besides, there are a couple of things left behind that I need, and I'm not going back there. I'll need your help," Lance told him.

"Sounds like you've developed a case of cowardice in the last few minutes," Butch teased. "You know what? I forgot to clear my personal items out of my office, too. I'll have to work for at least one more day."

Kait was actually cheerful at dinner. They both avoided the subject of the house and distress they experienced. Instead, they enjoyed Butch Logan's company, as did his mother. Butch was in rare form and kept the trio in stitches for hours until the proprietor had to ask them to leave, which they did semi-gracefully.

Janice and Kait reluctantly entered the house, but not without protest. The evening was young, and they felt like continuing somewhere else.

"A bit too much of the wine," Lance told Butch as he walked him to his car. "Seriously, Butch, if Silver asks you to reconsider, I wish you'd tell him 'okay'. You don't have anything to do anyway."

"How about my well-deserved retirement?"

"What's a couple of weeks?" Lance asked.

"Yeah. What is a couple of weeks? Tell me, what is all this secretive garbage? Fill me in, will you? What on earth would you need me around there for if you are not even going to be there? Give me a hint about all of this, would you?"

"Butch, let's just say you have always been on top of things because you're observant. I'm asking you to go back to the Union and be observant."

"I don't get it. I will have to think about it, but I will go in tomorrow to pack. If Silver approaches me, face to face, I will decide at that moment. Is that fair enough?"

Before they called it a night, Lance decided to give Kait full disclosure about his job. Kait actually took the news about Lance's forced retirement well. In consideration of all things, she felt bad for Lance having his career stalled, but the money Scott Silver paid him to go quietly, was quite incredible. There would be no worries for many, many, months to come, Kait thought.

Lance was at the kitchen table, a little worse for wear. He had gotten up early—unable to keep from thinking about Silver Bullet, how he could expose it, and connect it to Silver without jeopardizing anyone. He came up with a solution for the immediate future but hadn't been able to decide how to tell Kait. She had been through enough, and he had to end this nightmare.

BOTH HAD THEIR own agenda that morning. Kait came into the kitchen and poured herself a cup of the coffee Janice made before she left for the store for one of her perpetual trips to "pick up a few things."

The sun was streaming through the windows and even with the last few days of horror, and disappointment they had suffered, both felt some sense of hope with nature's brightness. Kait sat down at the table tentatively. "I'm sorry, Lance," she said simply.

"You're sorry? What on earth do you have to be sorry about? You wouldn't be involved in any of this if I hadn't taken the job. I never dreamed it would turn out like this."

"What are we going to do now?"

"I'll look for another job. We have enough money to live on until I find something. Once the insurance claim is processed, and the repairs are complete, we can list the house for sale. I was thinking something a little smaller would be more suitable anyway." Lance was not lying, just laying the groundwork to reveal the next step.

"I think the first thing we should do is get you to San Antonio. I'd feel a lot better if I knew you were safe and right now; you are safest with your family and friends."

"Wait," protested Kait, "aren't you going to San Antonio with me? I don't want to go without you!"

"I'll be right behind you. I'll stay here at mom's and hire a property manager that will handle everything from the repairs to the sale of our home. I have to open an escrow account so the insurance company can direct deposit the claims check into that account to use for repairs and the management company's fees. I'll use my severance to open it and cash out the rest. We'll use cash for every purchase until we have a permanent address. Don't forget to give me your credit cards, believe me, everywhere you will need to buy anything, takes cash. What do you think?" Lance knew she'd agree and was pleased with himself for avoiding too much discussion about why he needed to stay back.

"You know I think it would be wonderful, but what about you?"

"I think I want to do anything that would make you happy. It doesn't matter where I live. I've been all over the place. Besides, I liked San

Antonio. I can send resumes out of there just as easily as anywhere else," Lance told her, squeezing her hand.

"What about your mom? She'll want you to stay."

"If I didn't know better, I'd swear you are trying to find an excuse to stay here. My mom always wants me to stay, but we agreed a long time ago that I grew up and had my own life to live. Anyway, that doesn't matter because I thought she might enjoy going to San Antonio with you for a while. She'd have fun helping you find a place for us. Wouldn't you feel safer having someone you trusted traveling with you?" Lance hoped that he was not lying. He had not ask his mother yet.

"Yes, I'd feel a lot better," she paused, "you know? You're a good man Mr. McKnight." Kait leaned over and kissed him gently on the lips. "I'm so glad I married you," she smiled at him admirably.

"I'm glad you married me, too! I feel awful that I got us involved in this mess. The sooner we put this all behind us, the better."

Lance purposely avoided any discussion about Silver Bullet with Kait since their discovery of the financial statements in the safety deposit box in Buffalo. It would only upset her, and the less she knew, the better off she would be. Lance was sure that if he told Kait the whole story, she would refuse to go to San Antonio, and insist on standing by him through the rest of whatever came to be. There was no way he could allow that to happen. By withholding information, he could avoid the argument altogether.

It did not take long to convince his mother to close up her house for a while and accompany Kait. She thought it was a marvelous idea, with one stipulation. She did not want to fly. Lance would have to book two tickets on a passenger train with sleeper, dining and lounge cars.

Before Lance researched train times and fares, he made a list of items he would have his mom pick up while she and Kait were running errands and shopping. While they were busy, he would pick times, ticket options and take notes to make arrangements in person to pay in cash, after he finished his banking.

The Dinner hour was drawing near. The McKnight's were hungry. Janice surprised Kait and Lance by a casual suggestion they invite Butch to dinner.

Kait teasingly said, "I think there is someone who would like to say good-bye to Butch."

Janice blushed but said nothing.

"Okay, I'll call him but let's not make a long night of it."

The foursome enjoyed their dinner out, sharing stories about San Antonio and the good old days. Janice and Butch paid particular attention to each other. At the end evening when the time came to say their goodbyes, Butch held his moms hands together and gave the back of one of them a quick peck. Lance and Kait looked at each other and smiled.

The McKnight household rose early the next morning to get organized and review the plan Lance formulated over coffee and donuts. Everyone was around the table wide eyed like teenagers on Christmas morning. The table had a pile of brand new tech toys and gadgets Janice and Kait had purchased yesterday, per Lance's list. The only items not on the list, was in the large shopping bag on the empty seat.

They all had new phones and air cards placed in front of them as Lance explained the temporary telephones and extra minute cards they would use while making the transition from Chicago to San Antonio. This could keep them in touch until they settled into a new home, so no one had to worry about the other.

From the bag, Lance added to the lot on the table, three 4" GPS systems with charging cables, three, reserve battery packs with a vehicle charging socket for multiple recharging when a computer or automobile charger was unavailable. The GPS' he gave to Kait and his mom were enabled with the connect application giving Lance the ability to live track their phones. The product identification numbers were loaded into Lance's GPS. He told them both to be sure to keep their phones on and charged at all times. He was grateful they were focused on their gadgets, and not asking him why they could not track his global position.

Janice noticed twin bulky brown leather carryalls, side-by-side, one was a visible shade darker. "Lance, do you really think those are big enough for our phones and GPS'?"

Kait looked at the table, next at Janice, and the two of them started to laugh.

"Actually, you might be able to fit your purse inside there too, but it might be a tight fit," he responded.

Lance had a similar leather bag in his lap, a duffel style. He reached in and removed three stacks of cash, placing them in the space he cleared on the table. They were wrapped in mustard, violet and red currency straps, in denominations of one hundred, twenty and five dollar amounts.

"Take a cab from the train station to the Extended Stay by the airport and book two adjoining double, double bed suites. You'll be comfortable there. They have a kitchenette, parlor area, work desk. You have to pay in advance by the week." Lance picked up the four strapped stacks and gave each of them two.

"Here is one thousand in fives, and two thousand in twenty's, each," he grabbed the only mustard strapped stack that contained one hundred, one hundred-dollar bills.

Lance carefully peeled to open the paper band and cut it lengthwise. Then he eye split the stack into two piles. He split one of them again, secured each with the mustard strap he'd cut, handing one to each and said, "and this will cover the suites and train fare. I was going to get the tickets for you until it occurred to me; I had to pay in cash, and I didn't have the time to get there yesterday, but here are the schedule and times."

Everything that had been on the table was stowed, and everybody knew what to do. All had the same items in different colors except Lance. He was the only one with twice as much cash as the women combined. He also had a second burner phone that was a chrome finish, to use for talking to Butch, Mike, . . . anyone that was connected to Silver Bullet directly or indirectly.

The rest of his kiss-off pay he put into a certified bank check and sent by FedEx to Mr. Falco. They arranged for Falco to deposit the funds into another escrow account and arranged to get copies of the paperwork when he had an address.

Janice cooked breakfast feast and made one last pot of coffee. All three pitched in to clean up.

Everyone was packed and ready to leave. The cab was loaded; waiting for the last minute goodbye hugs and kisses to stop. Lance told them he would get there as soon as possible.

Part of his plan required everyone to believe that his only concerns were settling the house affairs to leave Chicago. Lance used the new chrome cell phone to dial Butch's home number. There was no one answered, not even an answering machine. Then Lance remembered how Butch felt about them. Butch did not like answering machines. Too many people would use the recorder to get even with him—quips. Most were callers without the guts needed to insult him to his face.

Lance decided to take a chance and call the office.

Surely, he could not be back there already. To his surprise, Butch answered the phone. "Yeah?"

"You're there. That's great. It sure didn't take Scott long to realize he needed you, did it?" Lance said to him rhetorically.

"He called very early this morning, acted like nothing happened and asked when I'd be in the office. I told him I would come back just so I could get some sleep. So, what is so great? Now I have to put up with this bloated toad. I'm not in a good mood. What do you want?"

"I just wanted to see if you were expendable. I'll call at a better time. But, if you need to reach me for anything, this is my new number."

"I fire you and you still think you're the boss! Anything else I can do for you, your majesty?"

"Not at the moment, Butch. I'm just beginning to get everything accomplished with the insurance company and all that other stuff. By the way, my mom told me to say goodbye to you, again. I think she's smitten. Kait said to thank you, again, and that 'you'll know' what she means. Kait is very happy that we are moving back to Texas."

Lance thanked Butch, said good-bye and told

him he would check in with him in a few days.

Lance hoped the news would get to Silver somehow to convince Silver that his problems were over when it came to him—the threat of his snooping, therefore buying Lance the uninterrupted time to act upon information he acquired that would eventually nail Scott Silver.

The best shot Lance had at bringing down Silver was exposing the rigged finances, but even better would be to expose where the money was coming from, and where it was going. The bigger problem now was how to have everything in place when he connected all the dots.. He needed the right people ready to move in on Silver. Taking it to the police would be useless with the evidence he had. Lance was sure it would not be enough to warrant charges if he told a detective in Fraud the entire story; they simply will not believe him. They would consider him a "hostile" with a grudge to bare.

No. The evidence he needed was the kind that'd put Silver behind bars for a long time. The evidence also needed to be presented by someone with influence, and willing to stay the course, . . . someone he could trust. Lance thought he knew just the person.

When Lance was at the university, he studied hard and was a top student in journalism. In the summer between his junior and senior year, as a reward for his hard work, he won a fellowship to study in Europe, he and nine students. Among them was an extremely talented woman, Marsha Windsor. An absolute genius, who Lance was sure, would end up as the CEO of a Fortune 500. As it turned out, she was fascinated with tax law. She went to law school. Unlike most others that used their law degree to get into a big firm or work for a District Attorney; she went to work for the Internal Revenue Service.

Marsha was now an IRS manager in corporate tax. She turned down numerous promotions because she simply enjoyed what she was doing. She hated the bureaucracy of the IRS but loved dealing with corporate tax law.

Marsha was highly respected for her flawless work and unique approach. Lance knew all of this because they kept in touch over the years with phone calls and dinners. After Lance left Illinois, their communication dwindled to Christmas cards and Birthday talks. Marsha never left Chicago.

Lance decided to call her. She would believe him, and without question, use every power of her office to uncover admissible evidence. Marsha would not cower away because of the name printed on a warrant. Justice was her resolve. Lance asked for the corporate law division after dialing the Chicago number for the IRS. Several minutes later Marsha's secretary answered.

"Corporate, Jenny Patterson speaking."

"Marsha Windsor, please."

"She is on another line. Who's calling?" Windsor's secretary asked.

"Tell her it's Whimpy." Lance earned the nickname in Europe, for his numerous visits to the Whimpy burger stands to indulge in the only European coffee he found, that remotely tasted like American brew.

Moments later, Marsha was on the line. "Good to hear from you Lance, how are you?"

"I've been better. I'm hoping you'll improve the quality of my misery."

"You always did get right down to business. I heard you were remarried in Texas. I would love to meet your wife sometime. Was it a big wedding?"

"Kait's on her way back to San Antonio. Besides, she is not the type that understands men having any kind of an informal relationship with women, unless they are going steady, engaged, or married. Kait's the jealous type, but a gem nonetheless." Lance did not address the comment about the "big" wedding. He got the reference, and had to wonder, was there anyone in the entire United States that did not know everything in Texas is big?

"Kait sounds very lovely, Lance. What do you mean on her way back to San Antonio? Have you been in Chicago? And you haven't even called?" Marsha asked with some disappointment.

"Sorry. As you said, I get right down to business. That's what I've been doing since I got here. I haven't really talked to anybody except newspaper people."

"But now you need something, so you decided to call. Some friend!" Only slightly jesting this time.

"Don't make me feel any worse."

"I am just giving you your deserved ration of

B.S. What do you need?"

"I thought you might be interested in a high-visibility tip."

"What are you talking about? We're the IRS, not the FBI."

"I know. Marsha, could we meet for a late lunch today?"

"Hang on a sec," Marsha checked her schedule and said, "how about three o'clock?"

"Great. See you at Schaller's?"

"Bummer alert, Schaller's pub closed in 2017. What about Billy Goat Tavern off Michigan?"

"No good. I might stumble into someone in the paper biz there. Okay, I know, The Village?"

"Good choice! See you at three, Whimpy!"

See you then, Marshmallow!"

THE NEXT CALL was to a number in Buffalo he recently acquired.

"Falco, Falco and Baine, how may I direct your call?"

"Claudio Falco, please."

"One moment, sir."

"Claudio Falco's office, may I help you?"

"Is Mr. Falco available?"

"Whom shall I say is calling?"

"Lance McKnight, I'm from Chicago."

"One moment Mr. McKnight."

Claudio Falco's secretary came back on the line and said, "He'll be right with you, Mr. McKnight, please hold." Lance verified that Mr. Falco received the packet of documents he mailed. The last time they spoke, he had not decided to talk to the IRS. Lance thought it best to run it by his Silver Bullet attorney, before he said too much to Marsha.

Lance was glad he was making headway. There was a lot more that had to be resolved, but so far, he was fast tracking and may get out of Chicago much sooner than expected. He also needed to talk to Mike.

After Marenski answered, Lance launched right in. "M squared, things are about to get dicey for me here, and may trickle your way. Remember where 'Jan' lives? Can you swing by on your way home? 'Bout five o'clock tonight?"

"Well, good morning to you too," Mike said, and agreed to stop by on his way home.

Lance looked at the time and realized he needed to go meet the adjuster at the house in forty minutes.

The house was a disaster. It was the first time he'd seen the damage in broad daylight. The only thing important right now was the precious evidence hidden in his office. Somehow, the commotion was so distracting he forgot. Lance managed to get to his office without getting full of damp char, but when he opened the door, it came halfway off the hinge of the door's frame. His office was a total disaster. Lance's heart sunk, and he almost started to cry. The prospect of finding the wooden box, or the metal case inside it, storing copies of Silver Bullet files and both sets of FEI files was nearly impossible. He could forget about the backup he made of Scaletti's hard drive. As Lance admitted defeat by giving up, he heard a loud pounding at the front door.

Backing out, a misstep caused a series of acrobatics to avoid falling, he landed face-first into a large pile of soggy debris. Lance had to use his throbbing hands to push himself up, and as he did, one hand slipped on something making Lance fall once more, revealing the wooden box he needed. To his surprise, he made it to the door in time.

"Hello, I'm Lance McKnight. Come in, please watch your step."

"I'm Mitchell Debora, Old Towne Insurance." Handing Lance his card, the adjuster looked around. Debora could tell the damage was extensive. "From what I can already see, your home will require some structural repairs as well as the cosmetics to make the place sound and livable again. It's something, I'll say that, but don't worry, we've got you covered," he said trying to ease the client, that was understandably upset.

"'Well isn't that special,'" Lance said facetiously, "The whole damn house is a charcoal pit. I'm supposed to wash and paint that?"

"Yes. Well, your content's insurance should cover the expense of replacement and cleaning where possible." Again, in another attempt to calm Mr. McKnight, the claims adjuster whistled, "I've seen some damage, but this is something. I am surprised no one was hurt badly. From the street, you can see damage to the roof, it's something"

"You keep saying 'It's something,' it's something? What is it?" Lance asked impatiently.

"Toasted!" Debora smiled graciously.

Lance held back his laugh wanting to stay irritated. "I could have told you that. Listen, you can ditch your comedy routine and tell me what you need from me, right now. I have an appointment to get to."

"Well, for now, we'll need a brief explanation . . . ," said Debora.

"Try the police, they have it." Lance fired back at him.

"And a verifiable list, of everything that you lost, that you have an extra rider on. If there are items not included in your content's coverage or rider, recent purchases like jewels, expensive art, that sort of thing; I'll also need the receipts of anything not currently listed."

Lance just rolled his eyes wondering how he was expected to find a receipt for anything.

"Okay. What else, Mitch?" *Sounds like . . .* he thought to himself.

"Mr. McKnight, if you would rather we not pay your claim; we'll be happy to give you a waiver to sign." Debora replied with some distaste.

"Look. I'm sorry for being so rude. I'm just distraught and overwhelmed, Mr. Debora, my apologies." Lance gave the agent the quick version of the fire and a telephone number to reach him. "We aren't sure where we will be during repairs, but if you leave a message, I'll call as soon as I can. There really wasn't anything outside of the policy as it is, so we'll settle for the amount of the claim as was insured."

"Yes. Well, we are not going to cut you a check today, Mr. McKnight, or one based on your own authority. Once the fire investigator submits his report, providing the case is officially signed off on, we will cut you a check for the full adjusted amount." Mitchell Debora was amazed at the folks who mistreated insurance adjusters. *How soon do you want your check?* A question the insured should ask themselves before meeting with an insurance claims adjuster.

Lance shook Mr. Debora's hand, and thanked him.

Now that he had accomplished what he came for, he checked to make sure he had everything and headed for his car, then decided to continue using Kait's BMW and drove toward The Village in The Italian Village Complex on West Monroe St.

Butch Logan pulled into the driveway, surprised to see it empty. Lance was supposed to meet with an insurance adjuster, but it looked like no one was around, so he did not cut his engine. Butch got out of his car, went to the front door and lodged something in branches behind the closest bush next to the stoop, got back in his car and left.

Securing an easy place to park would be tricky. The closest spot would be risky but decided to chance it and took La Salle to Monroe to park at Hyatt Centric. It was a miracle, there was a spot to purchase, even if he didn't need it for the entire day.

Lance pilfered through his briefcase and made sure everything he may need to show Marsha Windsor, was at hand. The chrome phone started to ring a tone that didn't register right away.

"McKnight! Where in the heck are you? Aren't you supposed to be with the insurance guy?"

"I'm all finished and had to run a few more errands before I skedaddle." Lance was tired of lying, so he did not say more.

"Well, you better get back there as fast as you dare to drive your wife's car, and look to the left side of the stoop, laddie!" Butch did not wait for a response and hung up.

Given that order, Lance would keep his meeting short, and go back to the fancy ashtray he once called home after his meeting. The years had been kind to Marsha Windsor Lance noticed as he made his way to the table she chose.

"I'm sorry we won't have the time to catch up properly. What I got here is a bit complicated, and there are a few sketchy movements on my part that may or may not have to come to the surface. I'm hoping not, but what I have here involves tax evasion, laundering, co-mingling of corporate assets—the list goes on."

"I am all ears but remember; I have the ethics of my profession to consider so extra caution should be taken in every word you use, Lance."

WITH THAT UNDERSTANDING, Lance promptly began a brief rendition starting with the FedEx he received to the attempt on Kait's life. He told her he thought that the IRS should audit Scott Silver, FEI and his personal holdings. To get warrants for every bit of data from every computer he owned, every file out of every cabinet, and in every storage closet. That his investigation to date, pointed directly at Scott Silver.

"I believe you, not because you are a highly regarded investigative reporter, and know how it all works, because I know you, but where is the physical proof?"

"I have copies of all the proof you need. Exact images of the laundering system and every related file and then there are these," Lance fished out copies of the accurate and dummied expense reports taken from Scaletti's safety deposit box in Buffalo and slid them across the table to her. "Scott Silver has a safety deposit box with originals of some of these. Only one little problem Marsha, the way the proof was obtained is questionable." He did not want to explain the files and transferred data he had on the thumb drives inside his briefcase, unless he had to.

"Busting Scott Silver would make the front-page story for the newspapers. Even for the papers he owns, but what do you want me to do? Go arrest this guy because you said he was cheating on his taxes?" Marsha asked facetiously and did not want an answer.

"On the surface, FEI is spotless. I imagine it is the same with his records. But, Marsha, I have proof that Silver is hiding more than money from the IRS and just like these documents I gave you, the evidence is inadmissible. The only way this works is if you gather the evidence officially. Can't you do some kind of audit or something? Get the financial records; subpoena the actual job tickets from the corporate offices? You already have his tax returns. I'll guarantee the two won't match. Some will be the originals of the document's I just gave you. You could get a hold of FEI records at the same time you raid the safety deposit box. The key is the differences in the records between the advertising revenue and newsprint expense. The bottom line will be the same," Lance explained.

"Don't we give away something when we waltz in and demand these records?"

"No more than walking in. Does it matter? Just make sure you're not dealing with Silver when you present the demand letter, and don't let the people out of your sight. The bank in Buffalo should be easy. FEI will be tricky. I'm not saying you don't know how to do your job, just that I know these people—watch them closely. Make them get the financial stats for you while you wait. Keep them in full view, so they are unable to alert Scott or forewarn him."

"You know we could make this a lot simpler by getting these records and prosecuting Silver as the CEO," Marsha suggested.

"No. A good lawyer could spring him on those charges. I want to show conspiracy to murder along with everything else. I want Alexander Scott Silver behind bars!"

"All right, Lance, but in order to get those documents, I'll need you to sign an affidavit. Not for me, my superiors are going to want something more solid than 'a friend told me so.' It's just a formality, and you won't need to be identified if all goes as planned. After that it will have to go through the approval process, not that we do things slowly here at the IRS,"

"Marsha, Thank you. You have no idea how relieved I feel. Well! I have a little shopping to do, then I'm off to join my wife." Lance stood and picked up the table check.

"Oh! Great! I do the dirty work while you vacation."

"Dirty work is right. A bit splashed on my hands. It'll rinse off."

"Just swing by my office before you go, hot shot. I'll have the paperwork ready. And Lance, no more mud pies. We need spotless evidence, the kind the IRS office will get tomorrow."

Lance wasn't going to worry about it anymore. He would do as Butch suggested and go by the house.

He was not sure what to expect to discover as he parted branches away to look behind the shrub until he removed a nondescript brown bag, wedged between branches. Lance felt exactly what it was when he took the paper bag. Out of habit, he checked the mailbox, then he decided to make sure the house and garage entrance doors were locked, thinking how silly it was to lock up the house, and drove to his mother's. There was just enough time to wash up and eat something from the fridge before Mike showed up.

Mike Marenski didn't give Lance a chance to greet him. the minute he crossed the threshold he said, "I told you that things took some time you know! Good things come to those who wait. Since you're not big on waiting, and haven't behaved well, I'll just get right to it. I know I told you that I told my phone company contact to cease, and I did," Mike handed Lance a little yellow square piece of paper, "he came through for us, anyway. They located the satellite tower used, eliminated employee and company cellular phones, then they had to cross-reference with a 'foreign' signal, but would have . . . ,"

"Okay, okay, I get it Mike, like you said; I'm not big on waiting. What did they come up with?"

"Geez Man! 'Bite the hand' why don't you? The top one is a pay as you go cellular capturing a call to Louisiana, the second number, and last three numbers are in the Miami area code. Two are similar to Silver's as far as being registered, and one is a wireless account from a FEI Wire Service dedicated to arm's dealing and duals as a tip line for information to stories printed, and the other one happens to belong to Jeff Bayer."

"Jeff Bayer? I don't recognize any of these numbers. Louisiana? A wire service in Miami, huh? Mike, do you think these all belong to FEI and Silver, or perhaps Bobby?"

Mike could tell by the expression on Lance's face, he was scheming something in his head. For a minute, it seemed as though Lance was finally committing to wrap the house matters up, and head off for San Antonio. When he started tapping on the paper, his demeanor shifted slightly. Knowing Lance, it was a sign that the other shoe was about to drop.

"Kait's on her way to San Antonio and I'm supposed to go shortly, but this may be the connection that'll take him down. It may prove to be the 'keys to our success' so I've got to go to Miami, Mike. It's the only way. I'll tell Kait I'm going on a job interview," he told Mike.

"You're going to get your head blown off! That's what you're going to do," Mike protested.

"I'll have protection," Lance insisted.

"You mean that hunk of metal under your coat? I am not even going to ask. I sure hope you know how to use it," Mike said, then he asked, "How are you going to get that thing on the plane with you?"

"I'm not," Lance replied. "I'll drive," he said flatly.

"Are you crazy? Fourteen hundred miles?" Mike raised his voice.

"I need some time to think."

"Two and a half days? You should be brain dead by then! Lance, you're obsessed with this thing. Just turn it over to the authorities and forget about it. I'll come with you. Then, go to San Antonio, be with your wife and forget all of this."

"I have gone to the authorities. To the IRS. They're going to get the documents to prove there is fraud on the tax returns, and I'm going to get the evidence that links Scott Silver to fraud! Are you going to help me, or not?"

"Of course, I'll help you. I just don't want to see you getting hurt. Why don't you just let the IRS take it from here?"

"Because they won't necessarily tie in the attempted murders to Silver, and I want Silver! I'm almost there."

"Okay. Just call me from the road tomorrow, and I'll text the information on the phone numbers. And Lance, please be careful!"

After Mike left Lance took a few minutes to regroup, trying to piece together the interesting information Mike gave him, that was pulling him to Florida, and away from San Antonio.

HIS WIFE WOULD have a coronary; his mother would have a cow. That entirely aside, the worst part was leaving Devon behind, just when they were starting to get close again.

Lance awoke in the middle of the night. He was still in the same position he was in when he sat down earlier. He unintentionally fell asleep. He wanted to go out and buy some shaving and grooming necessities—such as soap, toothpaste, clothing, underwear, and socks.

His old clothes were snug. He decided to stay one more night and in the morning, he'd call Jill, to see if she'd let him have Devon for the day. He could use the opportunity to explain why he and Kait were leaving the area. His daughter would get a kick out of helping him pick out a few sets of shirts and pants. They could have lunch, and Lance had one more parting surprise in store for her.

The McKnight father and daughter duo fueled up in the food court after an exhausting morning shopping.

"Wow dad, I am wiped out. I had a great time, and now I don't have to worry about you looking like a dork in Texas giving us 'McKnight Women' a bad image."

Already, Lance noticed his chalkboard humor had not skipped a generation.

"Aw, it's too bad you're so tired, and can't be seen with me dressed like this. I had a special surprise for you, but I can see you're having difficulty holding up your fork."

Devon waited anxiously as Lance turned the key in the ignition and begged him to tell her the surprise.

"Well, when I was little, my parents took me to what she said was 'the best museum in the world,' right here in Chicago! The Museum of Science and Industry," Lance explained, turning onto Michigan Avenue. "It's about five minutes from here, and you'll love it. It has a real coal mine that you can go down into, and it has a spectacular submarine. There's also a huge train set!" Lance sounded like a twelve-year-old.

True to Lance's intent, they pulled into the parking lot of the Museum of Science and Industry in Jackson Park. The enormous pillared building having the lake as a backdrop looked, as architecturally comparable to the United States Congressional Capitol in Washington D.C. The site of it gave Lance the fortitude to put computer programs and life changing negotiations out of his head. He enjoyed the time with his daughter and explained in simple terms why he, and Kait were moving back to San Antonio.

Devon also understood why Kait was not able to say goodbye because Lance became an effeminate liar, having one handy for all occasions. He hated lying to all the McKnight women he loved but refused to fill them with fear for their own safety every waking moment.

The trip to the museum was a hit. Devon did love it, as Lance had promised, and he loved it all over again . . . so many years later. The afternoon passed too fast, Lance realized, but Devon, and he would register the day in memory banks at the ready, awaiting others to be added next time, Thanksgiving perhaps.

As Lance pulled into Jill's driveway, Devon said to her father, "I guess I'll enjoy visiting you in Texas. It's your's and Kait's Thanksgiving this year, isn't it?" Devon reached out and put her small hand on his right shoulder. "I know you're sorry. It won't be so bad, Dad. We can talk. I'll give mom your new number." Devon kissed him on the cheek. In turn, he kissed the top of her head, told her that he loved her, and would call as soon as he got to San Antonio.

The shopping and visit to the museum with Devon drained more energy from him than he thought. Lance took his time packing for the trip to Miami. The weather may not be as forgiving on the way there as it would be in Florida, so he packed accordingly. Lance used only one suitcase from the spare luggage set in a guest bedroom, knowing his mom would not mind. The lighter he could travel the better.

Kait would not mind if he took her car for the trip, as long as he drove within the posted speeds, did not squeal tires on the pavement taking off, or slam on the brakes, and Lance tried to remember the last thing she'd always say, every time he drove her car, whether with him or not. Then it came to him; he was not to raise the volume too high, so the speakers do not blow.

The 325i would be comfortable for a long distance drive and handled very smoothly on the road. The sooner he was finished with Florida, the better. Lance removed everything from the trunk to check the spare tire and changing accessories, then arranged the first aid case, winter kit, and spare blankets that were always in there. The trunk was small, but also accommodated the small packed suitcase and the retro boots and jacket taken from his old closet.

Lance was finally ready to leave, but by this

time, it was nearly nine o'clock in the evening. Nevertheless, he decided to go. He set the car's GPS, to the route he thought best; Interstate 57 South, to Interstate 24 East, for now.

The cell phones were charged and at the ready. Once on the open road, he set the cruise control to sixty-seven miles per hour.

It was unusually darker on the older interstates, but that was lost on Lance. He just started up with his reveries as always, which then made everything else relatively oblivious to him. All of this gave Lance a sense of déjà vu.

Years earlier, when he was a reporter at the Oakland Oracle, he hadn't spent much time on stories categorized as investigative reporting. Still, there was one story early on that fell into that genre. He remembered the thrill of going undercover. At least, that was what Lance called catching the great brick thieves leading to an expose about the group of traveling tradesmen that rolled into town, swindling everyone in their path.

Unlike their kin stealing from the elderly by way of performing unneeded repairs to roofs and siding, this band would steal bricks from the lower class areas. They would obtain addresses of houses; on a list the city is to condemn if code violations were not satisfied. Before the owners could get to the repairs, thieves would show up at the houses and strip every brick off the structure.

Generally, the rest of the house—left intact. Unless there was a crawl space and the home fitted with usable insulated copper plumbing. At the time, there were many transplants coming to Southern California and Texas from the East and the North. Home builders knew the newcomers liked reclaimed bricks for their homes. So, the brick thieves in Oakland had at least two markets for their wares, which they shipped by railways through an organization set up specifically to handle the hot building material.

Lance spent two months on the story, posing as a city inspector, a potential buyer, even a supplier, and enjoyed the role-playing. The unsettling fear of "being caught" somehow stimulated him; motivated him to take all the precautions to get the story published and come out of the ordeal unscathed.

That was how Lance felt now. He had to get enough evidence to nail Silver before Silver caught up with him, although he felt relatively safe since no one besides Marenski knew he was going to Miami.

The big difference between the bricks and Silver Bullet was that he was dealing with a bigger league of thieves, and murderers! Like most times in his life, Lance did not know when to quit.

Driving through the night, alternating flashes of optimism, fear, paranoia, and panic consumed him. It was nearly nine o'clock in the morning, and Lance was nodding off between the reveries. He had to stop and get some rest, so he could think clearly. Lance had a long way to go. He'd just drove past Chattanooga, Tennessee and was now on Interstate 24 East.

Lance decided to call Mike Marenski. Lance figured Mike would be in by now. He dialed the number and let it ring three times.

Mike answered with, "Yeah."

"I forgot how professional you were," Lance joked.

"Lance? I can hardly hear you. Where are you?"

"I'm just south of Chattanooga. I've been driving since I left. I think I'm gonna stay at this Holiday Inn I've been reading so much about plastered on billboards the last hundred miles. Say Mike, I appreciate all you've done. I want you to know that,"

"What?" Mike hollered in between crackles and zaps on the line. "I think I'm losing you. I'll talk to you later," and hung up.

After driving off the exit ramp, he could see the Holiday Inn signage in the distance. As the structure came into view, it certainly was not modern, but anything would do at this point; he needed sleep. The nine hour drive wore him down. Lance paid for a prorated room on the ground floor, so he would not have to check out in four hours. He parked his car in the space nearest the room, dropped his suitcase on the floor, and crashed on top of the bed. Lance did not wake up until six o'clock that evening.

Scott Silver felt only half relieved after Butch

fired Lance McKnight. Scott suspected McKnight must have stumbled upon Silver Bullet. Initially, he had thought the dismissal would end the issue. There would be no more worries of anyone trying to gain access to computers or anything else concerning FEI or the Union. Scott was so relieved when Butch told him that the McKnight's were trading in Chicago for San Antonio.

Naturally, Scott figured his plan worked and felt spry. He decided to go prod Butch with some friendly jabs; he was in an elevated mood. Scott wandered unannounced into Butch's office and sat.

"What brings you out of your Victorian hole? I thought you only left it when you were in search of food!"

"I should have left well enough alone after you quit and looked for someone else," Scott said wheezing from his walk over to Butch's office.

"Is that an offer for me to file unemployment?" Butch asked smiling.

"No, Butch. It's a nice way of reminding you it's always a possibility."

"What else is new? Maybe I'll quit again; join McKnight in Florida. I hear Florida is a great place to retire,"

Scott's demeanor grew very serious. With narrowed eyes, he tugged on his shirtsleeves. Scott's face turned nearly purple within seconds. "I thought you told me McKnight was leaving for San Antonio? Why is he going to Florida?"

It was obvious to Butch that Scott was furious. The signs were not lost on him. "I did tell you he was going to San Antonio because that's what he told me. Between then and now, Mike Marenski told me he was going to Florida for a job interview. In fact, he's halfway there at a Holiday Inn south of Chattanooga. What's the big deal if he's gone to Florida instead of San Antonio? You didn't want him around here! Scott, when are you going to stop worrying about Lance McKnight? It's going to give you a heart attack! On second thought, keep worrying about him!"

Scott stood and waddled out of the office, without a word. Butch was about to call after him, but instead said, *Screw it*, to himself, while shaking his head in disbelief.

Scott headed back to his office, tottering as fast as his weight would allow, with one thing on his mind—his hot phone and Florida connection. Before sitting down, the phone was in his hand. Gasping for breath, he dialed Hafez Fakhouri's number. It rang three times before voice mail answered. Abruptly hanging up, he dialed the number for Abe Baten. He hated to talk to him, but he had no choice.

Abe's familiar, raspy voice greeted him. "We've got a big problem. McKnight is on his way to Florida! If he shows up anywhere near the wire service, we're in trouble. Take him out. No more, 'scare tactics,' Hafez will agree; this is the only way to protect our mutual interests. Kill him dead!"

Baten was silent. Scott did not know if Baten was going to rip into him, afford the solution, or hang up. Finally, Abe spoke very slowly and deliberately, "Where is he now?"

"At a Holiday Inn, south of Chattanooga, on his way to Miami. I want this taken care of!"

"As do we, Mr. Silver. We risk much more than FEI." Baten sensed it was all Scott could do to bite his tongue, but managed to, even when he said, "Send the jet down. I think I'll take a trip to Chattanooga, after I talk to Hafez."

"Don't bother, I just tried calling him and got his voice mail," Scott said flatly.

"I know."

Scott ignored Abe's implication. "Let's not count on finding McKnight on the road, again. It might be best to prepare for his visit in Miami."

"You will send the plane now and let me handle the details!"

Scott was ready to explode. He wasn't used to being given orders. Scott needed Hafez and Abe too much to snub the order. "The jet is on the way Abe."

When this was all over, the next thing he would send Abe, were flowers for his grave in a Miami cemetery.

Lance shaved, showered, changed his clothes, and repacked. He put a sports coat on. He left the gun inside the paper bag stowed in the duffel bag with most of his money. Lance put the suitcase into the trunk and placed the duffel bag underneath the passenger seat and drove to the lobby entrance to check out. He was driving at night to avoid travelers, and the desire to arrive as soon as possible. He wanted to get the information Marsha would need and get back. Unwilling to waste precious time, he would push on.

Into the night he drove, still worried. This leg of the journey the time was spent thinking of Kait's safety. Would she be okay? He talked to her after she arrived in San Antonio, but not since, and made a mental note to call her in the morning. She'd be worried sick! Had his ploy worked? Did Silver think he had abandoned the cause and moved to San Antonio?

He knew money poured into FEI was funneled into a shell company and flushed back out to where? Or, into what? It was so unclear to Lance. He knew Scaletti lost his life over it. He knew he was in way too deep to dig out by himself. Lance knew he had to get Silver before Silver got him. What he had established was that he didn't know where the money initiated and what the end use was. Maybe the answers were in Miami.

Interstate 75 was rather scenic through Georgia, but it was all lost on Lance's moonless night drive. Mindless driving peppered with Silver Bullet carried him over six hours before he remembered, he hadn't even bothered to use the cruise control. He was on the outskirts of Tifton Georgia. Before setting the speed governor to 67 mph, he glanced into the rear view mirror to see if anyone else was behind him in order to safely change lanes. Sparks and fire were spitting out of the tail pipe! His first reaction was to careen to the side of the road and stop. He was shaking so fierce, he was barely able to keep ahold of the steering wheel. Don't lose it! He shouted, "Hang on! . . ." At a speed of forty miles per hour, tires screeched with the forced application of the brakes. The car finally came to a halt after what felt like an eternity. He pushed to open the door, grabbed his briefcase and duffel bag, jumped out, and started to run across the road to the left lane's embankment; hoping traffic wasn't coming as the back end of the car exploded into flames.

The explosion spewed fire everywhere over the divided highway igniting the grass and shrubbery close to the road, and everywhere flaming projectiles landed. The force of the explosion blew something that grazed his back as he dove down into the ditch. This time he felt Lady Luck. Had Lance hesitated a second longer, the hurling object would have decapitated him. Lance tried to ease up from the ground. Feeling extremely dizzy, he clutched the only possessions he had left.

Lance couldn't put much pressure on his leg because his knee felt dislocated. He had enough presence of mind, to know he was partially on the roadway and had to keep moving. He hobbled across the lane to rest against a car that stopped to offer help.

A SAMARITAN WITH A thick southern drawl cried out, "Mister! Are you all right?" Stacy Norton was almost as shocked as the man whom she saw nearly blown to bits.

"Yes, um . . . no, not really . . . sort of, I think," Lance blurted breathlessly. After a bit he asked, "Do you have a phone I could use?"

"I already called 911, hun. They'll send the police and Tifton fire department. They'll be here any minute now."

Lance looked at the car. "Doesn't look like the firemen will make much difference, does it?

The sway of her head back and forth answered Lance's keen observation, then she said, "You still want the phone?"

"There's no one else to call, now, thanks."

"Listen, you need to sit before you fall over." Stacy got out of her car and helped him into the back seat to sit and rest. "I saw the whole thing . . . oh my word! Someone up there likes you! My name's Stacy, Stacy Norton. I was born 'n raised in these parts, seen plenty of miracles, none like this one, though."

"Must be one," he mumbled quietly. Lance was still dazed, becoming more unconfused as he watched the lights and heard the sirens coming at top speeds. In the distance, both departments were approaching the area from the same direction as the paramedics.

Lance clutched his belongings in one arm and exited her car. He came to Stacy's window and thanked her sincerely. Reaching out his hand to shake hers, Stacy extended hers, and they shook as Lance said, "Listen, you get out of here, Ms. Norton. You did everything you could by reporting the accident and helping me. You don't want to get tangled up in this." Lance was smiling and nodding yes for her. As they withdrew from their handshake, Stacy felt his hand press a thick wad of folded paper into her palm, which she clutched as he thanked her again. Lance hobbled toward his wife's smoldering luxury car to wait for the emergency teams.

He told them exactly what happened to cause an emergency stop. The firefighters made sure all flames were out.

The car was grey. It could have been a Volvo or a Mercedes instead of Kait's BMW by the looks of the remains. All four tires melted off the rims, and the vehicle's paint job was vaporized—everything else melted or charred. Inside, the only things that were recognizable were the steering wheel and steel framing. Lance eyed the mess with total discouragement. He looked down around the scene and saw a circular piece of charred metal. He picked it up, wiped it off, and sadly shoved his wife's BMW emblem into his pocket.

"It was probably your gas tank that exploded," one of the firefighter's said after he finished talking to the police officers. Then the Squad Captain joined the others on the rig and left the scene.

The State Trooper came up to him, handed him some papers to sign which he did while in a trance. The trooper informed him where they would impound the car for the insurance adjuster.

Lance assumed it was all on the report, so he

paid little attention. When the trooper offered Lance a ride to a Tifton motel, Lance nodded his head in agreement. It was almost one-thirty in the morning.

Thirty minutes later, Lance was in tiny motel room. Exhausted and unable to think, he was grateful he had the forethought to grab his brief case and duffel bag. Lance was happy to be alive. At once, it dawned on him. The gas tank did not erupt; Scott Silver made an attempt on his life! . . . Marenski. It had to be him! Mike Marenski was the only one he told about his detour to Florida, and the room in Chattanooga! Mike sold him out! That's why he stalled, Lance thought. That is why he kept talking about stepping back and giving it to the authorities. Why did he give me the telephone numbers' information?

Did Mike set me up? All the questions clamored in his head, which was doing enough of it on his own.

McKnight wondered if he was just being paranoid now; however, if Mike was in on it, Lance played right into their hands. He kept him informed every step of the way. Can I trust him? He asked himself, and then asked, can I trust any of his information? He must be feeding it to me for a reason. He surmised Mike was leading him down the primrose path. Lance finally fell asleep.

Dawn came too soon; Lance thought as he woke and noticed the sun was just beginning to rise. His dreams had made for a restless nap, as did the realization that he was now completely on his own, at least for this part of the operation and drifted off again.

When Lance got up for the day, he looked at the clock and called Kait, using the blue phone.

"Hello," Kait's voice sounded distant.

"Hi, Babe," Before he could say another word, Kait was all over him.

"Where have you been? We've been calling, leaving you messages. We're worried sick," she howled.

"I'm sorry, I was going to call after I got on the road again. I'm on my way to an interview in Florida."

"What? Lance McKnight, did you say Florida?"

"Well, I'm not quite in Florida. I'm around Tifton, Georgia on the way to Miami. I drove straight through to Chattanooga, pulled into a rest stop for some shuteye," then hit the interstate again. The Miami Hurricane has an opening. We scheduled an interview, so I thought I'd drive down to rehearse everything I'm going to say. This way, I don't have to mess with rental cars, loud passengers or hijackers."

Lance ended with a nervous chuckle. He didn't like lying to Kait, but knew it was necessary.

"What about the insurance and repairs on the house?" Kait spoke formally in an even tone, which indicated she was either extremely happy or very upset.

"It's all taken care of. Now, we sit back and

wait. I sure miss you, Babe, I really do."

"I miss you, too, but I wish you'd let me know what's going on."

"I have. Look, I'll be in Miami late tonight and should be on my way to San Antonio tomorrow night. How's mom?" He asked, attempting to steer her off the subject.

"Lance. Are you all right? You sound tired and strange," "I'm fine. It's a harder drive than I thought it would be. That's all." Lance promised to call back soon and hung up before Kait could say more.

Marsha Windsor was next on his call list. If Marenski told Silver, they would shred everything, everywhere. Since Marsha had no idea he was going to Miami, he felt obligated to at least warn her of the possibility, a coworker he confided in could tip off Silver, and that he was sorry. Marsha told him she hoped the files were available, that they're set to swarm in the following day. Lastly, Marsha said if it all turned out hunky dory, and no wrongdoing was found, she may have to look for a new job.

Lance told her not to worry; the raid was going to prove worthwhile.

Lance, freshly showered and shaved, had nothing to wear other than clothing he wore the day before. Another quick shopping spree was necessary. Devon was going to be devastated; her tasteful clothing selections were ashes, Lance, not so much.

Once dressed, he called the front desk to find out where the nearest car rental agency was.

THE CLERK TOLD him every agency had pick up service. Lance chose Hertz. A Toyota Camry would do nicely; with loads of space since he was traveling a little lighter than when he had started out in Chicago. Lance shopped at a local department store for clothing. Once redressed, he drove to the city impound lot behind a colonial complex, serving as a police department, county jail and municipal courthouse. He signed the paperwork that would have the car scrapped out.

Looking at the map traded for Kait's roasted BMW, Lance figured he had another ten hours counting stops and tolls to reach Miami. Interstate 24 South to Interstate 75 South, was the quickest route. If he left now, he'd get there around one o'clock P.M., give or take. Well, at least no one knew he was in Tifton. In fact, they probably thought he was dead. That should create some advantage in Miami.

Abdul Baten was back from Chattanooga, convinced again, he'd taken care of the problem that plagued Silver.

Abe hadn't spoken to Hafez, so early the next morning he went to his Miami Beach mansion. Hafez led him to the covered terrace housing an infinity pool and overlooking the Atlantic Ocean.

They sat at a round table that matched the polished, Italian marble bar. The chairs and lounge seating were covered in a stylish, plush, water resistant fabric situated between the bar and private sun deck.

Hafez and Abdul sat and drank coffee that was brought fresh from the "homeland." Abdul smiled for a moment but then turned somber. "Hafez, I know I traumatized McKnight this time, but I don't think this guy's going to quit."

"Do you think we need to find out what he knows?"

"I think that we may have a hard time getting to him now, before he gets to Miami anyway."

"That is a pity," Hafez said, shaking his head, slowly running his fingers through his hair as was his habit. "I would like to meet this 'McKnight' that you have been toying with recently. Excuse me while I take this call."

Abe couldn't clearly hear what was being said to Hafez, but he didn't want to—tinny sounds of screaming through the small speaker could be heard. Abe noticed the growing disdain on Hafez's face and in response.

"Mr. Silver, I am not accustomed to functioning in a state of panic. You were warned and had no authority to order Abdul to kill anyone. To be clear, killing him was not in our best interest at the moment. Neither of us can afford the exposure. I think it best we discontinue our arrangement, temporarily. I know where to find you when it is safe to resume our business together." Hafez hung up.

"Mr. Silver has become far too dangerous for us, and since we can't predict his next move, I think we need to take control of the situation a different way. I want you to level the wire service. Destroy the entire block if necessary; make sure the all content is damaged beyond forensic analysis. FEI Wire Service is the only traceable connection with Mr. Silver. The time has come to sever ties."

Abdul Baten was busy that evening building a unique explosive device with enough impact to level the place. He would plant the bomb in the furnace room. And as a precautionary measure, he would also place smaller charges in strategic locations.

Lance's trek from Tifton was long, but uneventful. Although, it seemed strange at the beginning driving in daylight. He had gotten used to driving in the dark for two days. He pulled into Miami at about 1:15 A.M. and worked his way over to Biscayne Bay to check into the Omni International Hotel across the street from the Miami Hurricane; the paper Lance said he was scheduled for an interview that morning.

The Hurricane had a virtual monopoly in Miami yet lost its stronghold in Ft. Lauderdale and other Northern coastal cities over the years. Nevertheless, it was still a good newspaper and Lance somehow always felt more comfortable close to a property of the Fourth Estate. That was all he knew.

11
REAL FAKE NEWS

LANCE WAS EXHAUSTED from the events of the past few days. He decided he could do no more tonight than work out a plan as to how he would get into the bureau tomorrow. With more sleep, he might have a better chance of formulating a plan to wrap up his investigation. The fog of confusion surrounding the FEI bureau and its purpose was beginning to become clearer. Lance could not think any longer. Tired from the short nights, and the stress of the trip, he slept soundly.

He got out of bed, showered, and shaved and put on his old clothes once again. He ordered a pot of coffee from room service and watched Good Morning America until he was sure he would be able to reach someone at the Chicago office. By eight in the morning, he was bouncing off the walls, and grateful he didn't have to wait longer.

He needed to make sure that the FEI Corporation in Chicago had the Miami wire service under its corporate umbrella—making the FEI Wire Service in Florida's legit, on the surface anyway.

The first number he dialed transferred to the national desk. The phone bounced to the news desk, and he asked the women who answered if she could connect him to the manager of the wire service in Miami.

"I'm sorry, sir; our wire service hotline is the only one I can connect you to."

"Well, my name is Lance McKnight, and I'm with the Chicago Union and am in Florida, on assignment, and I need to speak to Mr. Bayer, who I thought was my contact in Miami." Lance told her, knowing that would be one of the best lies of the day.

"I'm sorry Mr. McKnight. I can't transfer you to their offices directly or give out their information; we rely on the strength of our anonymity for the accuracy of our tips, and the safety of our staff."

"Ma'am, I have vital information I came into while in Miami, that my boss, said I should give to Jeff, but in my panic, I seem to have misplaced his number and address of the wire service where I'm to meet him."

"One moment please."

Lance was not sure what to expect when she came on the line again and started getting a little warm under the collar waiting. Was she checking on his employment? It was not so early in Chicago. Many facets of the newspaper business started much earlier. When she returned to the call, she gave him the address and the only number she could find for Mr. Bayer.

"Thank you for all your help and have a good day."

Okay, Lance thought. The editorial staff was aware of the existence of the Miami wire bureau and thinks it is legit. Now he had a number to cross-reference.

Upon reflection, Lance realized he had to continue the investigation low key. He was making real progress, and close to forming a coherent outline of Silver Bullet.

Silver or someone was always one step ahead of him. He did not know if anyone knew if he was alive or dead. And wondered how could he get into the bureau without the wrong people finding out? He could not just break in; nothing taken would be admissible. No mud, he clearly remembered Marsha's words. He did not know who may recognize him—he did not know the face of the person or persons, Scott Silver hired to kill him.

Driving by, the call center's workstations were not at all visible because every window had been covered with a reflective coating. At the end of the block, kitty-corner to the service, was a small twenty-four hour restaurant with a good view. He turned on the next side street and parked his car at a meter, dumping loose change into it to fill the meter to the maximum time; two hours. Lance selected a booth by the window and sat down. The server brought him coffee and a glass of water and took his breakfast order.

Lance carefully watched the storefront. Not a single person went in or came out. The establishment did not appear to be open. Maybe, the wire service was a fully automated system needing minimal monitoring and an answering service. Of course, Lance knew the wire service was a front, but did not know what for.

Watching patiently, hoping something would come to him, it finally did!

The server was happy to see Lance leave, not because he was monopolizing a table since there was hardly a sole in the place, but because she thought anyone who would come into a restaurant and stare out the window at a shabby storefront for hours on end had to be the law or a private eye. When Lance asked for the check, the server cheerfully slapped it down onto the table.

"Thanks! You can pay at the register."

When Lance went to the register, it was his turn to wonder. The server was there ready to collect. Lance just smirked. When he got to the rental car, a parking ticket was in the wiper. "If it wasn't for my bad luck, I'd have no luck at all," he said to himself repeating one of his mom's mantras.

Lance decided one of the best ways to get

into the building was to waltz right through the front door, as if expected. In order to pull it off, he would have to prepare. He needed to know everything about the operation from the owner of the building to include the inner workings.

County records buildings always seemed bustling to Lance. He could never figure that out. All those people sitting at rows of desks were busy doing something. Dade County was no exception. Lance knew immediately he was probably going to be standing in several lines before getting what he came for. Of course, he was right. He was directed to the property tax records terminals to search for the information with the city lot number or physical address, revealing who owned the building housing FEI Wire. Frank H. Trey owned the building.

Lance called directory assistance and asked for the phone number for Frank Trey at the address he took from tax rolls. He called the number and asked for Frank, as if he were a long, lost friend. It did not work. Apparently, the phone number was an office, and Lance was dealing with a receptionist or secretary.

"I'm sorry, Mr. Trey is unavailable. May I take a message?"

Lance expected the automatic response and said, "Well, perhaps you can help me. I'm a reporter for The Chicago Union, which is a FEI newspaper . . ."

"We don't talk to reporters," the woman curtly

cut off Lance.

"Oh, no Ma'am, Mr. Trey leases us our space, and I just needed to know how I might get a copy of a key to the building," Lance lied this time with such earnest, "I've lost my key card and can't locate anyone who can help me! I'm on a deadline! I don't know what I'm going to do if I can't . . ."

"Sir, Sir, please, calm down. We employ a property management firm to handle leasing and repairs. We use Miami Property Managers. Would you like their address and telephone number, sir?"

"Really? Yes, I would, thank you." Lance jotting down the number as she gave it.

Before ending the call she added, "Speak to Billy, and tell Billy that Maia sent you. Okay, Sweetie?"

"You're a lifesaver, thank you, Maia."

Lance called the property management company and did exactly as told. After a brief description of his needs he mentioned that Maia referred him. Billy connected him to Mr. Stubbs, who was responsible for that property. Mr. Stubbs asked him to come to his office, gave him the address, informed him, the suites were located in Bayside Marketplace off Biscayne Boulevard South, and to take Miamarina Parkway. Lance decided that the real estate that housed the property management company had to be a premiere location in Miami being on the waterfront. Their office was as plush and tropical as the vegetation landscaped throughout the walkways.

The meeting with Mr. Stubbs went easier than he could have anticipated. He did not have to lie feeling a tinge of disappointment. Mr. Stubbs looked at his Chicago Union identification badge. Lance handed him what amounted to no more than his old building pass with his name and picture on the card. Lance held his breath hoping Stubbs would not know the difference between a press card and a building pass.

Stubbs gleefully handed back his pass and gave him a keycard. After he instructed him how to use it, Stubbs also told him it was their policy to prosecute for failure to return temporary access cards, within twenty-four hours. It was only until he got back in the car that Lance felt he could breathe normally, but the adrenalin still surged.

Having the front door access card was ideal if the entrance door happened to be locked. Now he had to get permission to see files, and make copies of documents, which would make the proof admissible.

Lance concluded he needed some rest before he could finalize the field trip to FEI Wire Service, AKA—Silver's Laundry and Gun Emporium. He drove back to the hotel, key in hand all the way.

LANCE RESTED SOUNDLY until he heard the phone ring. The computerized wake-up call squeaked in his ear. When he got out of bed, he felt refreshed. It was only one o'clock in the afternoon. He rinsed off in the shower and dressed in a set of new, typical reporter garb.

He called the number for Jeff Bayer. After a convincing lie about needing transcripts for Mr. Silver, Mr. Bayer let Lance know the service was not open for the day, due to monthly pest control scheduled for that morning. With the insects and Palm Rats, Lance was told they sprayed regularly to protect the wiring and sensitive equipment. Jeff Bayer said Lance, could go by there and get what he needed, if he had a key, and if the pest control folks were gone. Otherwise, he'd have to wait until the following day. He checked his gun, which he suddenly thought might be useless since he was not sure whether his hands had the ability, or the guts, to use it. Nevertheless, it still made him feel safer, so he put it in his coat pocket.

The computer terminals were all new. Every station had large flat screens and the towers were fitted wireless connections for the Internet, keyboards and printers. The operating system was the same as the Chicago terminals, so it would be easy to find the transmission files; stories that have already been electronically wired to various newspapers, magazines, and other media affiliates.

In the middle of his tinkering, he realized that so far, the stories he came across related to terrorists, suspected arms dealers and the spectacular busts, or raids on their homes and businesses, until the recent weeks.

Those issues donned front page stories about Senator Andre Gaston's agendas for the United States in an early bid for the presidency. "Now that's odd," Lance spoke out quietly with a curious tone, "all this interest in guns and out of the blue changes to a presidential candidate from Louisiana." Louisiana? Silver's burner phone called a number there.

All the stories seemed to go to FEI newspapers, and to a hundred newspapers owned by Excelsior. He decided to print out the transmission files. They might come in handy somewhere down the road. There may or may not be a connection to Silver Bullet, but they might end up being more important than perceived.

The printer kept churning out the files as Lance turned his attention to an unexpected noise. Lance froze. Did he hear something in the back hallway? He switched off the printer and tore the paper from the carriage, shoving the printed material into the wastepaper basket he emptied out onto the floor. Motionless, his heart was pounding so furiously he wasn't sure if he could hear anything. He reached over and turned off the terminal.

Then Lance remembered his gun. He pulled it out, his hand shook nearly out of control. He stepped against the back wall and edged his way along it to the hallway.

As he peeked around the corner he saw the back door being pushed; it was stuck. He looked around frantically. Where could he go? He didn't have any time! He rushed down the hall the few feet to the restroom door and lunged into the room, praying that whoever was coming in the door hadn't seen him.

Lance could hear the back door open and close as he stood against the wall behind the restroom door. He was sweating profusely, wishing he had hidden somewhere other than the washroom. He was sure he heard the back door to the alley close, but then he heard another door. Open or close? He strained his ears trying desperately to hear someone pass the restroom and walk up the hallway to the office. Nothing!

The pest people left long ago; the odor left behind was unmistakable. He began to think that whoever it was had left. Maybe he should go out and check. After all, there was a gun in his hand, hopefully he would not need to use it because he was not sure he could pull the trigger. Lance put his ear to the outside wall and tried to listen for any activity.

He heard a muffled clanging, the sound of sheet metal. A furnace made the noise. Someone was in the furnace room! Furnace repairs were not likely to be scheduled for the same day as interior and exterior bug spraying.

Abe Baten entered the FEI office from the rear entrance with his key. The lock always stuck and had to be jimmied a certain way to open. Instantly assaulted with a subtle, sickening odor. Making his way to the furnace room, he removed the protective housing and went to work. Abe wasted no time and was about to close the furnace room door to place the rest of the charges, when a curious noise distracted him. Was somebody here?

Lance was feeling impatient and with that a little nervy. He hadn't heard anything more, and he had to find out what was going on. He shuffled as quietly as he could to the restroom door and opened it ever so slightly. He couldn't see anything. He opened the door further and saw Abdul coming out of the furnace room.

Lance panicked, but while retreating back into the restroom, the gun slammed into the door. At that very moment, Abdul turned in response to the noise.

That's it! Lance thought. I'll have to make my move now. He jumped out of the restroom, extending the gun in front of him gripped with both hands. Lance thought he should yell 'Freeze' or something, but he didn't. He was too scared to say anything.

Abe stared at Lance, first with surprise and then with calm contempt. "Mr. McKnight?" Abdul asked, staring into Lance's eyes, never even looking at the gun as he continued slowly toward Lance.

Lance stepped backwards as slowly, and when he looked around, realized he had been pushed back into the front office. The storefront was feet away. "No more moving!" Lance ordered.

Abe smiled at him for one second and then charged forward with loathing in his eyes. Lance pulled the trigger twice. One struck Abe in the chest, the other grazed the wall, and Abe dropped his phone as he fell to the ground and wasn't moving. Lance thought he had better not waste any more time. After wiping the gun free of his prints, he tossed it down the hall toward the man he shot, and fled toward the front door, grabbing hold of the bin of admissible evidence he'd printed.

Peripherally, he saw movement. He turned, and saw the assailant reaching out—doing something that made a beeping noise then was simultaneously engulfed into an enormous ball of fire heading Lance's way. Lance turned around and dove head first out the door in the nick of time, skidding across the sidewalk on top of a plastic trash can clutched to his chest. It was somewhere between the fireball, and the pavement that everything went blank.

The room was foggy or just very blurry, out of focus and spinning. Was it a room or was this one of the place's people went after they die in an explosion?

Lance tried to move his head, but the pain was nearly unbearable. He reached up to hold his head only to find it bandaged like a cap, wrapped down to his brow. How could he get rid of the headache? 800 mg of ibuprofen was not enough. Slowly, his eyes were beginning to work. Objects were starting to come into focus, like the nurse who was standing over him, watching and waiting for him to come back to life. He looked at the nurse and then around the room. He must be in a hospital emergency room, he thought.

There were little cubicles made with curtains the staff pulled to come in and go out.

"Don't move that head too much! It was probably very painful when you just shook your head a minute ago, wasn't it?" The nurse didn't expect an answer, and explained, "You have a concussion. We did an MRI and there doesn't seem to be any permanent damage, but you need to rest quietly for a few days and try not to move your head. You have a very persistent visitor waiting for you to waken."

"I don't know anyone in Florida," Lance protested.

"Relax. This guy doesn't know you either, but he still wants to talk to you. He's with the police and just wants to find out what happened to you," she reassured Lance.

"Just what I need!" Lance half said to himself.

The nurse left. Five minutes later she came back with a guy who looked as if he came right out of the casting studios of Miami Vice. He looked about thirty-five, wearing a linen sport jacket with two days of stubble on his face.

THE MAN APPROACHING was no Don Johnson but did cause Lance to check his head again to make sure this wasn't just another crazy dream, making the pain come back. "Don't shake your head," he remembered. So much for following orders! Why start now?

"Hello, Lance. Is it okay if I call you Lance, isn't it? I am Lieutenant Rick Wilcox with the Miami police force. Would this be a good time to ask some questions?"

Lance looked at him oddly. He wondered if this guy was who he claimed to be, then deliberated about how much of which story he would tell the guy, growing tired of telling stories. "Do you have any identification?"

The lieutenant reached into his linen jacket and pulled out a leather wallet, flipped it open and showed Lance his shield. It looked official. Lance shrugged. Lieutenant Wilcox looked at him and shook his head. "You're awful, lucky and cynical; you must be a newspaper man."

"How did you know I was a newspaper guy?"

"I just followed the clues! Some guy narrowly escaped an explosion and is admitted with an ID that's from the Chicago Union newspaper; I figure he's a newspaper guy, but that's just me."

Lance already had half of the story pieced together; the same story he told the management company to get the key. Now all he had to do is embellish on it a bit. "Sorry," Lance apologized, "I'm still a little confused."

"Just take your time and do the best you can to tell me what happened, and we'll be done for now," Lieutenant Wilcox said.

Lance hesitated; he did not want to lie to the police or tell the entire story, yet. "I came to Miami on a lead for a story about arms dealing and working on the research. Although our offices were closed for the bug people, I went down there to review some files and make copies. Jeff Bayer gave permission. While I was printing files, I heard a noise coming from the back, so I went back to look. Someone in a room further down the hallway opened the door, saw me, and pulled a gun. I turned, and ducked, then ran to where my work was and shoved it all into a wastepaper basket. I was about to make it out the front door when I heard a loud boom."

"Why do I have the feeling I'm not getting the whole story?" Rick rubbed his stubble. Lance smiled for the first time during their discussion. "Stick around Miami for a couple of days—we'll need to take down your official statement," the Lieutenant told him, still looking slyly at the wounded newspaperman.

Lance frowned, which made his head hurt again. "I have to get back to Chicago to wrap up my story. Can't you use the statement I just gave for now, and go from there?"

Lieutenant Wilcox looked at him seriously for a second and shook his head. "You probably can't even walk, but if you can get by the Doc', feel free. Just let me know where you'll be."

"Ah, Lieutenant, you don't happen to know what's happened to my trash can of files, do you?"

"We got it. You were found on top of it."
"Well, I need it for my story!"
"No way, that's become evidence for now, anyway. Sorry McKnight."

Lance smiled again. "You are right it is evidence. I have a feeling that in the next couple days, you're going to have a lot more to do than at this very moment."

"Stay in touch until we close the case, McKnight."

After the lieutenant left, Lance tried to get up. He struggled to sit up, his head pounding pain to his brain. He managed a sitting position, where he stayed for three or four minutes hoping, the dizziness would go away. He finally swung his legs over the side of the gurney and waited for the side effects to go away again. He inched his butt over the side of the table to touch his feet to the floor.

Slowly putting his weight down, Lance could tell that his legs were going to collapse. Pulling himself back up he turned entirely around using the gurney to support him. This time it worked much better, except for the pain in his head, which he tried to ignore. Finally, he was able to stand, free of support.

His entire body ached, and had no idea which parts would work, and which parts wouldn't. He hobbled around the privacy curtained cubical three or four times before declaring out loud to himself, he was ready.

"Ready for what?" the nurse said, as her patient turned to face her. "I'm ready to go," Lance announced.

"You're not going anywhere, young man," the nurse told him.

"You must be mistaking me for someone else. I know I'm not a young man. If you could feel what I'm feeling right now, you'd probably put me at eighty plus," Lance joked. "But, I have to go."

"You're in no condition to do anything but continue resting in bed," the nurse insisted, "we'd like to have you for at least twenty-four more hours for observation. You do have a slight concussion and why you were admitted."

"Well, you'll have to mark my chart unadmitted. I promise I'll go back to my hotel and rest, but I have to get out of here."

"I'll get your doctor." The nurse ran off in a huff. Lance's conversation with the doctor was nearly identical to the one with the nurse, but neither the doctor nor the nurse had the legal right to force treatment on him while he was cognoscente. As long as he'd sign a waiver, he was free to leave.

An attendant wheeled him down to the emergency room reception desk. Once release papers were signed, the receptionist called a taxi. Lance was also wheeled to the cab. Now seated in the back seat, he asked the driver to take him to the police station.

During the ride, he remembered the rental car he'd left at the wire service and was sure he was unable to drive it. In fact, he wasn't sure the rental would still be there. Cars abandoned in alleys did not stay whole, very long, and made a mental note to inform the rental agency.

When finished with Wilcox, Lance took a cab back to the Omni. The driver pulled up in front of the hotel. Lance asked the driver if he could help him into the lobby. The driver looked at him quizzically at first but then went around the car and pulled Lance out of the back seat.

He managed to hold himself up and work his

way into the elevator, supporting himself on the wall and sides of the car. I've got to do better than this; he thought as he rode up to his floor.

In the room, Lance decided not to lie down. If he did, he probably wouldn't be able to get up again. Sitting on the edge of the bed closest to the phone, he started to make his calls. The first was to Kait.

"Hi, how did the interview go?" Kait was much cheerier, and happy to hear from him, more so than the last time they talked.

"Well, I don't think I'm the right guy for the job, but last night we went out and had a blast." Lance just could not resist the pun—even if Kait didn't get it. Something inside made Lance blurt it out. Maybe, a little bit of Butch rubbed off on him.

"It's too bad about the job," Kait attempted to comfort him, secretly glad a move to Miami was off of the table.

Lance needed to change the subject to avoid having to explain what really happened, yet. He didn't want to worry her or dampen her cheer. "Everything quieted on the home front?"

"Yes. San Antonio is a lot better than Chicago! Your mom even thinks so. We've just been relaxing, having Margaritas . . . ,"

"Well, I'm heading back to the dark city tonight. I have to sign a few things for the management company. I'll be in your arms within a week. I love you and miss you! Give my love to mom, too."

"I will. I love you, too! A lot. Hurry up and get here. Your mom and I both miss you. Drive careful."

After talking to Kait, he called the rental car company and told them where they would have to pick up the car. The material in police custody was safe, it may not be everything from the office, but Lance took enough of it that would convict Silver for illegal arms dealing, money laundering, conspiracy to commit murder; exactly what he set out to do in the first place. He hoped Marsha had been successful obtaining the financial statements she needed from FEI and Buffalo National Bank. Combined, the evidence was staggering.

Another visit to Marsha would be necessary to fill in all the blanks he could, along with names, places, which would allow her the ability to contact the various police departments for the trail of evidence. His editorial would result in solving five crimes, including a billion-dollar money laundering operation. For a minute or two, Lance pondered the multiple options for publishing his story.

Presently, law enforcement officials don't understand what piece of the puzzle they had. Lieutenant Wilcox would ferret it out; Lance was sure of that. Everyone would look like heroes. The separate agencies involved would be commended for working so well with each other when it was all over.

None of that would happen until Lance wanted it to. He found the key by blasting right through the gateway to Silver Bullet. Now, Lance could present it all to Scott Silver, and get the satisfaction of watching his face as he understands his empire, will be destroyed by him. Silver's days of pushing people around, and cheating the system were over, once Lance got back to Chicago.

Focus was now on Senator Gaston. His role was taking a while to grasp. No one knew about the connection. Until Lance talked to the Senator, he wasn't sure anyone would. Lance called the airline and booked a flight straight to Chicago.

When he finished packing, he hobbled around the room several times to work out his kinks. The pain didn't subside much, but he could negotiate a lot better than he did in the hospital. When he was satisfied, he ordered a cab to take him to the airport. He had a twenty minute window to wrap up the rest of the calls he wanted to make before leaving for the airport.

The IRS office was not open, and he didn't want to leave a message, so he called Marsha's cellular number. Marsha was surprised to hear from him and could meet with him at her office tomorrow morning at nine o'clock.

Lance made it to the Miami airport with

ample time, since there was no luggage to check. Forgetting it will take an eternity to walk to the gate was an oversight. Halfway there—fifteen minutes later, he was exhausted and flagged down a courtesy cart. He reached the gate as they were preparing to close it. Lance had gotten sympathetic stares all day, but at the gate, he was treated brisk.

"You're lucky we're letting you on. You know, you're supposed to be here a half hour before flight time!"

"Well, I've been awfully lucky lately. I guess this is just one more piece of the thread that's holding all my luck together. I was here as suggested; I just couldn't make it to the gate in time." The agent didn't say a word. She simply looked at Lance shaking her head as she closed and locked the jet way door.

The flight attendants made up for the crotchety agent. Recognizing that Lance was tired and in pain, they fixed up his first class seat to rival most hospital beds. Pillows and blankets were everywhere, strategically placed for comfort.

The roaring motion of the plane landing woke Lance with a thud to the head. He thought it was going to burst. The throbbing wouldn't stop, and he grabbed his head as if that would somehow relieve the pain. That was the first time since the hospital that he realized; he still had the dressing on his head. Geez Louise! No wonder people stared at him with a myriad of facial expressions all day!

After working his way down the jet way into the busy terminal, Lance ducked into the nearest bathroom and looked at himself in the mirror. Yeah, that's why everyone gawked. Some of them must have been frightened; he looked like the beginning experiments of Frankenstein.

Grabbing the dressing near the bottom of the left ear with both hands, he yanked with all his might. The pain surged throughout his brain and down his neck, but he made no headway removing the dressing. He tried one more time with a similar result, except that it ripped enough for him to unwrap it and remove it . . . ever so gently. Now he needed a comb, which he didn't have. He spent at least three minutes running waterlogged fingers through his hair. Tinges of pain came with every stroke, but he finally had it looking a little better than a Yorkshire terrier's. Lance flagged down another courtesy cart to take him to ground transportation for a taxi to the Drake.

He remembered nothing until the following morning's wakeup call at 6:30 A.M.

Marsha's smile faded while watching him enter slowly, and carefully sit. When he was finally still, Marsha blurted out, "What happened to you? You look horrid. What's with the limp?"

"Do you know a good stylist?"

"Bad hair day Whimpy?" she asked staring in disbelief. He was a hot mess.

"What happened with the raid? Were you able to get all the documents?"

"Wait a minute . . . thought you left for San Antonio? What happened to you?"

"I'll tell you everything after you tell me!"

Marsha's grinned before saying, "It went as smooth as clockwork. We got the records in Buffalo and from FEI. You were right about Tyson. The first thing he wanted to do was to call Silver, but we did not let him. We stuck to him like glue until he handed over the financials. You were also right about the sets not matching. The doc's differed were where you'd said—newsprint and revenue, and there was never anyone so happy that you were right, than I was, Lance. It could have been a disaster. Anyway, did you ever think of working for the government? We could use someone like you!" Marsha was only halfway joking.

"Nope! I'd rather lead the dull life of a newspaper man. You bureau guys get into too much danger for me," Lance chuckled.

"Why do I feel you're pulling my leg? Lance, why are you really here? We could have discussed all of this over the phone. From the looks of you, you should be on a slab in the county morgue."

"Am I to take that as a compliment? It isn't far from the truth. I was almost beheaded when Kait's BMW's gas tank exploded and burnt to the ground, with almost everything I owned inside it. I had to ditch the rental car in a back alley. Then, I was blown into the street by another explosion. Oh, and the best part . . . I was able to repose half of a day in a hospital, totally unconscious. Outside of that, the trip was great, however, I wouldn't recommend driving to Florida; it's too dangerous."

"We have a solid case on tax evasion, racketeering, money laundering, wire fraud, all thanks to you." she picked up a box of papers and set it onto her desk saying, "So far, all of this seems to prove Mr. Silver personally, via FEI, was deep into it on his own, with Mr. Scaletti's help. We will go over all of this thoroughly and inventory this box of documents to submit as evidence. This is all that implicates Mr. Silver, but so far, the corporation doesn't appear to be culpable." Marsha stared shockingly. "You know, you're lucky you're alive, Lance McKnight."

"YOU KNOW, LATELY, everyone's been telling me I am 'lucky.' You are right. I am lucky to be alive 'cause I would not be if it was up to Silver and his cronies. Lance took a few minutes to explain how he had the permission to make copies and take whatever files he needed, from the Editorial Manager of FEI Wire service in Miami."

Marsha momentarily focused her attention on a stuck drawer. Lance seized the opportunity to slip the thumb drive into the handle cut out of the box of seized files on top of her desk, while he mentioned the evidence that Lieutenant Rick Wilcox had in custody that would help convict FEI. "I'm turning this all over to you. You take it from here and deal with the alphabet agencies you need to. I know there is a revelation, and I know the evidence is all admissible."

"Lance, why don't you just tell me why

we're talking here, now?"

"I want you to tell the entire story to Lieutenant Wilcox; give him the officer's contact information, for the Buffalo and Tifton police on this list. It is the only way, Scott Silver will pay for murder, and a few other felonies they'll handle." Lance handed her a tidy summary of the details of his entire investigation of Scott Silver from the FedEx to his flight back to Chicago from Miami. The names, telephone numbers and case numbers were all right there for her.

"What does Fakhouri and H.F. mean?"

"I'm not sure, but I think it's important and connected somehow . . . possibly Silvers laundry partner? H.F. and S.S. were the only secured file cabinets and were off by themselves hiding in an alcove. I was able to get the S.S., but not the H.F. files. The only thing I can't tie up in red ribbons for you is the banker. There's got to be a banker who was processing the transfers. I couldn't figure it out."

"What do you think Silver was doing with the money?"

"That's a whole other investigation isn't? Who knows?" He had a good idea but did not offer it up.

Lance's immediate problem now, was figuring out how to get into see Silver, without the guards or anyone else raising an alarm. That may take a bit of doing, since Lance was sure that Scott had put the guards on alert and were not to let him inside the building. Lance knew that Scott often didn't arrive to the office before ten in the morning. Therefore, if Lance could get into Scott's office before Scott did, he'd have the advantage of surprise.

It was already nine fifteen and Lance decided he had better hustle. The paper was only ten minutes away and limped as briskly as possible down Michigan Avenue. He stopped a block from the main entrance then cut around to the loading docks, behind FEI. Only a few vehicles were at the dock and no one in sight. Once on the docks, he checked several chutes.

The chutes were used by the bundled papers that were sent out from the tray system and then dumped into the chutes and out onto the dock. Two chutes on the end of the dock were still open. He stuck his head inside one. Two workers on the other side of the room had their backs turned toward the chutes. It appeared they were in a heated discussion about one of the pieces of machinery. If Lance was ever to make his move, now was the time. Lance climbed into the chute, over the tray system and jumped down to the floor. Pain racked his body and his head was still pounding furiously.

Surprisingly, neither man heard nor noticed him. Lance edged his way along the wall, working away from the men and toward a hallway that led to the pressroom. No one was in the pressroom, at least not visible to him. If the morning shift was there, they must be in the reel room with the paper rolls. The quickest way was through a room to his left, but if he went into the composing room, someone was bound to see him.

Lance used the freight elevator for two flights and walked out into a back hallway leading to Scott Silver's private elevator. He pushed the button to call the elevator, hoping no one was in it, or showed up before it came. Then he prayed, Scott Silver would not be in his office when he exit's the elevator. His wishes were granted on all three counts.

As Lance entered Silver's office, and walked past the restroom into his Victorian playground, he thought he had made it safely, and sat down in front of the oval desk. Only then, did he suspect that Silver was already there. An open briefcase was on the desk, and on the floor by his desk, a large suitcase and carry-on bag sat nestled together. Was Scott planning to go somewhere? I guess if I were Silver, I'd plan a little getaway, Lance surmised.

Sounds of a flushing toilet came from Scott's private restroom. Lance braced himself.

Fear paralyzed Scott Silver in mid-stride when he saw Lance McKnight staring right at him. Scott regained his composure, walked around to his platformed chair, and looked at Lance with all the hatred he could muster. His face turned crimson. He tugged fiercely as ever, at his shirtsleeves. "What are you doing here? Who let you in?"

"I let myself in," Lance said smugly. "I came to witness the fall of the Fourth Estate!" Looking over to the suitcase he nodded, "You planning a trip?"

"You stupid jackass! Who do you think you are?" Scott snarled.

"No, 'Alex', you're the Ass. I'm just the guy who will see to it, you're sent to jail for a long time if not forever," Lance answered calmly.

"You think a little IRS audit is going to put me away, do you?" Silver baited.

"Not in and of itself, Silver, but coupled with murder, wire fraud and money laundering, not to mention the attempted murder of my wife and I, and my dog?"

Scott's blood-red face turned white. He never looked so confused in all of his life. "You think you're pretty smart, don't you?"

"I think you're lucky Illinois doesn't have a death penalty. You see, I obtained all the other evidence needed legally, and turned it all over. Soon, the authorities will discover Silver Bullet!"

"Go piss off, McKnight!" Scott screamed as he started pulling a handgun out of the right hand desk drawer.

Lance's smug demeanor grew fearful. His mind raced painfully. Something had to be done to disarm Silver, fast. He eyed the briefcase and without thinking shoved it with every ounce of might, crashing into Silver's hand. The only thing this really did was buy Lance a little time, but Lance lost complete control. Enraged, he leapt over the desk, grabbing for Silver's right hand and the gun. Both men were locked together against Silver's credenza and bookcase behind the desk. He never considered it might be hard to manipulate Silver, not necessarily because of his strength, rather his sheer bulk. Silver was wheezing. Lance slammed Silver's hand up against the bookcase two or three times. The gun finally flew out and slid across the desk onto the floor. Lance grabbed Scott's neck with both hands and would not let go. He was nearly incoherent.

"You deserve to die!" Lance screamed repeatedly, as the pressure on Silver's throat turned his face a deeper shade of purple. Lance was choking the life out of Silver as he sensed another presence in the room and glanced into the mirror inside the bookcase. His eyes widened when he saw Mike Marenski holding a gun in the reflection. The butt end came crashing down upon his head and everything went black.

12
ALLS WELL THAT ENDS II

IT WAS HARDER to open his eyes this time. The pain seemed to exude out of his eyelids and shoot to his head. Nothing was clear! There seemed to be blobs of darkness surrounded by swirling whites and grays.

Every time he tried to focus; the pain would make him shut his eyes. When he shut his eyes, it would be too tight, and the pain became even more unbearable.

He practiced for what seemed forever, until the dark blobs became images. One seemed to be moving toward him, and he finally recognized Mike Marenski. Lance lunged, "You dirty . . !" He screamed, missing his mark.

Hands grabbed and pushed him down holding him there and he winced in agony, feeling the welt from the gun butt and remembering his former friend's reflection in Silver's mirrored bookcase, trying to finish the job.

"Calm down Lance, Please! You're in no condition to be jumping around," Marenski's voice echoed through the darkness.

Lance could barely speak but forced himself to eke out a response. "You're the one who put me in this condition," he whispered hatefully.

"I had to," Mike replied. "I had no choice. You would have killed Scott."

"Exactly! At least, I had a good reason. All you wanted was to protect your crooked cohort!"

"Wait a minute! Wait just a minute, you think I'm working with Silver?"

"I know you are, you told him I was in Chattanooga. Silver took another shot at me by trying to blow me to the moon from my car. That was why you stalled and wanted to cool it for a while, uh huh! And why you gave me the information on the numbers to set me up!"

"That's a load!" Lance could barely make out Mike's arms flailing with his objection. "Butch knew you were going to Chattanooga, maybe he told Silver, but I didn't tell him."

"Butch didn't know . . . and Butch didn't smash me over the head with a gun!"

"Look. Let's get this straight right now. The only reason I hit you was to protect you from yourself. I hit you, so you wouldn't wind up in prison for murder, and it was just luck that I got there when I did. We had gotten a call from the guard station telling us that the IRS was there with a federal marshal to arrest Scott Silver, and wanted me for questioning. I came to Silver's office to see if he was there and found you two mucking around like a Japanese Sumo Wrestler and Pee-Wee Herman! After disabling you, I held Silver's gun on him until the Calvary came. I'll tell you what, I don't appreciate your implicating me in this thing. I have done nothing but help you since you brought me in on this! I'm sorry I had to hit you, but it didn't seem to crack that hard head of yours anyway. So there's no harm done,"

Lance's head was spinning in every direction. Injuries due to attempts on his life, compounded by the tussle with "Shamu," and the news he just got from Mike was overwhelming.

AFTER WHAT SEEMED like over an hour to Mike, Lance stared at him as if to question his truthfulness, then he finally said, "I'm sorry I mistrusted you. I was sure you had given Silver the information."

"Humph," was all Mike said turning into a candy striper carrying in a dozen roses to place on the table next to Lance's bed. For the first time, Lance realized he was in a hospital bed, and not on the floor in Silver's office.

"What am I doing in the hospital?"

"Where else should you be when you're littered with multiple contusions and a possible concussion?" Mike pulled the card from the flowers. "Do you want me to read this?"

Lance nodded painfully, holding his head.

"Lance, thanks for the Silverfish. Sorry I didn't wait until the afternoon, as promised, but I thought you might do something foolish. I was right. Call when you're feeling better. All my best, Marsha." Mike smiled saying, "Fairly insightful lady, wouldn't you say Lance?"

"Yeah, but she forgot to mention how handsome I look."

Butch walked in on the two of them laughing. "It's old home week around here," he said coming up next to Mike and putting his hand on Mike's shoulder. "Guess what I've been doing?"

Mike looked at Lance and then back at Butch.

"I don't think he really cares. I think he has a headache."

Lance smirked and Butch laughed. "I've been talking to John Beecher. You remember him Lance. The better half of FEI—hired you in the first place?"

Lance moaned. "Does he want his boy back?" Lance asked flippantly.

"Not at all, but he's worried about FEI and its reputation after all this mess."

"He knows? Who told him?"

"I did!" Butch said dumbfounded. "What's with you, Lance?" Butch realized that Lance probably had not been brought up to date with the events that had taken place in the last several hours. "Mike told me the whole story and, frankly, I was surprised you didn't bring me into it long ago. Did you think I'd take Scott's side? That scum bag is finally going to pay, and I hate the fact that I could have helped bring this to light a lot earlier."

"I don't know, Butch. I guess I didn't want to involve anyone else. No offense, I had no idea who I should trust, and if I was wrong . . . well, I meant no harm. Don't feel special, everyone was misled, left in the dark, or plain flat lied to, just ask Kait."

"What has Beecher said about all this?" Mike asked.

"You know," Butch began in what everyone knew was his story-telling mode. "I used to think that old fart didn't have the guts or judgment to make anybody do anything, particularly when it came to Silver. Boy was I wrong. He obviously has outstanding judgments, because he asked me to be the publisher of the Chicago Union. We talked about what was good for FEI, and we both agreed Silver was not. John said he was just too old to fight him and Silver made them money, but he had nothing to do with Silvers other ventures. The Union's lawyers will cooperate fully and get through it with minimal losses. Anyway, I pointed out the credibility problems due to Silver; and I wasn't interested in turning it around. The guy who took the initiative to expose him should be his first choice,"

"Thanks for nothing," Lance replied.

"I thought you would be happy. What's the problem?"

"Why would I want to be a publisher of a paper that's, number one, temporarily suspended from operating, and two, going south faster than vacations in January? Not to mention, my wife would have a cow! I did what I did to nail Silver, not his job. Besides, you already gave me a year off, and I'm seriously thinking of enjoying it."

"No one's telling you that you have to take it! It just sounded like a logical suggestion to make to Beecher; that's all. It's up to you, Lance, you ungrateful leprechaun! Besides it's not official until the fat man's in 'Sing-Sing,' or something like that."

Butch's wit brought another painful smile to Lance's face. "I'm not ungrateful, Butch. I'm just tired and I really can't fathom going back to the Union right now. There are a lot of things I still have to do to wrap this whole affair up."

"And what's that Sherlock? You've done enough. Let the authorities handle the rest, whatever it is,"

"Yeah, sure. Let them do it. They've been doing such a good job."

"They might have if they were told the whole story," Mike injected.

"That might have gotten me killed." He turned to Butch, "I'm really going to miss you. You made life at FEI bearable, and never lost your sense of humor!"

"Ah, don't cry, Tig . . . laddie. You won't miss me, I'm going back to San Antonio, too. And looking forward to seeing you, Kait and, hopefully the other Mrs. McKnight, if I can get there before she leaves." Butch turned and headed for the door.

"Butch?"

"Yeah?"

"Did you tell Scott I was in Chattanooga?"

Butch thought a moment. "Yes, I did. I didn't know I shouldn't. I really thought you were going to Miami for an interview." Butch hesitated and then asked, "Is that all you wanted?"

"Yeah, why?"

Butch grinned his finest grin, "I thought you were going to tell me not to call you laddie . . . laddie!"

"A bad comic, but a good newspaper guy," Mike teased after Butch left.

"And a great friend to have, like you are, Mike. Well, I'd better call Kait."

Mike realized that it was his cue to leave. "If there's anything else I can do for you just let me know. I'll be home until business at the Chicago Union or whatever they rename it resumes as usual."

"Haven't you done enough?" Lance asked rubbing his head.

"It was for your own good," Mike insisted heatedly.

"I know . . . I know," Lance said smoothing over his dark humor. "There is one thing you can do for me," Lance told him seriously. "I need some airline tickets."

"You must be out of your mind! You can't go anywhere. You're half dead for goodness sake!"

"You always did exaggerate. Seriously, Mike, I really need to go to Toronto then New Orleans and end up in San Antonio, with as few layovers as possible. If I can do this all in a day it'd be terrific."

"I'm not about to ask why, but sure it has something to do with all this Silver Bullet mess. I will say again, leave it to the authorities, Lance."

"I can't."

"I don't like it."

"You don't have to like it. Please, Mike, just do it! Didn't they teach you that in the military?"

"Yeah and I didn't like it then either. Okay, Lance, but will you at least wait a few days to give yourself a chance to heal some?"

"The day-after tomorrow will work. My room key should be in one of my pockets here, and the money is hidden in my hotel room in a duffle bag stashed behind the bottom dresser drawer, closest to the bathroom. Will you tell the front desk, I'll keep my room for a couple more days without maid service?"

Mike nodded then shook his head, found his key and stomped out of the room without another word.

Lance looked around the room to locate the telephone.

It was mounted on the side of the bed, supposedly for the convenience of the patient, but he or she had to find it first. He picked it up, trying to focus on the instructions to dial, but he couldn't. So, he lay in his bed thinking of how he was going to unravel the lies to Kait so that he could still salvage some kind of credibility with her.

After the perfunctory greetings, he just told her. "Scott Silver is in jail, and I put him there!"

What are you talking about, Lance? You sound very strange and what you just said sounds even stranger. Where are you?"

"I'm in Chicago, in the hospital," Lance said flatly.

"What?" Kait screamed. "That isn't funny!"

"I know. It's fairly serious, but I'll be all right."

"Why are you in the hospital? What do you mean, you'll be all right? Lance, I don't like the sound of this. What's going on?" Kait was nearly in tears.

"Maybe I should start at the beginning, the end just seemed to make it worse. Remember the note from Bobby Scaletti and the papers from the bank in Buffalo? Well, they have become evidence against Scott Silver for laundering money through his corporation, having Bobby killed and trying to kill me and you to try to scare me off." Lance knew he wasn't doing this right, but it was over the phone. He would tell Kait everything, in greater detail in person, when his investigation was complete.

"I guess he didn't know Lance McKnight, did he?" Kait replied proudly.

"No, I guess he didn't. I'm not even sure I do anymore."

Kait's silence was concerning. Was she furious?

"Oh, Lance, quit making up stories and tell me what really happened? Did Mr. Silver hire you again? No, don't answer that, I don't want to know." Then she giggled and said, "Now tell me if you're alright."

"I'm fine, are you? You're taking this all very matter-of- factly."

"It scares me to death, but it's over, right? And I thank God, for that, and that you are Okay. I've been worrying about it all along, but I knew you weren't going to include me because you wanted to protect me. I accepted that and prayed a whole lot."

"I guess I still have a lot to learn about you, don't I?" Lance said with both love, and pain in the same breath.

"And I, you," Kait whispered. "But next time let me know what's going on. I can take it, even if I have to shed a couple of tears through the process."

"I hope there isn't a next time, but I think I just found out that anything short of the truth with you, is foolish. Kait, I love you," Lance meant it with all his heart.

"I love you, too and I want you in San Antonio, now."

"I have to spend at least another day in the hospital. Then I have to fly to Toronto and New Orleans to tie a couple of loose ends. Silver was up to something with the money he was washing through FEI, and he had another prominent publisher in his grasp, a guy named Excelsior. I need to deal with them personally." Lance stated the truth, and held his breath, waiting for the backlash.

"Is it dangerous?"

"I don't think so, should be pretty routine."

"Then do it, and hurry home, I miss you. Is it all right to tell your mom?"

After Lance asked Kait to break it easy to her, they hung up.

For the second time that day, Lance felt an enormous urge to cry, but held back the tears; at least the majority of them. He leaned back on his pillow and closed his eyes. His head was still pounding, and he laid there for what seemed like hours before he finally fell asleep. That's just what Lance did for the entire next day and night; rested, without interruption.

The following morning Lance had energy enough to harass every nurse in the place, informing his doctor twice—he was leaving with or without a release.

Mike Marenski came to the hospital and saved the day. "What's going on here?" Mike belted out as he walked into Lance's room. "Every nurse and doctor within two floors have asked if I could talk some sense into you. I told them I couldn't, but I'd make sure you were out of here today," Mike announced, waving the airline tickets.

"You are sure you want to do this?"

"I am so glad to see you, M squared! I don't want to, I have to. They aren't totally in the clear yet and won't be unless they do the right thing."

"Why don't you quit being so sanctimonious and take care of yourself for awhile?"

Lance stared at him for several seconds. "You know you'd do the same thing. Besides, I'm doing this for me as much as for anyone else. I couldn't live with myself if I didn't talk to these guys."

Mike rounded up Lance's clothes while Lance made a phone call to Excelsior newspapers' headquarters. Yes, Clinton would be in for the rest of the day, but it would not be possible to schedule an appointment on such short notice. As long as he was there, thought Lance, there would be a way to see him.

As Mike wheeled Lance through the automatic sliding doors, Lance seemed to have a revelation. "I didn't even ask you, I'm sorry, Mike. I just assumed you'd take me to the hotel, then to the airport."

"Well, I don't know. I have a lot of things to do . . ." Mike looked at Lance crunching up his face in frustration. "Of course, I'll take you," Mike said smiling. "And I promise not to hit you over the head."

Lance was in Toronto by mid-afternoon. The cab driver at the airport took him to Excelsior headquarters, which happened to be on the twenty-second floor of the Ernest and Young Tower, in Toronto Dominion Centre. Lance mused, I bet Clinton Excelsior wouldn't be happy to have the building's namesake taking a look at his books. The taxi dropped off Lance in front of the Tower, paid the rides fare and marched through the lobby to the elevators. As he waited for a car, he told himself this was going to be quick.

Once in the Excelsior suite, he walked confidently up to the receptionist. "I need to see Clinton Excelsior!"

"He's unavailable," the woman told Lance. "Can I take your name and number, and perhaps he could get back to you." She was visibly annoyed by Lance's interruption.

"Yeah, you can take my name. It's Lance

McKnight, an associate of Scott Silver, but he won't need my number because he's going to talk to me, now," Lance walked right passed the receptionist's desk and through the double doors into Clinton's office suites. He looked both ways and there were offices on either side of the halls running down several hundred feet. The image was daunting.

"Mr. McKnight," the receptionist scolded, following him. "You can't do this, sir."

"Where's his office?" he demanded.

She shook her head, "Please leave now, sir!"

"Where is it? Tell me, or I will open every door on this floor."

Finally, she pointed and said, "Take a right at the end of the hall. His is the third office on the right." She gave him a dirty look and fled to her desk to call security, and warn Clinton Excelsior, that a belligerent man named Lance McKnight had breached their executive offices.

Clinton Excelsior's office door was closed. When Lance turned the handle and thrust his body into the door, he burst across the room startling Clinton. Lance knew he was in the right room. He recognized him, but not the other two men.

"What's the meaning of this?" Clinton jumped to his feet.

"Scott Silver," was all Lance said.

Clinton's face turned white, but calming down slightly, he said to Lance, "Were having a private meeting here. How dare you burst into my office, like a maniac? Clinton turned toward the two men and apologized for Lance's rude behavior.

"I think you got that turned around, Mr. Excelsior! You and Silver are the maniacs. The U.S. Federal authorities already have Mr. Silver in custody. I believe you will be indicted once the Canadian authorities are alerted."

"Shut the door, Mr. McKnight," He said emphatically, and softened his voice, adding, "Please." Excelsior then introduced the two men as his attorneys, Gerald Kinney and James Marsden. When they stood to give Clinton and Lance privacy, Clinton asked them to stay.

L<small>ANCE TURNED TO</small> face the lawyers and said, "Yes, you better sit in on this. Mr. Excelsior is going to need you, once his connection with Silver is revealed. There is a lot of explaining to do about your 'associates' that I haven't quite nailed down yet, and the authorities aren't really seeing all the evidence for what it is. They do not have the benefit of my knowledge, yet. You have a few answers I want. You'll cooperate with me, Clinton, or face questions regarding Silver's 'other' interests and partners in crime."

"And why would I tell you anything, Mr. McKnight?"

"Well, I have the key to the gateway. I can direct the authorities away from knowledge of your connection to Scott Silver. So everything only lands directly into Silver's lap. I'm sure they would be happy to discuss a plea deal on your behalf in exchange for corroborating evidence."

Gerald Kinney, interrupted, "I think we should hear what Mr. McKnight has to say, Clinton. I am of the belief, Mr. McKnight is being sincere, and only wishes to see to it, Silver is prosecuted. You may not have known, but could still be charged, guilt by association. 'I didn't know,' is not the best defense to build from."

"Listen to your corporate lawyer. Don't worry, this won't take very long. Just don't feed me any of your righteous indignation. You aren't being compared to Silver, and probably shouldn't end up incarcerated." Lance was not going to show all the cards he had. Clinton's automatic connection to Silver's arms dealing would stay with him, unless Clinton reneged on the deal he was to propose.

"Alright, Alright. Scott Silver and I were combined benefactors in our goal to get Senator Gaston elected as president of the United States in the coming election. Our reach was unparalleled. Can you imagine the revenue generated by the combination of our newspaper houses? We're already seeing a return on our investment. I never pass on a legal way to make money, and if by chance I am given information, well knowledge is power. I happen to have business interests all over the US; Senator Gaston looked favorably on capitalism, issues Scott Silver also supported," Excelsior admitted. "But I do not know one thing about his money laundering operation or anything else. I swear!"

"I'm sure you know that in the United States,

it's illegal to commingle corporate assets and contribute campaign funds to political campaigns in the manner you both have."

"Commingle corporate assets? Again, you've lost me. I don't know anything about fraud," Clinton protested, now on the defensive.

"Somehow, I believe you. You never did strike me as the brightest guy in the journalism world."

"Who do you think you are? Coming in here, . . ."

"Don't!" Lance snapped. "I know who I am! I've been in this business all my life, and for the most part; I've met people who were in newspapers because they believed in them. Because they want to see readers get the truth. They wanted to be able to have people trust and rely on what they produce. People that believe journalists have integrity. That's changed a lot in recent years. We've slowly turned 'News' papers into opinion pages. You and Scott have also gone a long way to destroying all of their credibility in very short order."

"You're not going to turn me in now?"

"No. I just wanted you to know, that I knew about your involvement as an incentive to tell me how Senator Andre Gaston fit into it. I couldn't put it together and knew you would tell me to avoid messy charges. Just don't forget, any more missteps like warning anyone, and I'll unload every piece of ammunition I have. Believe me, whether or not, 'you didn't know' you will when you are making license plates. Now, tell me precisely where I can find Senator Gaston." Lance climbed down from his soapbox. His head was pounding, and he just wanted to find a place to rest. He accepted the slip of paper with Senator Gaston's address on it, turned and started walking out of the room.

"Mr. McKnight!"

"What?"

"Thank you!"

Lance flashed Clinton a cheeky grin and left.

The roar of the jet engines reversing as the wheels hit the runway of the Houston airport drowned out any other noise in the cabin of the plane. Prior to touch down, half the passengers began whispering to each other about an event that happened several months earlier, at the Houston airport. Many of the terminals were still under construction. The rebuilding effort had been a slow process.

As the plane taxied to its position at the gate, Lance could tell major renovations had taken place and had to wonder how an attack like that could keep happening in the United States of America. But, It happened . . . and happened again . . . and will continue to happen as long as the Fakhouris and Silvers of the world fall through the cracks, and sell arms to anyone with hatred for America, her people and all she stands for.

Weary and foggy from his adventures, Lance decided not to deplane. The flight continued on to New Orleans, his last stop on the Silver Bullet express. He just wanted it to end. He needed rest and couldn't wait to see his wife. Lance slept through the boarding in Houston, and the flight took him over the Gulf of Mexico to New

Orleans. Waking as the airplane landed, attempting to clear the cobwebs, he rubbed his eyes only to initiate shooting pains in several pockets of his brain. Lance was grateful Clinton disclosed the connection to the presidential race, for the whereabouts of Senator Gaston, as well as his own forethought to ask for his home address. He was also glad he read the wire transcripts and prepared articles in Miami. However, he had no idea where that address was in relation to the airport, deciding to question the rental clerk, as he followed the signs to ground transportation after he deplaned.

The rental agent looked at the address, then referenced a map. "It's a bit of a ways out, but no worries; we have a GPS in every vehicle. The shuttle to your car is straight out that door, sir; have a good day," the clerk handed Lance his copy of the paperwork.

The shuttle rumbled off from the curb. Lance was still groggy, and his eyelids opened and shut all the way to the car lot. Lance finally got to the rental and found his car from the paperwork he was carting. He got into the car, set the GPS for the address, and followed the route for about forty-five minutes until it took him in front of an enormous southern style home; the automated voice of the GPS sounded off, "You have reached your destination on the right." Let's hope so, Lance thought.

He finally reached the home of Senator Andre Gaston. Lance rolled down the window and pressed the intercom. The camera had his face in full view as he spoke into a metal box, "My name is Lance McKnight, and I'm here to see Senator Gaston."

A minute passed, and the voice through the intercom said an appointment wasn't found.

"Oh, I don't have an appointment, but my business is urgent. He'll want to see me. I assure you. Can you tell him it's imperative and pertains to Scott Silver?"

The gated entrance opened for him to drive through, and he parked in the crescent shaped driveway.

Once inside the Gaston mansion, a guard scanned Lance from head to toe, with a metal detector. Then he patted him down the old-fashioned way. With the rise of 3D printing, they took extra precautions.

"My name is Lance McKnight. I used to work for FEI, at the Chicago Union, under Scott Silver. I would like to see Senator Gaston, and as I said, I'm sure he'll want to see me."

"I am James Hillerman. The senator's campaign manager. I do not know what this is all about, but I do not believe the senator has any business with Scott Silver. So, if you don't mind . . ." Hillerman was about to shut the door on him, but Lance stepped forward and stopped it with his hand.

"If you're his campaign manager, then you know that he has had a lot of business with Silver," Lance informed him, "look; we can do this a whole different way. I'm from the Chicago Union. With Mr. Silver spending some time with the government, I don't need your 'story' to publish this. I just thought you may want the opportunity to get ahead of this. I would like to meet with Senator Gaston now," Lance told Hillerman, staring him down angrily.

Hillerman SIGHED, slumped his perfect, mannequin figure and stepped aside in a gesture that indicated Lance could follow him to the senator's home office.

Lance recognized Senator Gaston's distinguished look and thought it was somewhat ruffled from what looked like a study session, based on papers strewn atop the table next to the chair. The senator rose as the two men entered the room.
"Senator. This is . . . I'm sorry I didn't even get your name."
"Lance McKnight," Lance extending his hand out to greet the senator. They shook hands, Andre motioned Lance to take a seat on the sofa, as he sat back down in a leather chair. The senator looked quizzically at Hillerman and then back at Lance.
"What can I do for you, Mr. McKnight?"
"You can withdraw from your run for the presidency!" Lance said flatly, staring at Andre and then at Hillerman. Senator Gaston jumped up from his seat. In unison, both men yelped, "What?"
Irritated, Hillerman held up his hand in a motion to quiet Andre. "Mr. McKnight, you must be joking! The senator has unquestionable adoration of the majority of Americans. Even

though it is far too early to determine outcomes, I doubt there is a candidate who can bring to the table what Senator Gaston brings to the table. Why, on earth would the senator withdraw?"

"Mr. Hillerman," Lance began calmly, "with all due respect, please, I came here to speak with the senator. I do appreciate your zeal in protecting his position. Granted, the senator is immensely popular, but he had some other backing, the nature of which would send his ratings plummeting to a record low, if the public were to discover it." Lance turned to Andre, "I'm sorry senator, but you must withdraw. I know about you, Scott Silver, and also Clinton Excelsior. I know it all, Senator Gaston, and then some! I'm the one who uncovered it. I haven't reported the connection I uncovered between you and Silver yet, because I believe you were not culpable and thought there may be some extenuating circumstances. All that aside, he was using your campaign to launder money. Did you know all of this?"

"No Mr. McKnight. We merely accepted the campaign financing and newspaper coverage nationwide, through Excelsior and FEI newspapers. I was allowed to get my message out in my choice of words, not an editorial of my stance, which can often skew meaning, having a negative impact on readers, rather than the positive message from our camp."

"You had to know he would use the financing and advertising against you, to control you, somehow. If not, you do now. Your career would end most ungraciously. What you do not know, and I am reluctant to tell you, I do want you to survive this. Mr. Fakhouri and Mr. Silver were responsible for selling the arms to the terrorists who killed your daughter in the Houston hijacking."

"Mr. McKnight, how dare you . . . have you no shame?"

"I'm sorry."

"When Silver came to me, I believed it was a way to run for the presidency with an even playing field with all the free advertising I was promised. Do you know how many campaign dollars that saved? To know that my campaign budget was unlimited, financing for all costs related to the campaign paid throughout the entirety of it." Andre gave himself a minute and said, "Our party has a realistic opportunity to restore what has been lost for some time now. Almost as quickly as I got involved with Silver, I cut all ties, and our campaign is running on my money, and that of legitimate contributions. I believe we still have a good shot at this."

"Senator, you have to drop from the race, the sooner the better," Lance said sincerely, "you may make a great president, but not now. I haven't said anything about this to anyone in the media, and I don't plan to, if you withdraw. It's up to you. I know it looks as if I'm blackmailing you, but I prefer to think of this as a negotiation."

"You're right, young man, and I'll tell you what, If my health holds out, and I'm still sane in four years. I might make another run at it legitimately. If so, I hope I'll get your vote."

Andre stood up as Lance rose and extended his hand. "Count on it, senator!" he said and shook the politician's hand. Lance nodded to Hillerman, who nodded back in woeful disbelief.

"Good-bye gentlemen, I'll find my way out. Thank you, Senator," he said turning back to Senator Gaston.

Epilogue

When Lance finally got back to San Antonio, and joined Kait and his mother, he felt at home again, even if home was just a hotel room on the River Walk. Home is where the heart is, Lance thought, and both were with Kait. After getting to the hotel from the airport, they hugged and kissed, both euphoric in each other's arms.

Lance then embraced his mom and thanked her for all she had done for him and Kait. "Mom, I know we've been through a lot of trials and tribulations over the years. Still, this Silver episode takes the cake," Lance observed.

"You're right dear," Janice replied. "All this has made me think that maybe it's time for me to explore places to live rather than Chicago. I heard Mr. Logan is moving back to San Antonio as well. It would be nice to see him again."

Kait and Lance looked at Janice, surprised by her comment, offering a sly smile in return.

"You know," Lance said, changing the subject, "when we first got to Chicago, I was seriously considering getting out of the newspaper business. The deeper I got into this Silver mess, the stronger those feelings became. On the way home, I realized that Scott Silver did not represent the industry. If anything, people like Butch Logan and Mike Marenski represent what newspapers are all about, and I'm proud to be part of that. Well, I'll be proud to be part of it again, when the time comes," Lance pronounced. "Right now, now I just need some rest."

Kait faced Lance and agreed that he should rest for a while. She also noticed something in Lance's face changed from tired to weary. Lance stared at her for a second, then took one of Kait's hands and held it palm up as his other hand came out of his pocket and cupped over hers. "I'm sorry Kait; this is all that's left of your car." Lance removed his hands, leaving Kait holding a roasted BMW emblem.

Kait took the emblem and tossed it in the trash. "I don't need that. All I need is you," she declared as she kissed him.

Made in the USA
Columbia, SC
13 April 2020